*Shauna's
Great
Expectations*

Kathleen Loughnan

Shauna's Great Expectations

ALLEN&UNWIN

SYDNEY · MELBOURNE · AUCKLAND · LONDON

First published by Allen & Unwin in 2019

Allen & Unwin
83 Alexander Street
Crows Nest NSW 2065
Australia
Phone: (61 2) 8425 0100
Email: info@allenandunwin.com
Web: www.allenandunwin.com

A catalogue record for this
book is available from the
National Library of Australia

ISBN 978 1 76063 157 4

For teaching resources, explore www.allenandunwin.com/resources/for-teachers

Copyright © Cover portrait illustration, Cass Urquhart 2019
Additional cover images by Franzi / Shutterstock
Cover and text design by Debra Billson
Set in 10.5/16 pt Janson Text by Midland Typesetters, Australia
Printed in Australia by The SOS Print + Media Group

10 9 8 7 6 5 4 3 2

For Stephen

For Stephen

By the time the speeches start, a dozen social justice warriors have been stretchered out of Hyde Park due to the heat. It's forty-two degrees this Australia Day, but no one who lives west or north of the Great Dividing Range would call it a scorcher. Nothing that a hat and a pair of sunglasses can't fix.

This is the first 'Change the Date' rally I've ever been to. My favourite cousin, Andrew, who I've dragged along for the ride, has been spouting smart-arse remarks since we arrived half an hour ago. I can tell he's having a good time.

He smirks every time some pink-faced, blue-haired university student passes out. Andrew hates university students. He says they do nothing but complain about how hard it is to study while living off his hard-earned tax dollars. I think Andrew secretly wishes he'd gone to university. In our family, no one goes – next year, I'll be the first.

'Check out Captain Cook,' says Andrew, pointing to the statue of the man who 'discovered' Australia, looking down on us from the security of his plinth. 'You don't hear him whining about the heat.'

'Or the bird poo,' I add.

The great explorer's head and shoulders are resplendent with a white crust of pigeon excrement.

'Do you think they should tear the statue down?' I ask cautiously. Apart from the occasional bitter barb, Andrew stays out of Indigenous issues. We're both Kamilaroi – my dad and Andrew's mum are brother and sister – but Andrew just gets on with it. I used to do that too, but it never got me anywhere.

Andrew considers the question for a moment, brings the brim of his black Akubra down further over his eyes.

'You know what I reckon, Shauna?'

'What?'

'I reckon they should tear the bugger down and replace it with a statue of Captain Hook.'

For an electrician from Bathurst, he's pretty droll.

I smile faintly, fishing for a good enough response, trying to remember *Peter Pan*.

'Captain Hook with his ticking crocodile?'

'Time's chasing both of them, isn't it?'

He guffaws at his own joke – it's a family trait. He's so loud that the people in front of us turn around and give us dirty looks because a Greens MP is on the podium, mid-speech. He's telling us how Australia Day should fall on a day that doesn't cause hurt to Aboriginal Australians. And that Captain Cook has to go.

I imagine a Captain Hook statue and burst into giggles, drawing more death looks from the social justice warriors blocking our view. I guess we should be more respectful to the people championing our causes.

It's not as though we are the only black people here. A large mob of Kooris marching from Redfern arrived around the time we did. But they're not the ones making the racket. I can't speak for everyone, but I think we just want to be acknowledged, not as Aboriginal Australians but as Australians. I'd be satisfied if someone whipped out a Sharpie and scribbled over the word 'discovered' on Captain Cook's plaque. You can't discover a country that's already groaning with people.

When a *tear it down!* chant goes up, Andrew rolls his eyes and I know it's time to go. He's no activist. He came reluctantly to this event. He turns to me with a grimace.

'Why don't we float? I don't want to waste a day in Sydney talking about statues and dates. Let's go down to Circular Quay and do something important.'

'Lunch?'

'You could twist my arm.'

We have an awesome seafood lunch at a flash restaurant by the harbour. It's Andrew's treat because he's got a great new job at Country Energy in Bathurst. He started off as an apprentice electrician when he was sixteen, and now, at the age of twenty-three, he's practically the boss. Well – not quite, but he gets paid a lot.

Andrew gives me a lot of grief about the school I board at, Oakholme College, because it's seriously posh. Of course I'm there on a scholarship. There's no way my parents could afford to send me there otherwise. They have to draw down on their mortgage every year just to buy the books. I'm not kidding.

There are all kinds of scholarships on offer at Oakholme – music, sport, nerd. I'm the holder of an Indigenous scholarship, which the school gives to one girl a year, usually in Year 7 or Year 8. My best friend Lou-Anne and I are the only girls from the recent crop who've survived. Lou-Anne's in Year 11 now. She got the scholarship a year after I did, and I don't think either of us would still be there if it weren't for the other. This year there's a new Year 7 girl who I've been asked to 'mentor', a job I'm not looking forward to because I'm not exactly the maternal type. However, starting the year with a 'friend' is supposed to make things easier for the poor kid. I'm in favour of the new mentorship program – I just wish I wasn't leading the charge.

'Any hotties in your year?' Andrew asks me over dessert. The reason he and I are in Sydney together is that he's dropping me off at school for the beginning of first term. Even though he teases me about Oakholme I can tell that it's from a perspective of disgusted fascination. He often asks me questions about what goes on at school on the pretext of running it down.

'Well, there's Lou-Anne.'

Andrew groans. He's met Lou-Anne a few times. Sometimes she stays with my family during the holidays.

'What's wrong with Lou-Anne?'

'She's not my type, Shauna.'

'As if *any* private school girl's your type. You'd run a mile if I introduced you to a typical Oakholme princess.'

Andrew looks down at his dessert. The fact is that he's repelled by anything that smacks of privilege, but embarrassed by anything that reeks of poverty. Somehow I just know though, that when he has kids, they'll go to private schools.

'Look,' I continue breezily, 'seeing as you're asking, there's a really beautiful girl in my year called Keli Street-Hughes. She's peaches and cream. Porcelain skin. Strawberry blonde hair. Curvy.'

'What about her personality?' asks Andrew, his eyes narrowing. He knows when he's being played.

'*Great* personality. She's an absolute delight.' I try not to smile but Andrew must pick up on the laughter in my eyes.

'I can't wait to meet her,' he says. Then, with a hop of his eyebrows he adds, 'She sounds almost too good to be true.'

'Oh, she is. *Almost*.'

★ ♥ ★

Keli Street-Hughes happens to be the bane of my existence at Oakholme College. She is *not* beautiful, she does *not* have a great personality, and she certainly is *not* a delight. In spite of being an inveterate racist and general ignoramus, she's managed to scale the heights of Oakholme social life by dint of extreme yet seemingly baseless confidence. Keli's never experienced a shaky moment and somehow that's been enough to make her very popular. She's even a hit among the teachers, an amazing feat for someone who always gets such crap marks.

I'd never introduce any member of my family to Keli. It'd be a gold-plated free kick in her favour.

Even so, as Andrew pulls into the Oakholme car park, I can't help but call his bluff.

'Are you coming in to meet Keli?'

He *um*s and *ah*s and makes excuses about having to get back to Bathurst to help my uncle Mick set up some backyard lighting.

'Behave yourself this year, Shauna,' he says knowingly, with a peck to my cheek. I guess he's referring to New Year's Eve. We camped together at a music festival, but I escaped his supervision and did not behave myself. Let's just say it involved some alcohol and a swag belonging to a very gorgeous guy by the name of Nathan O'Brien. Andrew was meant to be keeping me out of mischief and he obviously didn't do a very good job.

'I will,' I reply, my arms around his neck.

With an overstuffed sports bag slung over each shoulder, I watch my cousin drive away, swaying under a wave of homesickness. Andrew came all the way from his place in Bathurst to my parents' place in Barraba to pick me up. Usually I catch the train from Tamworth because my dad's busy with work and my mum's not up to driving long distances, but today I got the silver service. Not for nothing is Andrew my favourite cousin.

Of course the start of a new term at Oakholme does have its advantages. I never get tired of that first walk through the tall sandstone gates and then seeing the chapel gardens. Flame trees and jacarandas have showered carpets of red and lilac over the expansive lawn. Inhaling the scent of climbing rose mingled with warm sea air, I head past the white sandstone chapel with its cloud-spiking spire and stained-glass windows towards the dormitory building, a two-storey

Federation-style monolith with wraparound verandahs. Beyond the school buildings are the cliffside sports fields that give way to sheer, sparkling waterfront. This is some of the most valuable real estate in the country. This is my school, but every time I come back here after a break, I feel like an invader.

As I head up the sweeping staircase to the dorm rooms, I hear hungry, raucous laughter and hope that some of my friends have arrived already. I share my dorm room with a great group of girls: Lou-Anne, Indumathi and Bindi. I don't expect Indu and Bindi will be here today, but Lou-Anne's coming all the way from Eumundi in Queensland. Like me, she'll probably need a day before school starts to recover from the trip, mentally and physically. Lou-Anne's the baby of a huge family and she's usually pretty homesick for the first few days.

'Keli, you cow!' I hear a familiar ocker shriek echo through the stairwell. It's Annabel Saxon, Keli Street-Hughes's permanent sidekick from Albury. She's more or less the same as Keli, but washed out and sucked in. A few seconds later the diabolical duo comes hammering down the stairs wearing pillowslips on their heads. I guess they must have let the excitement of making their beds get the better of them.

I turn side-on and squeeze my belly against the rail, but Keli slams into me with her shoulder and clatters onto the landing three steps below.

'Oh, sorry,' she says through haws of laughter before removing the pillowslip. Sprawled on the tiles, long ginger hair akimbo, she looks up at me red-faced and grits her teeth. I guess she's not sorry after all.

7

Sycophantic Annabel skids to her knees at Keli's side as though she's just fallen down three flights rather than three steps.

'Are you *okay*, Kel?'

'I'm fine,' Keli replies stoically.

Annabel's pinched, mousy face turns to me. Her eyes burn with accusations infinitely worse than those that fall from her lips. 'You should watch where you're going.'

'You were wearing pillowslips on your heads.'

'Yeah,' retorts Annabel, 'and you weren't. So you should have seen us.'

She helps Keli to her feet. I turn to leave this ridiculous situation before they say anything else stupid.

'Is that a "Change the Date" badge you're wearing, Shauna?'

I'd forgotten about that. Someone handed it to me at the rally and I'd pinned it to my t-shirt. I don't really care if they change the date or not. The rally didn't change my opinion. I just want to be treated well when I'm in my own country.

'Wow, you learned to read over the holidays, Keli?'

Keli scoffs and shakes her head in disgust. 'You people. So ungrateful. If it weren't for us you wouldn't even exist. Your ancestors would have starved to death. You should celebrate Australia Day by thanking every real Aussie you see today.'

'Yeah, Shauna. Have some pride.'

Where to start? That's the problem with taking on Keli & Co. No sane, reasonable person would know where to start. Sometimes they make me so angry that I come out with extreme statements that I don't even believe.

Like, 'There's no pride in genocide, Annabel.' I regret it as soon as I say it.

They exchange raised eyebrows and burst into peals of laughter.

"'There's no pride in genocide,'" they mimic. And they keep repeating it as I bound up the stairs to my dorm room, hot-faced and brimming with all the excoriating one-liners I didn't think of at the time.

What a great start to the new term! I've already been mocked, blamed for something I didn't do and racially vilified! If I didn't think that Keli Street-Hughes was such a joke, I might even take it personally. The moment I walk into our dorm room, I rip off the badge and chuck it into the rubbish bin. I fume, furious at myself for fuming about Keli Street-Hughes.

Keli, like me, is a boarder from the country. Almost all the boarders are country girls, or 'scrubchooks' as Lou-Anne and I call them behind their sunburnt backs. Keli's from Cole-ambally, and her dad is a seriously rich intergenerational cotton farmer. He's the Tampon King of the Riverina, as Keli herself once joked.

If you could look up 'scrubchook' in the dictionary, you'd find a picture of Keli Street-Hughes at the races. She's a flame-haired, pearl-choked, saddle-bag-with-eyes. She's one hundred per cent freckle. I don't have a problem with freckles per se – only malignant ones. To put it bluntly, because there is no other way of describing Keli's feelings, she hates Aboriginal people with a passion. It's got something to do with a friend of her mother's who was raped and murdered by two Aboriginal men before Lou-Anne and I were even born.

Like a lot of white country folk, Keli has decided to hold the misdeeds and shortcomings of every bad Aboriginal person in history against us. Lou-Anne's a Torres Strait Islander, for Heaven's sake. For years Keli has been coughing and spluttering racist words at us from just within earshot. *Boong. Coon. Gin.* All ugly, all one syllable, and all cough-able, so that were we to report Keli's behaviour to a teacher, she could always claim that she'd just coughed. She's learned to refine her behaviour after a couple of dobbings-in.

When I was in Year 9 I gave someone in authority the full details of her nonsense. It was our down-to-earth school chaplain, Reverend Ferguson. By then I'd been having weekly counselling sessions with her for over a year and I'd begun to trust her. The harassment stopped dead for about six months before starting again in subtler – for Keli – ways. I thought I had her nailed to the wall in Year 10 when she stuck a sign on the door of our dorm room that said:

OAKHOLME DETENTION CENTRE
WARNING: ETHNICS SLEEP HERE

I handed the sign to Reverend Ferguson, who passed it on to Mrs Green, our small, single, serious principal, who for some reason to do with respectability persists with the surname of her ex-husband. I really hoped that Keli would be crucified, or at least yelled at. Instead I was called into Mrs Green's chic, modern office (one of the walls is an aquarium), where she told me that Keli denied posting the note and without any proof there was not much that could be done about it.

'I wouldn't worry about it if I were you, Shauna,' she said in her cold, cultivated, near-English accent. 'Whoever wrote this is an ignorant little philistine.' (Like, duh.) 'You're not even an ethnic.'

I suppose I was so shocked that thin, neat Mrs Green (she looks like a vanilla pod with the seeds scraped out) also thought the word 'ethnic' should be used as a noun and not an adjective, that I was struck dumb. I just didn't have the confidence to say *but what about all the other stuff?*

At my next session with Reverend Ferguson, I told her what had happened and asked her whether she'd spoken to Mrs Green about all the other nasty comments.

'The school does have a strict anti-bullying policy,' she told me, 'but I suppose Mrs Green's worried about creating a legal situation with Keli's parents over things that are difficult to prove. Next time something happens, come and tell me straight away.'

Well, I thought that was exactly what I'd done! I found it harder to trust Reverend Ferguson after that, but I'd never quite trusted Mrs Green, so that was no loss. All that happened was that *all* the boarders got a lecture from Mrs Green about bullying.

A few years before I arrived at Oakholme there was a student who was almost bullied to death. I mean she was literally suicidal after finding a webpage set up by fellow students dedicated to mocking and denigrating her. The legacy of those morons – they remained at the school and the victim left – is a ban on using mobile phones and social media at school. Everyone grumbles about it, and there's certainly a lot of covert online activity, but as the only boarders who don't own mobile phones, Lou-Anne and I don't give a hoot. Some of the boarders' parents complain, too, because they can't contact their kids as frequently. Still, the policy has, in theory, stuck. Any boarder who wants to make a phone call has to use the landline in Miss Maroney's office.

As far as I know, Keli has never set up a webpage committed to my denigration. She prefers to air her gripes the old-fashioned way. She coughs, splutters and scoffs racist taunts in Lou-Anne's and my direction. I'm a bigger target, I think, because, as a Kamilaroi on Dad's side, I look more like the kind of black that Keli speeds past on the main street of Coleambally in her mum's Rolls. I'm tall and rangy, with big, flashing eyes. Lou-Anne, whose people are from Thursday Island, is more of a gentle, benign island princess, even though she could probably kill you with a well-placed headbutt if she chose to.

I must admit that although Keli's harassment is galling, the longer it goes on, the more idiotic her hatred and snobbery seem. Last year we started to bite back. Lou-Anne had always been the one to tell me to calm down and ignore Keli, but even she retaliated.

One of Keli's many well-aired grievances is that we're here on scholarships whereas her parents have to pay school fees. She was complaining stridently about it in the row behind us during assembly one morning.

'... and our parents are paying for these *freeloaders* to be here.'

'And our tax pays for their parents' welfare,' added one of the coven.

I couldn't help myself. I whipped around.

'My parents aren't on welfare,' I pointed out. 'My dad's a truckie and my mum's an artist.'

'Drink driving and dot paintings don't count,' said Keli, and everyone giggled.

Then Lou-Anne turned around too. 'My parents *are* on welfare,' she said, grinning and looking Keli right in the eye. 'So say thanks to your dad for us, Keli.'

'Yeah, Keli,' I said. 'Say thanks to your dad. We'll pay him back one day.'

Keli fell silent and blushed so badly that her skin matched her long, fiery plait and even her ears turned red. She never mentioned her father's dollar again, but we do. Now, practically every time we see her, we coo, 'Say thanks to your dad, Keli!' She always turns to her friends and they gather together in conspiratorial whispers before erupting into carefree laughter. They're pathetic. I can hear their grubby squawks from my dorm room.

Most of the girls at Oakholme College aren't like that. Most of the daygirls are falling over themselves to be nice to us. I have one real daygirl friend and her name is Jenny Bean. Jenny's very intelligent and will probably be dux of the school. Although we were in some of the same classes when I arrived at Oakholme College in Year 8, we didn't become friends until a school trip to Toulouse in Year 10, when we got billeted by the same French family. We're both nuts about the French language and culture and, ever since the trip, we've been planning to travel to France together after the HSC. This time: Paris. Forget schoolies week on the Gold Coast, we're hitting the Champs-Élysées! For the last two years we've been reading books and watching films set in Paris, and we just can't wait. It's one of the roots of our friendship.

Jenny isn't one of the 'nice' girls who go cross-eyed pretending that they haven't noticed I'm Aboriginal, or act like it doesn't matter. She's always been curious about my family and what I do during the holidays. She never tries to sweep the differences between her and me under the carpet and make out like life's the same for both of us. Though we attend the same school, I'm a boarder and she's a daygirl. Friendships across this divide are pretty rare.

To me, the daygirls get liberties that we boarders can only dream of, like free time and privacy. The life of a boarder is strictly regimented, and that's why I enjoy arriving at school a day early at the beginning of term. When there are just a few boarders around and no daygirls, Oakholme feels like a luxury holiday camp. When school's in full swing, it seems much more like the institution that it is, with a Monday-to-Friday routine enforced to the minute. Showers, breakfast, roll call, school, prep. (a posh word for homework), recreation, dinner, private study, bedtime. We muck up when we can but there's not much wiggle room. Even the weekends are structured, with an early morning prep. session on Saturday for boarders like me who don't do sport and don't want to cheer the others on. Sunday afternoon there's chapel, like it or not. From Year 10 onward, we are allowed to go out unaccompanied on Saturdays and Sundays. We usually go to the city to look at shops and eat takeaway in the Botanic Gardens, but we have to be back at school by 6 p.m. Only during school holidays are we truly off the leash.

I unpack my clothes from my bags and place everything neatly in the wardrobe I share with Lou-Anne. By the end of term, all our clothes will be rolled together in an unholy jumble at the bottom. Nothing will be folded or hung. Garments will be sniffed to check whether they're dirty or clean. We always begin the term with such fine intentions and end it such incurable slobs. In spite of weekly inspections, which we anticipate by kicking stuff under furniture, our dorm tends towards pigsty.

For the moment, though, our room is pristine and actually very beautiful. All the dorm rooms are gigantic, with wide, oak floorboards and high, ornate ceilings. They're pretty plush, and even with the beds, wardrobes and a couple of Chesterfield lounges, they don't feel cramped. Once everyone arrives, the deluxe feel will be destroyed by doonas, photos, toys and ornaments, but it will feel a lot more like home.

As boarders at Oakholme College, we're in the minority. Most of the students are daygirls – rich eastern-suburbs princesses, either from stuck-up old Anglo families or from new Greek, Italian or Chinese money. There are only about forty boarders spread across eight dorm rooms.

On the pinboard above my desk I always stick the same old photo of my family and me. I'm about ten, and we're standing out the front of my *real* home. The house where my brother and I were raised in Barraba, in northern New South Wales, is a three-bedroom fibro cottage on cinder blocks with a view of the back fence. It's about as far from fancy as it gets, but apart from Oakholme, it's the only place I've ever lived. It's weird to be back at school after the school holidays. For the first few days, whenever I close my eyes, I see my mum in her scuffs in the kitchen and my dad walking across the backyard from his man cave. Then I accept that I'm just not there anymore.

In summer, it's stinking hot in Barraba, and there are hardly any trees for shade in the suburban area, but Dad keeps the lawn sprayed so you can walk around the whole yard without shoes. That's one thing I miss about home during the warmer months – the feeling of trodden, brown grass on the soles of my feet on a sunny day. I almost never go barefoot at school.

Still, I don't think student accommodation comes much flasher than the Oakholme dorms. I remember the first time I walked into the building, when the grandest establishment I'd ever set foot in before was the Barraba courthouse. It was like entering an expensive shop full of stuff I could never afford to buy. On the wall alongside the staircase, there was a life-size painting of the school's founder, the Reverend Doctor Sterling McBride, that just about scared the life out of me. He's still hanging around the staircase looking thin-lipped and disapproving, but he doesn't scare me anymore. In fact I'd like to ask *him* what those beady little eyes are doing in a girls' dormitory house!

My dorm buddies and I are always cutting up about Reverend McBride, even though he's long dead. The other dead guy we poke fun at is Sai Baba, Indu's spiritual master. It's his image she pins above her desk. His eyes are kinder than Reverend McBride's, but they still seem to dart around the room watching us.

Indu has an outrageous sense of humour and is in on our joke, but you can only push her so far. Hinduism is her religion, after all. She literally worships the bearded Sai Baba, who sits cross-legged, barefooted and naked from the waist up (in the image). Back in Year 8 she got called into Reverend Ferguson's office one day for religious counselling because the school didn't approve of her worshipping false idols. Yes, incredibly, this is the kind of thing that can happen at Oakholme College.

According to Indu, Reverend Ferguson was super-embarrassed to even broach the issue, which tells me that our dear principal was the real one behind the intervention. Reverend Ferguson's full name is Reverend Sally Russell-Ferguson – Lou-Anne and I call her 'SRF' or 'Self-Raising Flour' because she's so puffed-up, flustered and theatrical. She's a notorious softie. Following some hot licks from Indu about Sai Baba being a real historical figure and not just some statue, symbol or holy spirit, Reverend Ferguson actually apologised. The tapestry of Sai Baba was never mentioned again by the powers-that-be.

Indu's parents are both doctors in Mumbai and she would be almost alone in Sydney if it weren't for us. She has an aunt here who she stays with during the shorter school holidays, but she's admitted more than once that she feels closer to us than to her aunt and her aunt's family. This is kind of strange, because at school she stands out as being different even more than Lou-Anne and I do. She speaks with a very un-Australian accent that screams of her native India but also hints at something more English than English itself. Her vocabulary can be odd, too. Every now and then she'll come out with a word only a great-grandmother would use, like 'cross' (when she means angry) or 'nonsense', or a phrase like 'until and unless'.

Bindi, whose dad is Greek, is the final quadrant of our 'ethnic' circle. She's very shy until she trusts you, but once she does trust you, you get too much information. There's really nowhere she won't go. Though she can be invasive at times, the upside is that she's staunchly loyal. You can have a flaming argument with her one moment, but the next she'll be defending you to someone who's gossiping about you behind your back.

The four of us oddballs look after each other, and we're virtually inseparable out of school hours. On my pinboard, along with the photo of my family, I stick a photo of us on the night of the Year 9 and 10 formal. We all thought we looked so great at the time, but now the image is just funny because it's so embarrassing. There's way too much of everything that was important to us back then – make-up, push-up bras and trout mouths.

Out of nowhere, a perfectly sung arpeggio comes echoing from the direction of the staircase. I hang one more blouse in the wardrobe before sprinting up the hall and down the stairs. The arpeggio turns to a squeal when Lou-Anne spots me. She drops her luggage and leaps up the stairs, arms outstretched.

We meet on the landing by Reverend McBride and hug amid a volley of shrieked greetings. Then we go upstairs together, start making our beds, and end up running around the dorm with our pillowslips on our heads.

2

OLIVIA PIKE IS waiting for me in the withdrawing room. It sounds like she's in rehab, I know, but at Oakholme all the rooms in the admin. building have official names like that. It's totally Old English and wanky, but still, when you get invited to one of those rooms it makes you feel like you're part of some hallowed class.

Anyway, I get the note at roll call:

Shauna, your mentee, Olivia Pike, will be waiting to meet you in the withdrawing room at 9 a.m. sharp. SRF.

After roll call, I head down to the admin. building, which is Victorian-era, three-storey, the original boarding house back in the day. I make my way to the withdrawing room and there's this blue-eyed, blonde-haired kid sitting at the board-room table. She has an air of confidence about her, so I know right away that she can't be Olivia Pike.

Olivia Pike is this year's recipient of the Indigenous scholarship. I sat in the very same chair in the very same with-drawing room four and a half years ago, wondering if they ever used the fireplace, because it seems really real. (It is.)

After one glance at this prissy blonde chick, I click my tongue and stalk right back out. I'm missing my French class to be here and we're working on the subjunctive, which totally confuses me. I really wish I were there and not here (an example of the correct use of the subjunctive, I *think*).

Annoyed that my time's being wasted, I go to Reverend Ferguson's office to tell her that Olivia Pike's not in the withdrawing room.

'She seems to have withdrawn,' I say, never short of a joke, even when the circumstances irritate me.

Reverend Ferguson clasps the end of her desk in panic. 'Oh, don't tell me…'

Even though the Indigenous scholarship is competitive (you have to do an exam and provide references), the recipients have a habit of going AWOL. You know, walkabout. The school board thinks they're doing this great thing for the Aboriginal community by plucking a cute little button-nosed black girl out of her unwholesome environment and giving her a proper education and upbringing. What they don't understand is the pull of home and family that drags us back, the way the moon drags the tide. For a while there were rumours that the school wouldn't hand out any more Indigenous scholarships because of the failure rate. Since the program began ten years ago, seven out of the ten scholarship recipients have taken off for home within the first twelve months.

Olivia Pike has set a record though, scarpering in the first five minutes.

I follow Reverend Ferguson as she races to the withdrawing room.

'Olivia?' she cries in a pained voice as she flings open the door.

'Yes, Reverend Ferguson?' the blonde girl says calmly.

Reverend Ferguson half-screams, half-laughs, grabbing my upper arm as if she's drowning.

'Oh, Shauna, you had me scared to death!'

'*That's* Olivia Pike?'

Reverend Ferguson lets go of my arm and straightens herself up. She's a larger lady, our Self-Raising Flour, and like self-raising flour she tends to get bigger when heated up. Her forehead pops sweat beads and her clothes seem suddenly too small. She opens her jacket, adjusts her skirt and finally exhales. Sometimes it's hard to believe that Self-Raising is one of God's earthly vessels.

'Olivia, this is Shauna Harding. Shauna's going to be your mentor this year.'

Olivia Pike smiles for just long enough to show dimples and a dental plate.

'Hello, Shauna,' she says.

'Hi.'

I'm still in shock. I can't believe they've given the Indigenous scholarship to a piece like this. Jesus Christ. She's not even black. I guess she must be one of those confused souls who identifies as Aboriginal but doesn't have a black gene in their body. I mean, she's practically albino.

'I'll leave you two alone to get to know one another,' says Reverend Ferguson, closing the door behind her.

There's a seat at the table opposite Olivia Pike, but I don't sit. I had a nice speech prepared in the vein of 'if you ever have any problems or need any advice, don't hesitate' but I don't deliver it.

'Look, I have to get back to class, but, um, I'm Shauna Harding and I'm in Year 12.'

Olivia Pike blinks at me like a camel, then her pretty face twists. 'I don't want anything to do with you,' she says nastily.

'What? What do you—'

'I don't want anyone to know about my background. I've told Reverend Ferguson and she's promised not to tell a soul. So if word gets around, I'll know who let slip.'

'Fine with me,' I say, completely bowled over. Usually there's no announcement about who has won the Indigenous scholarship. It's kind of obvious because a random Aboriginal girl pops up and everyone knows how she got here – her rich parents! (joke). I'm happy not to make a big deal of it, but crikey, the *attitude* on this girl!

'So don't ever come and talk to me.' She looks at me in disgust, like I'm something stuck in the tread of her shoe. 'Don't even *look* at me, all right?'

'Fine with me,' I say again. I've got my hand on the door handle, about to walk out, when I think of something to burst her bubble.

'People will find out,' I say. 'They always find out.'

'Maybe in your case, Jedda.'

'My name's Shauna.'

'Well, you're as brown as a walnut, Shauna.' (Which is not true, but I am darker than her.) 'I'm passable,' she says.

'That's what you think,' I reply icily before leaving the room.

Reverend Ferguson's hovering in the hallway.

'That was quick,' she says uncertainly. 'Now, you do know that Olivia wants to keep her background confidential...'

'Olivia doesn't want a mentor,' I tell her, leaving her mouthing like a goldfish as I head to the language lab.

Jedda, I mull furiously, trying to remember how to conjugate *être* in the subjunctive mood. How dare she! That little Year 7 shit!

Of course the first thing I do after French is tell Lou-Anne all about Olivia Pike.

'Passable,' repeats Lou-Anne. 'What does she mean by that?'

'Well, she obviously thinks she can pass for white.'

Lou-Anne takes a minute to process that. She never says anything she doesn't mean, not even to be nice, which she always is – sometimes painfully so. I know she's not going to say something like *Why would she want to do that?* We know damn well why she would want to do that. We're not ashamed of our heritage, but we've both had the feeling at times that life would be a lot easier if we could just turn white for a few hours. We've talked about it before. How only white people can be Australian. How everyone else, including us, the originals, needs to justify themselves with an adjective. *Chinese Australian. Greek Australian. Indigenous Australian.*

Shit, man. Forty thousand years and we're still not just plain old Australian.

White people are colourless, adjective-less and unremarkable. Aboriginal people, though, are always black. It would be nice to take a break from living in colour.

24

Lou-Anne shakes her head. 'You don't have to talk to her.'

'I'm supposed to be mentoring her.'

'Maybe you can do it by email?'

I start laughing, because Lou-Anne is being perfectly sincere and serious.

'What, Shauna? I'm trying to come up with solutions here!'

Lou-Anne's right, of course. We all have school email addresses and I could, theoretically, send Olivia emails. *Theoretically*. I suppose I should give her another chance, considering how scared and alone I felt when I first arrived at Oakholme. What would I have done if Lou-Anne hadn't arrived? Who will Olivia Pike have? The other white girls, I think nastily.

The bell rings for our next classes. We're in our dorm room but we're not meant to be here. More often than not we come up here between classes, just to decompress. And to break the rule.

'So what do you think the go is with Olivia?' I ask Lou-Anne.

'Maybe her colours ran in the wash?' she says, before laughing raucously at her own joke.

'You know what I mean. How did she get here?'

'Probably the same way you and I did. She sat a test to make sure she could spell her own name and then did an interview to make sure she looked the part.'

'Obviously she was interviewed in a very dark room,' I remark.

'What are you saying, Shauna? That she pretended to be an Aboriginal or Torres Strait Islander so she could get the scholarship?'

I shrug.

'Come *on*,' says Lou-Anne. 'Who'd pretend to be black if they weren't?'

'Maybe she's trying to squeeze the last few dirty drops from the identity politics dishrag. People do that kind of thing, you know. For attention.'

Lou-Anne puts her hand on my shoulder. I must look upset or something.

'But didn't you just say that she wants everyone to think she's white?'

I shrug. 'I guess you're right. You'd only want everyone to think you were white if you weren't.'

'Shauna, you're making my brain hurt. Stop.'

Lou-Anne sings an arpeggio, which is what she does when I make her brain hurt. Along with rubbing her temples and scrunching her eyes shut. When my best friend sings an arpeggio, though, it's music. She's a classically trained soprano and wants to become a professional opera singer one day. Every second schoolgirl dreams of becoming a professional singer, a model or an actress, but Lou-Anne's the only one I know who's actually in with a chance at stardom. She's a supercharged type of soprano, a coloratura, which means she has a light, agile voice that can pull off high trills and leaps you wouldn't think a human was capable of. She's applied for a place in Opera Australia's Young Artist program. It's really competitive, but her audition video, filmed by yours truly, got her through the first round and she has a live audition later in the year. One of the music teachers here at Oakholme, Miss Della, is giving her lessons four afternoons a week, so it's obvious that I'm not the only one who believes in Lou-Anne.

Though her family knows how talented she is, I don't think they have any idea how hard she works or how close she is to succeeding. No other member of Lou-Anne's family has excelled at anything much other than reproduction. One of her sisters, Beth, gave birth to twins when she was just fifteen. Now all three generations live in a ramshackle house near Lake Weyba. They're a lovely family – I've stayed there heaps of times – but they're also chaotic. When Beth had the twins, Charlotte and Chelsea, their family became known to the dreaded social services, and that's how Lou-Anne found out about the Indigenous scholarship at Oakholme. Her family, especially her mum, didn't want her to come to Sydney, but once Lou-Anne heard about the music department here, there was no stopping her.

I remember seeing her for the first time. Built like a rugby forward, pigeon-toed and followed by a frizzy, black ponytail that spanned the width and length of her enormous back, Lou-Anne did not seem destined to last. Another scholarship recipient who'd been in Year 10, Elodie, had just left the school to work in her uncle's sandwich shop in Dubbo. That's what she told everyone, anyway. I knew she'd left because she just wanted to go home and never come back to this strange place. I thought Lou-Anne would realise she didn't fit in and leave for similar reasons. I still have the same feeling myself sometimes. The scary thing is that I have it when I'm in Barraba as well.

At the time I started at Oakholme, at age twelve, my family was a bit chaotic, too. My big brother, Jamie, had just died in a car accident and my parents were really depressed. They'd stopped looking after me and the house, and I'd stopped going to school so I could look after them. My school at the time called social services and we got a caseworker, who turned out to be a decent person. She gave me information about the Indigenous scholarship.

All the girls who get the scholarship seem to have sad backstories, but Olivia Pike? Seriously? I wonder what kind of bad luck could have befallen her. She doesn't look like the kind of person who's gone through anything worse than a slight headache.

'I'll talk to her,' says Lou-Anne finally. 'I'll find out what's going on.'

'Don't do that. I don't want to give her the satisfaction of snubbing you.'

'At least Self-Raising Flour didn't put her in our dorm room.'

'I hope they put her in with Keli Street-Hughes.'

'I wouldn't wish that on anyone.'

'It'd be a fitting punishment.'

'And Olivia deserves to be punished?'

'She should be careful what she wishes for, Lou-Anne. You can't just solve all your problems by pretending to be someone you're not.'

'Maybe not, but do you blame her?'

I don't respond, because I'm actually pretty sure I do blame Olivia.

Our housemistress, Miss Maroney, comes blustering into the room and gives Lou-Anne and me a Red Mark each for being in the dorms during class time. Three Red Marks and you have to stay back on Wednesday afternoon for detention. It's not a big deal when you're a boarder and you spend the afternoons at school anyway.

'Sorry, Miss Maroney,' we say as she writes down our names in her diary.

'What will it take to get you girls to *listen*?' she growls.

'I would definitely listen if you paid me, Miss,' says Lou-Anne.

Miss Maroney tries not to smile.

'Get out before I give you another Red Mark.'

'Oooh!' Lou-Anne and I purr in mock terror.

Miss Maroney makes a lot of noise, but she's not very terrifying. She's only about twenty-five and she looks like Barbie. She teaches maths and sport in the same steely voice. She thinks that we don't know that she has parties in the school's indoor pool during the holidays. If Mrs Green ever found out about it, Miss Maroney would probably lose her job, and a plum job it is too. Oakholme's sporting facilities are state-of-the-art, thanks to alcohol-laden fundraising soirées hosted by Mrs Green in the school ballroom. Yes, Oakholme College has a ballroom.

'What subject have you got now?' asks Lou-Anne as we skip down the stairs and out of the dormitory building.

'English. You?'

'Music in the auditorium.'

We pass Keli Street-Hughes & Co in the quadrangle. Annabel Saxon and Keli's other twangy cronies always travel in a group, and when they stop to talk they stand in a perfect circle, elbow-to-elbow, so that no one else can edge in.

'Say thanks to your dad for me!' Lou-Anne and I sing in unison as we glide past the circle of wisdom.

Keli's tinkling laughter floats after us and glances right off us to the ground.

3

A GROUP OF Year 12 girls have been invited to a meeting in the withdrawing room. We're the gluttons for punishment who completed an HSC subject last year. Most of us did 2-unit maths, and will continue maths at a higher level this year. Oakholme has begun to encourage its top students to complete an HSC subject in Year 11, based on the theory that spreading the stress over time maximises ATARs.

This meeting is about the HSC University Pathways program, which gives Year 12 students the chance to complete a first-year university subject. It's only been offered to the students who, in Mrs Green's view, can cope with it. This is the first year the program has been open at Oakholme College. We had to apply last year, and most of the girls, including Jenny and me, chose to study Introduction to Legal Systems and Methods online at the University of New England. It'll be useful for me because I want to study journalism at uni and to do that I would have to take some law subjects anyway.

Mrs Green had to push for the HSC University Pathways program to be introduced. It was a few years before the powers that be – the ancient Oakholme school board – gave in. She obviously has grand ambitions for improving the school's academic reputation, which I'm not sure its student body has the ability to back up. Not all rich kids are smart. They're pretty much the same as the rest of society. Some of them are intelligent, some of them are dunces, and most of them are just good old average.

Reverend Ferguson was against loading a university subject on top of the HSC because she thinks we're already under too much pressure. I know her opinion on the matter because, although we don't have regular counselling sessions anymore, she always accosts me to chat about this or that. I think she misses me.

Of course I told SRF that I was all for HSC University Pathways, because it opens up options for me once I've finished school. In the end, there was a compromise – only the girls who were already excelling academically would be recommended for a place.

Mrs Green stares at the excited occupants of the with-drawing room. She has bright, piercing eyes that seem to be able to see everyone at once. When the room falls silent, she clasps her hands and leans back onto the mantelpiece.

'If you're in this room, it's because you're already good at sitting exams...' she begins. She gives a spiel about how the university units on offer are respected by other universities across Australia.

'This is new territory for Oakholme College, and we weren't sure exactly how we'd support your extra studies. But we've come up with a solution. There will be extra classes on offer to support the online work, but they won't be held here at Oakholme. They'll be held at St Augustine's.'

An involuntary *whoop* goes up around the withdrawing room. St Augustine's is a *boys'* school, about ten minutes drive away! Embarrassed giggles quickly descend. As anyone who's been to an all-girls school knows, there's nothing apt to render girls boy-crazier than sequestration from the male gender. I went to a regular povo government school, Barraba High, until halfway through Year 7, so I'm not quite as under the boy spell as some of my friends. Jenny, for example.

Jenny is one of those girls who's ordinary looking until you *really* look at her and realise just how delicate and pretty she is. The glasses and puppy fat are deceiving. If you talk to her for five minutes you can't help but notice her gorgeousness – dark eyelashes, clever, hazel eyes and the cute smatter of faint, pinprick freckles that run over her little ski-jump nose. But there are some people, boys especially, who don't make it through the five minutes because Jenny can be a bit intense.

There's this one heartthrob at St Augustine's who Jenny's been mooning over for about six months. His name's Stephen Agliozzo. He's been unfairly blessed with curly, black hair *and* blue eyes, and he turns every girl and her mother inside out. I'm not joking. I've been to combined Oakholme/ St Augustine's social events and actually seen middle-aged women blush around him. Of course, he doesn't deserve any of it because he's an arrogant little prince. There's not a girl alive who would last a month with him. A girlfriend is like a haircut to Stephen Agliozzo, but probably less important. Jenny, thank God, doesn't stand a chance. I suppose there's no harm in dreaming, though.

'Can I see a show of hands if revision classes are something you'd be interested in?'

Every single person raises a hand. Jenny puts up both of hers.

'Right,' says Mrs Green triumphantly. 'I'll send permission slips out to all your parents.'

After the meeting, Jenny and I go to the Year 12 common room for hot chocolates. About the only useful thing the Student Association's ever done is install a coffee and hot chocolate machine there. It must spit out a thousand hot drinks a day.

Jenny's excited, *really* excited, about doing the University Pathways support courses at St Augustine's. The only thing that can get her as high as those clean-cut boys do is Paris. She has the same shine in her eyes when she's discussing the city of light, as if it's a new lover. And if Paris is her lover, it's mine, too. It's as if we've fallen for the same guy, but we're both so rapt in him that neither of us minds that he's seducing the other.

Jenny's managed to convince her parents to put up for some cheap digs, so all I have to do is come up with money for the flights, sightseeing and getting around. It's got to be doable somehow, though I've yet to raise it with my parents. They wouldn't share my exhilaration, and it's possible that they won't share their money. I remember the pained look on my dad's face when he had to contribute to the Toulouse trip in Year 10. He just could not fathom why I had to travel to the other side of the world. So I may end up putting the hard word on my cousin, Andrew. I think he'd loan me at least some of the cash. There's also the night shift at the

Barraba servo. A couple of weeks of that mind-numbing job would be worth it for Paris.

'Imagine being in Paris! We could go to the theatre every night. Imagine, Shauna!'

The wonderful thing is, I *can* imagine. The terrible thing is that I just can't quite imagine how I'm going to pay for everything. Theatre *every* night?

The two of us in a little studio apartment in the Latin Quarter. Buying pastries in the morning. Eating ham baguettes on a bench by the River Seine at lunch. Meeting some gorgeous French guy and zooming around Paris on the back of his motorbike...

'Shauna? *Shauna?*'

'What?'

'You look about a million miles away.'

'I was. I was in Paris.'

Jenny grabs my hand and squeezes it. There's light dancing in her eyes. We both laugh.

'What about Stephen Agliozzo?' I ask her with huge eyes full of mock-sadness. 'Do you think you could bring yourself to leave him behind for a whole month?'

Jenny can't help but blush as she rolls her eyes. She's never been one for carefree breeziness.

'We'll have to book our flights pretty soon,' says Jenny, between sips of her hot chocolate, which is fogging up her glasses.

'Thinking about Stephen?' I ask her cheekily.

'It's the steam from the hot chocolate, Shauna! I've already forgotten about him.'

35

'Oh, sure.'

Jenny was a late developer, and while she's very smart, there's no hint of the knowing, catty sophistication that would give her a pass into one of the 'popular' groups at school. It's one of the things I like about her. Sass, hormones and boy craziness have only just pulled into her station. I just wish she'd fixate on someone nicer and more attainable than an in-demand pretty boy like Stephen Agliozzo.

I'm not one of those really boy-crazy girls, but I do have a lot more experience than Jenny. I had a few boyfriends back in Barraba, but not much action since I first donned the bottle green Oakholme tunic. At Barraba High, it was all taken much less seriously. Kids hooked up and broke up on a week-to-week basis and most of them didn't cry into their social media accounts when it was all over. Some of the older students had longer, more serious relationships and it was well known that a few of them had sex.

I had sex this summer with Nathan O'Brien at the country music festival I went to with Andrew. Nathan's not even a schoolboy. He finished school last year and now he works on his parents' farm at Kootingal near Tamworth.

I don't quite know how it happened that night. We just stayed up talking about music and school and how annoying Sydney is. Then we ended up slow dancing to a bad cover of Keith Urban's cover of 'Making Memories of Us', both of us wishing the song would never finish. One thing led to another – believe me, I *wanted* it to – and I woke up the next morning in Nathan's swag with my sweaty, naked legs tangled in his.

Jenny almost needed oxygen when I broke the news to her. You'd think it was she who'd just lost her virginity the way she carried on. Lou-Anne, on the other hand, didn't flinch. In spite of her sister's glaring example of where sex can lead – the maternity ward followed by years of drudgery – Lou-Anne is quite seasoned between the sheets. Of course, all the smut unfolds up in Eumundi, where the kind of men who interest her live. At Oakholme people have no clue about Lou-Anne's sex life, or indeed anything that might explode the narrow boundaries of their rigid minds.

Nathan did hunt me down on social media in the days following our steamy night wrapped up in his swag, but I'm not sure what our 'status' is. If you'd told me that morning that I was going to lose my virginity that night, I never would have believed it. It came as a shock to wake up in a paddock entwined in someone I'd only met the day before. At dawn my eyes slammed open onto dry blades of grass and a broken – yes, *broken* – condom a few centimetres away from the swag. The first thing I did after locating my cousin, whose side I was meant to be plastered to (according to my mother's pre-festival instructions) was to find a pharmacy. After a dose of the morning-after pill, I was nauseous for days. So it was a mixed experience. The earth didn't move. The condom did. But Lou-Anne had always warned me not to expect too much.

It felt good to get Nathan's message, though, and to know that it wasn't just a one-night stand for him. When I read his words, my stomach dropped, and then fluttered around my body like it was not attached to anything. He said that he was coming to the Easter Show to exhibit his family's cattle, and that maybe I should swing by. *Too bad. I'll probably be back in Barraba at Easter.* That was my nonchalant reply, which I kind of regret now.

When Jenny and I are done salivating over Parisian fantasies in the common room, I go back to the dorms. After a ten-minute wait in the eternal queue for the phone in Miss Maroney's office, I ring home. My dad answers in his usual chipper tone. Still excited, I tell him about the plans for Paris, but he doesn't really get it.

'What about university, Shauna?'

'I'm still *going* to university, Dad. I'd go to Paris during the holidays.'

'You don't even have a passport.'

'I can apply for one at the Barraba Post Office.'

'Don't you think you should be concentrating on your HSC?'

'Paris would be *after* the HSC.'

Dad's silent for a few seconds. Then he says, 'What do you want to go to Paris for anyway? You've already been to Toulouse.'

Aaaaargh! I could scream at him, but I don't. God, it drives me crazy that he has so little understanding of my life. He has no idea about how things work, even when they're basic, and even when I spend time explaining them. He may be in Barraba and I may be in Sydney, but we are a universe apart. He and Mum live in a jar with the lid screwed on tightly, and if I still lived with them, I'd never go further than the lid.

'Come on, Dad…who *wouldn't* want to go to Paris?'

'Well…I suppose if you had the money…' He tries to rally some enthusiasm. 'Yeah, I s'pose it'd be an interesting place to visit. I'd like to have gone, if I'd had the opportunity.' He clears his throat.

My dad's a nice bloke, a softie, a pushover even. He may be a big, burly, bearded truck driver, but there's nothing tough about him.

'How's Mum?'

'Oh, she has her spells. She still sleeps a lot.'

'Has she been doing much painting?'

'She finished a beautiful tropical fish painting last week. It's huge. I'm taking it into the bank tomorrow to see if they'll buy it. They'd be crazy not to.'

Lately Mum's been selling some of her work to local businesses. She makes the most amazing paintings, using tropical colours, a lot of blues and greens and purples. She never painted much before Jamie died, but she's obsessed with it now. I guess she has more free time because I'm at boarding school.

'Do you want to speak to her?' Dad asks.

I don't know exactly why, but I find it hard to speak to Mum on the phone when I'm at Oakholme. I always get emotional, on the edge of tears, and there's always this queue of impatient, aggressively sighing boarders waiting just outside the door. Sometimes they knock and yell exhortations to hurry up. (Sometimes I do, too!)

'Nah, don't worry. I don't want to bother her. Tell her about Europe, though?'

There's a short pause. Then: 'I thought you wanted to go to Paris?'

Oh my God...

I tell him I love him and hang up. I fling open the door of Miss Maroney's office and see that Olivia Pike's next in the queue. She looks shocked to see me, then afraid, and finally airily contemptuous. I stalk past her and trot up the stairs past the painting of the old perv Reverend Doctor Sterling McBride.

It's been a few weeks since my first meeting with Olivia and we've managed to avoid eye contact since then, in spite of living, studying and eating in the same building. Sure, I've seen her around, watched her try to but not quite fit in with the other young boarders she bunks with, but I still haven't made any attempt to talk to her. Bugger her. The other day I noticed her heading into the sick bay with the nurse, Mrs Davis. She looked over her shoulder in terror at me, but said nothing. It probably won't be long until Olivia scuttles back to wherever she came from.

When I get to my dorm room, I sweep up an armful of French books and head back downstairs to the prep. hall. The whole top floor of the building is dedicated to dorms, and downstairs are 'service' rooms, like the dining room, the rec. room, the offices and good old prep. hall. Prep. hall is a theoretically quiet, peaceful place where boarders can go to do their homework. It has all the outer dressings of study – desks, chairs, computers and printers – but precious little actual homework ever gets done there. It's more of a place to congregate with friends and rake over the daily muck before dinner.

Almost everything at Oakholme – the rooms, the decor, the furniture – is old. There's some nasty synthetic-looking blue carpet in the library that must be from the eighties, but everything else is antique and ornate. In the prep. hall, there's a magnificent crystal chandelier hanging overhead, but no one ever looks at it. The good taste that the Oakholme parents pay for is largely wasted on its students.

This is the conversation I walk in on when I enter prep. hall to join my posse – Lou-Anne, Indu and Bindi: 'One day I just decided where my eyebrows would go and I had the rest of my face lasered.' Bindi raises the highly arched, impeccably sculpted eyebrows in question.

'I detest the very idea of it,' says Indu, who has a basic philosophical objection to depilation. 'What if one day in the future you decide you want to regrow your eyebrows?'

'Why would I want to do that?'

Indu looks pensive for a moment. 'What about when you're a granny?'

'You think I'll want a monobrow when I'm a granny?'

'I think that perhaps you'll want to look a little less quizzical than you do right now.'

Everyone, including Bindi, cracks up. I plonk my French books on the table.

'Bindi, you are over-groomed,' declares Indu, leading to more uproarious laughter.

'She means naturally beautiful,' adds Lou-Anne.

They're both right. Bindi is naturally beautiful, with huge eyes, high cheekbones and an elegant, aquiline nose. But she also has eyeliner tattooed on and she straightens and lengthens her naturally curly hair – all of which she gets away with in spite of the school rules against make-up, perms and hair

41

extensions. I suppose the school can't force you to wipe off things that are semi-permanent or irreversible.

Still chuckling, I open my French novel, *L'Étranger* by Albert Camus.

'I don't know how you can read that,' says Lou-Anne.

'I can't read it while you're talking to me.'

'Why would anyone want to read a book written in French?' Lou-Anne continues.

'Well, it doesn't get into my head through osmosis,' I tell her. 'I have to read it.' I glare pointedly at her Christian Studies textbook. 'I think you'll find the same applies to the study of religion.'

'What's osmosis?' asks Lou-Anne seriously.

Indu and I share a subtle eye roll.

Indu's in Year 11 like Lou-Anne, and she's pretty bright. Sometimes I wonder what will happen to Indu and Lou-Anne when Bindi and I leave at the end of the year. Will they become best friends? Will they take to their new dorm buddies? I try to imagine what it will be like for Lou-Anne to suddenly lose me. Next year I'll be at university during the semester and, hopefully, overseas with Jenny during the holidays.

Jenny and Lou-Anne have a frosty relationship – more of a non-relationship actually. They don't have a thing in common except me. Lou-Anne is my all-time best friend, but during school hours Jenny often trumps her. I downplay the friendship with Jenny to avoid Lou-Anne getting huffy. Jenny, on the other hand, seems to understand that I'm closer to Lou-Anne and doesn't hold it against me.

I go back to *L'Étranger* and try to read, but Paris creeps into my brain.

Jenny and I had the time of our lives in Toulouse at the end of Year 10. Even though it was the middle of winter and freezing like we'd never known, we loved it. Jenny said that she felt glamorous, like the star of an old movie. I fell in love with the city for different reasons. In France, I had this feeling of being unknown, and I liked it. No one knew me or anything about my past. No one made any assumptions about my character. Shopkeepers didn't follow me around the shops. Commuters didn't stand in the aisle rather than sit down next to me. I felt free. I liked the indifference, the sense of being just another foreigner. Being a foreigner in a foreign country, as opposed to being a foreigner in my own country.

I read the same paragraph of *L'Étranger* six times before surrendering again to my daydreams.

4

In French this year we're reading a short story called *Boule de Suif* by a nineteenth-century French writer, Guy de Maupassant. The title literally means 'Ball of Fat', and it's about a group of people who flee the German-occupied city of Rouen in a stagecoach during the Franco-Prussian War. Among them is the *Boule de Suif* herself, a chubby prostitute called Elisabeth. All the other 'respectable' passengers look down on her and ignore her until she produces a basket of beautiful food, which she generously shares with them.

The group is then captured by a German officer, who agrees to release them only if Elisabeth has sex with him. At first the other passengers support Elisabeth's refusal to sleep with him, but as time passes, they put more and more pressure on her to do it so they can leave. When she finally goes to bed with him and they're allowed back into the stagecoach, the respectable passengers go right on ignoring her and in the end refuse to share their food with her.

Only in French class would the pristine minds of Oakholme College students be exposed to a book about a prostitute who does the wild thing with a German officer for a leave pass. I think that Mrs Green and the other high-ups would be shocked if they knew. *I* was shocked when I read it over the weekend.

'What's this book really about?' asks our French teacher, Mademoiselle Larsen. She scans the room, looking for shrinking students to terrorise. 'Tell me – in one sentence.'

A few words about Mademoiselle Larsen – she's the J-Law of the Oakholme staffroom. She's a leggy, shapely glamour-puss who rocks a platinum blonde bob, but otherwise doesn't try too hard. Jenny's mum heard through the grapevine that Mademoiselle was more or less forced to resign from another Sydney private school because she invited her girlfriend to a musical performance. I don't know whether it's true and I really don't care. Oakholme would care, though, believe me. Religion is a big part of school life. We have several chapel services a week and Christian Studies is a compulsory subject until the end of Year 11. Saucy business, especially if it's homosexual, is frowned upon, to say the very least.

Mademoiselle Larsen's great value if you take her in the right spirit. She rules our French classes with *un poing de fer* (an iron fist), but never raises her voice or punishes anyone. The worst you can expect from her is ridicule or some scathing and probably vulgar comment muttered in French. Somehow that's even worse than Red Marks or detention.

'Keli Street-Hughes, you're looking particularly guilty this afternoon.'

Everyone turns to Keli. She trots out her nauseating gap-toothed grin. In spite of still not being able to speak French convincingly after five years of classes at a very expensive private school, Keli annoyingly manages to maintain her status as one of Mademoiselle Larsen's favourites. She has a drawling, bogan charisma whose appeal I'll never understand. The one thing I'll concede is that her French accent is pretty good. She seems to get by just by pronouncing English words like Inspector Clouseau. Even I grudgingly admire that brand of sass. Very grudgingly.

'Mademoiselle Larsen, I hope you're not suggesting that I haven't read the book.'

Last year, when we were reading *Les Liaisons Dangereuses* (Dangerous Liaisons), Keli made the mistake of confessing that she'd only ever watched the movie.

'I wouldn't dream of it, Keli. So tell me, in a nutshell, what the book's about.'

'It's about a whore' is Keli's deadpan response.

Everyone except me cracks up. Even when I think Keli's funny, I can never bring myself to laugh. I dislike her too much.

'That's a literally correct answer,' says Mademoiselle Larsen, 'but it's not very insightful.'

'You asked for a nutshell. There's your nutshell.'

Mademoiselle's withering gaze comes to rest on me. 'Shauna? What do you think? In one sentence.'

I know I'm not going to get a laugh, but I give it my best shot.

'It's about a group of people who consider themselves morally superior to someone unpopular, but when it comes to the crunch they're they ones who turn out to have lower moral standards.'

When Mademoiselle Larson smiles, her crooked overbite breaks through her painted lips. I know that I've delighted

46

her, and that's almost better than a laugh from the class. Pleasing Mademoiselle is kind of important to me. Possibly it has something to do with my early days in her classes, back when I was a sullen little turkey. I was spectacularly rude, and if there's one thing Mademoiselle can't stand it's bad manners. When I decided to be polite to her, though, it seemed like she'd decided to give me another chance. I suppose I want her to keep her good opinion of me, knowing she doesn't just hand it out no matter what.

'Bravo, Shauna. *Exactement*. It's a critique of French society at the time, isn't it? The people in the stagecoach are a macrocosm of French society. The political class. The clergy. Business people. They all consider a prostitute to be so far beneath them, but in the end they use her to get what they want.'

Mademoiselle grills a few more girls before throwing a question to the whole class. 'Consider some unpopular groups from our own society and how they're used by the media, politicians and others in power to advance their own interests. Can anyone give me an example?'

Jenny puts her hand up. 'Boat people. Refugees. Every election cycle they're used as a political football.'

Across the classroom Keli's gripped by an eye-rolling frenzy. Mademoiselle doesn't seem to notice. Keli's sour little flunkpuss, Annabel Saxon, puts her hand up.

'Yes, Annabel?'

'What about farmers, Mademoiselle?'

'I'm not sure about that. Farmers seem to be a fairly popular group in Australian society.'

'But Greenies accuse us of damaging the environment.'

'Climate change,' groans Keli with another eye roll.

'But if it weren't for farmers,' says Annabel, 'then *no one* would have food on their table. Greenies included.'

'They'd be eating witchetty grubs,' giggles Keli.

'Girls, you're on the wrong track,' says Mademoiselle with a note of irritation in her voice, 'and I think you both know it. Farmers are a well-loved and powerful group in Australian society. I'm asking you to consider people who are looked down on and discriminated against. Like boat people, as Jenny pointed out.'

'But boat people come to this country illegally,' says Keli. 'They commit crimes and chew up resources. Don't they deserve to be unpopular?'

Class discussions involving Keli always follow the same path. Everything boils down to her virtuous family and other people like them shouldering the burden of undeserving folk, like Greenies, boat people and *moi*. I'm getting really sick of it. As if Keli Street-Hughes's ever worked a day or paid a cent of tax in her life.

'Keli's right,' I say calmly, but inside I'm beginning to seethe. The rest of the class looks at me as if I've just lost my mind. In what circumstances would I be on the same side as Keli Street-Hughes?

'She's absolutely spot-on about boat people. Just look at the lowlifes, leeches and criminals who've landed on our shores since 1788.'

Keli fixes her narrow, yellow eyes at me. I fold my arms, refusing to break eye contact.

'Maybe we should *change the date*,' drawls Keli. 'Maybe we should change history, change reality, so that some people don't get their feelings hurt.'

'What about acknowledging the reality of Australia's history then?' I shoot back, my voice tremulous with anger. 'The decimation of my people by criminals from England!'

'How dare you call *my* people criminals!'

'Girls,' sighs Mademoiselle, 'this discussion has gotten completely off track, okay? Please turn to your novels and—'

'First of all,' preaches Keli, 'they were *convicts*, not criminals—'

'It's the same thing!'

'—and second, without us you'd be starving to death in the dust!'

Jenny grabs my arm and squeezes hard, just as I'm opening my mouth.

'Keli. Shauna.' Mademoiselle's voice is dangerously low. '*Ça suffit comme ça*.' (That's enough.)

'She's not worth it,' whispers Jenny.

Keli and I exchange homicidal glares for a good minute after everyone else has opened their novels to page thirty-six. When I look down at my book, my hands are shaking. Why, oh why, do I let this stupid bigot get under my skin?

When the bell rings, I wait until Keli and Annabel have left the classroom before sloping off to the dorms. I walk around in circles for a while, wishing I'd kept my mouth shut. Usually I ignore the scrubchooks, even when they're baiting me, but sometimes they make me so mad I can't help myself. Now I feel like I need to take a shower, and that's the problem

41

with getting into a fight with a pig. You get dirty, the pig gets dirty, but the pig enjoys herself.

About the only thing that makes me feel dirtier than confronting Keli Street-Hughes is cyberstalking her. It's a shameful habit, made only slightly less shameful by the fact that I occasionally do it with Jenny on her smuggled-in phone. Otherwise I do it on my parents' phones when I'm home during the holidays. It makes me feel pathetic and gross, but for some reason I'm compelled. I guess it's the thrill of getting a behind-the-scenes glimpse of someone who's seemingly bulletproof. I know people don't usually upload bad or incriminating photos, but I'm still hoping for a slip-up, a chink in her Tampon Princess armour. I haven't found anything yet, just a range of images of her blockish, ginger self pulling trout mouths and jug-jawed grins in various glamorous locations. *Keli Street-Hughes in the owners' box at the Melbourne Cup. Keli Street-Hughes at Tetsuya's for her nanna's birthday. Keli Street-Hughes in the Italian Alps at Christmas.*

Cyberstalking Keli Street-Hughes is like watching porn. It's titillating at first and then it just makes you feel sick and bored and like you never want to lay eyes on the real thing again. Yet in quiet and sometimes unhappy moments, when a phone is available, I find myself clicking on Keli's profiles. Instead of finding social proof of her inherent despicability, I find that she's got a zillion friends and followers who make overly kind comments about her mediocre looks and abilities. It's very vexing. And if she ever discovered the level of my online interest in her, I'd never be able to show my face on Planet Earth again.

From what I've been able to garner, Keli doesn't have a boyfriend, but she's often pictured online in the vicinity of her handsome, boofy-looking neighbour from Coleambally, Matt Adler. Matt goes to St Augustine's and is often spoken of in Keli's circles. He's a rugby hero and I get the impression that it's cool to drop his name. There are girls who follow the St Augustine's rugby teams around Sydney to watch their matches, and Keli is among them. I personally can't think of anything more boring than loitering on the sidelines like that, pretending to be interested in football when all you're really interested in is boys in little shorts. It's pathetic.

The bell for the next class rings in the distance, so I sling my bag over my shoulder and head for the staircase, determined not to let Keli or anyone like her get the better of me. It's ridiculous to care about the opinions of people I don't even like, let alone think highly of.

Later that afternoon, someone I do think highly of, Lou-Anne, gives an opera performance in the school chapel. She's practising for her live audition for Opera Australia, which will take place at the Sydney Opera House at the end of the year.

Unfortunately Lou-Anne suffers from stage fright and when she sings in front of more than a few people she gets the sweats and the jitters. This is obviously a problem she needs to get over before her big audition, so her singing teacher, Miss Della, is getting her to practise in front of small audiences first. The 'small' audience this afternoon is the whole of Year 12.

Lou-Anne's so big-boned and her speaking voice is so deep that you'd never think she could sing at such a high pitch. It's stunning to hear her produce sounds that should make the stained-glass windows shatter. It's times like these that the existence of God seems beyond dispute. Lou-Anne's voice is supernatural.

She's singing from Bellini's *Bianca e Fernando* with her back turned to the pews. For the moment, that's how she's coping with all the people. But near the end of the song, Miss Della takes her by her big shoulders and turns her around. She grimaces and closes her eyes but keeps on singing.

I can't help but glance across the aisle to Keli & Co, who are doing their utmost to avoid looking impressed. Arms crossed. Eyes studying the ceiling. Annabel says something to Keli and Keli sniggers. Talentless scrubchooks.

After the final note, Lou-Anne opens her eyes and says in her normal, deep voice, 'Was that okay, guys?'

The chapel erupts into laughter and applause. Miss Della frantically shushes us.

'We're in a chapel, girls!' she shout-whispers, as if Lou-Anne hasn't just tested God's ears and every pane of glass in the building.

The applause fades into murmurs, muted enough for me to clearly hear Keli make this comment: 'You can see the beads of sweat in her moustache.'

I know that she's talking about Lou-Anne. It makes me so angry that I want to throttle the lot of them, right here in the chapel. All the awe I felt listening to Lou-Anne sing leaves my body like breath after a good winding. Lou-Anne comes down the aisle, smiling, wiping her face dry with her shirtsleeves. I force a smile.

'My ears have died and gone to Heaven, Lou-Anne.'

5

I GET ANOTHER note in roll call. It's from SRF:

Shauna, see me now in my office.

I hope it's about the support courses at St Augustine's.
Maybe she wants to tell me that my parents have finally sent
in the permission slip.

'Shauna, where have you been?'

'I came as soon as I got the note.'

'No. I mean, where have you been as Olivia Pike's mentor?'

'Oh.'

'I met with her yesterday and she told me you hadn't
spoken to her since that morning in the withdrawing room.
And that was weeks ago.'

'Well, she told me she didn't want to talk to me.'

'And?'

'I assumed she wanted to do things under her own steam.'
I sound flippant, though I don't really mean to. I can tell that
Reverend Ferguson doesn't like my tone one bit. The soft
lines of her face have hardened. Her mouth is small and set.

'Why on earth would you assume that?'

I can't answer, and I don't think she wants me to.

'When you arrived at Oakholme College, you were just as brittle and abrasive as Olivia. You were just as closed off from people, from help. But that didn't mean you didn't *need* the help, did it?'

'No, Reverend Ferguson.'

'You've gone from a sullen introvert who couldn't spell or recite her times tables to one of the top students at the school. Did that happen because you were left to your own devices?'

'No.'

'No, it didn't. We worked hard to get you to come out of yourself. To think about something other than your own sorrow and your own problems.'

'I'll talk to Olivia,' I say, now feeling quite embarrassed. 'I promise.'

'You'd better, Shauna. Even though you're busy with your studies and about to get busier.'

'The revision classes? Did my parents sign the slip?'

'They sure did.' Finally she smiles.

At lunchtime, I scour the canteen queue for Olivia Pike. She's with a group of Year 8 boarders.

I don't beat around the bush. I wade through the queue right up to them.

'Olivia.'

'Yeah.' Her blue eyes flash icy daggers that aren't reflected in her voice, which stays light for the benefit of her friends.

'Come and talk to me once you've bought your lunch. You can come into the common room if you like.'

'No thanks.'

I stand over her, really *loom* over her. The icy daggers glow brighter.

I decide to play my trump card. 'If you don't come with me, who knows what might come shooting out of my mouth?'

'Okay,' she says, suddenly jelly-backed at the prospect of being outed. 'Just let me get my sandwich.'

Her tweeny friends huddle around her. *What does she want? What was that all about? Are you in trouble?*

She buys a ham sandwich and walks with me to the common room. We find a table in a quiet corner. She unwraps her lunch slowly, looking around the room as if it might swallow her. One thing I know about Olivia Pike: her veneer of aggression and arrogance is baking-paper thin. Between terrifying and terrified is a fraction of a millimetre.

'So how's Oakholme treating you? You seem to have made some friends.'

She bites into her sandwich, chews, swallows and scowls before responding. 'And I'd like to keep them.'

'I don't want to turn your friends away from you, believe me.'

'So leave me alone.'

'That's not possible.'

'Look, I'll tell Reverend Ferguson that we've been talking, okay? She put me on the spot yesterday. I didn't know what to say.'

'SRF wasn't born yesterday, my friend.'

'Who?'

'SRF. Reverend Ferguson's initials. Self-Raising Flour. That's what Lou-Anne and I call her.'

Olivia's dimples sink into her cheeks. What's that? A little smile? Some evidence of a sense of humour?'

'She'll know you're lying,' I say. 'She'll ask you what we talked about and you won't be able to lie quickly enough.'

'Try me.'

Now she's beginning to remind me of myself.

'Well, why don't I throw you a bone by covering some topics? Help you along with your fabrications.'

'I don't even know what that means.'

'Your lies, Olivia. Let me help you.'

She shrugs. 'Okay. Fine.'

'Where are you from?' I ask her.

'I'm from the Black Forest. Where are you from?'

'Barraba. New England. But my mum's people are from North Queensland. Now tell me where you're really from.'

She takes a long pause, as if silence could kill me. Then she blinks quickly.

'Bourke.'

'Bourke?'

'Yes,' she hisses. '*Bourke.*'

'I don't know anyone from Bourke.'

'Thank God.'

I could give up now, really I could. But then I think about that bright spot. The spark of humour. Where there's humour there's intelligence.

'So, Olivia . . . are the boys hot in Bourke?'

There's no smile, just an upward flick of her eyebrows. Then her face darkens. She looks down.

'I don't have a boyfriend,' she mutters. 'I've never had a boyfriend. Probably never will.' Her blue eyes move up to mine. 'You?'

I immediately think about Nathan O'Brien and start stammering. 'Well, not really. I mean, I've *had* boyfriends, but... I can't really be bothered with boys right now because I'm going to Paris next year. That's in France.'

'I know Paris is in France.'

I notice Keli Street-Hughes & Co saunter into the common room. They line up at the coffee machine and they all get the same thing. A cup of black coffee. They really are the biggest try-hards God ever put on this earth.

Keli surveys the room and Olivia cringes as her eyes settle on our corner.

'Hey, Ollie!' calls Keli stickily.

'Hey, Keli.' Olivia's smile is tight.

Buxom Keli comes up to our table armed with her long black and her long-black swilling crew.

'My buddy from Bourke!' She hugs Olivia's shoulders lightly and glares at me. I'm not quite cute enough to give her the 'Say thanks to your dad for me' line, but I wish I could.

'What are you doing in the common room with this article?' Keli says to Olivia. 'Is she lecturing you about identity politics?' She waggles her finger in Olivia's face and croons, 'Check your white privilege, Olivia.'

Olivia looks scared and lost. She clearly has no idea what Keli's talking about, but one of the Tampon Princess's pet bitching topics is identity politics. Apparently people like me take particular political positions just because we're Aboriginal or African or gay or whatever group we've decided to 'identify' with. As if someone who looks like me has any choice about which group they belong to. I don't get to decide! Usually other people choose for me the second they clap eyes on me.

I smile sweetly at Keli. Keli smiles sweetly back and shakes her head. She wants to say something crippling, but she's afraid of my response. I can tell. She's not in control anymore, and she knows it.

'You know the common room's for Year 12 students only,' she says eventually.

'I was just about to leave,' says Olivia, standing up. I stand, too.

Annabel coughs 'coon'. The rest of them snigger.

'Did you just call me a coon?' I ask.

Annabel looks suddenly terrified.

'She just coughed,' says Keli.

'You know guys,' I begin, holding onto self-control by the ragged tips of my fingernails, 'some of us were invited to a meeting in the withdrawing room last week to discuss HSC University Pathways. I was truly astounded to see none of you there. *Astounded*.'

'As if you were there for any reason other than affirmative action,' says Keli.

'As if I was there for any reason other than the fact that I've completed an HSC subject early.'

'They feel sorry for you because you're a...' She coughs.

I walk out, knowing I won't be able to stop myself from smacking her if I stay a moment longer. Olivia follows me, her eyes blazing with hurt and fear.

'Sorry about that,' I tell her.

'That's why I don't want you talking to me,' she says. 'Keli's my friend.'

'So next time we don't go to the common room.'

'There's not going to be a next time,' says Olivia, and she storms away, blonde ponytail swinging furiously behind her.

6

TODAY IS A shit pie. A tasty but thin pastry encasing a crap-tastic filling. I always walk around with a chest full of lead on this day, looking for something or someone to distract me, because a shit pie with no pastry is just a bucket of shit. It's the day of the first introductory support course at St Augustine's (pastry) and it's also the anniversary of the death of my brother, Jamie (filling).

Jenny Bean is crazy-excited. She hopes that the highly sought-after Stephen Agliozzo will be there. I hope he's not. I hate it when every girl and their sister flock around the same handsome guy.

In English class, Jenny keeps looking at the clock. Like, ten times a minute. It's really making the period drag.

She must have washed her hair this morning, because it smells strongly of apples. I can tell she's trying to make herself as appealing as possible to attract Stephen Agliozzo's attention. But attraction doesn't work like that, does it? If a guy likes you, he likes you, and apple shampoo makes no difference. Shit-flavoured shampoo might not make a difference either.

Finally the lunch bell rings.

'Only four hours to go,' chirps Jenny, with a final glance up at the clock.

'I don't think that Stephen Agliozzo's going to be there,' I say. 'I doubt that he has what it takes to do a uni subject *and* the HSC.'

Jenny pouts. She's going to defend the smug little prince, I just know it. She's such a fool for him.

'You're only saying that because he's so good looking,' she huffs. 'You're judging him by his appearance.'

'So are you.'

'What do you mean?'

'Well, you're not going gaga for his ugly friends, are you?'

'I'm following my heart, Shauna. Is that a crime?'

'You're following *something*, but it's not your heart,' I mutter.

'Shauna!' she gasps, clasping her hand to her mouth as if she were the one who made the off-colour joke.

'And no, following *that* isn't a crime either,' I add in a whisper.

Above her clenched hand and behind her smudged glasses, Jenny's eyes shine and crinkle. I can tell that she's up for a gossip-filled lunch together, but I excuse myself. I have a phone call to make. I have to call my parents and talk about Jamie, like I do every year on this horrible day.

I sneak into Miss Maroney's empty office. Well, to be honest, I don't sneak. I just walk the hell in because I don't care how many Red Marks I get today. I'm always reckless on the anniversary of my brother's death. It's a day when anything short of death doesn't seem worth worrying about.

By the time I've dialled my parents' number, there are tears running down my face. My voice is potholed when I speak to Dad. I've planned what I'm going to say, but it's hard to get the words out.

Two years ago, when he'd already been dead for three years, I decided that I would only tell funny or happy stories about Jamie on this day. We've raked over all the other stuff enough. Whether it was an accident or suicide. Whether Dad should have let him take the car out. Why the staff at the hospital told us to come and see Jamie without letting us know that he was already dead. How his face was unrecognisable.

'Do you remember when he put the box of rocks under the Christmas tree?'

Dad laughs. 'Yeah. How could I forget?'

Jamie liked to mess with my mind on occasions of gift giving. One year he put this beautifully wrapped present tied with curly ribbon under our tree.

'It's for you, kiddo,' he said.

Even though my eight-year-old self had total confidence in Jamie's fifteen-year-old self, I just had the feeling that the expensive-looking gift was nothing but a pretty box full of rocks.

'Is it a box of rocks?' I asked him.

'Oh no, kiddo. It's not a box of rocks.'

'What is it, then?'

'If I told you, it would ruin the surprise.'

In the week leading up to Christmas, my curiosity ran wild. I could spend an hour at a time handling the box, shaking it,

63

listening to it, weighing it in each hand. I fantasised about what it might be. Jewellery. Maracas. Amethyst crystals.

When Christmas morning arrived, I shot out of bed at dawn and ripped open the box. Lo and behold, the box was full of…

Not jewellery. Not maracas. Not amethyst crystals.

Rocks.

Jamie almost pissed himself laughing.

'I guess I shouldn't have thrown that rock at him, Dad.'

'It wasn't easy finding someone to stitch his lip on Christmas Day.'

'How's Mum?'

'Sleeping. She got up for a while this morning. Then she looked at some photos and went back to bed.'

The photos of Jamie are all we have left of him. Of his overbite my parents never had fixed. Of his eyes that sparkled when he smiled. Of his cherubic nose and lips. Of his coltish, caramel limbs. What's Mum to do but look at photos and cry herself to sleep? What can anyone do?

'Can you wake her up?'

'I reckon it'd be better if I didn't.'

'Okay.'

I really do love my parents. I suppose almost everyone does. You love them even when they're on the disappointing side. It's shameful to admit that my parents have disappointed me, that I do blame them at least a bit for letting my brother's life go to hell, but that's the truth. They never stood up to him. They never said no. After the age of about fifteen, he was never told, 'No, you can't do that.' *No, you can't leave school. No, you can't stay in bed until midday. No, you can't have sleepovers with girls. No, you can't steal from us. No, you can't get pissed every night.*

All he had to do was slam the door or start swearing or punching the wall and my parents would throw their hands in the air and give in. It seemed like nothing was more important to them than keeping the peace and being liked, no matter what the price. My parents both had the crap beaten out of them as children, and they wanted Jamie and me to grow up without violence. We had happy childhoods and they never hit us, but they never really confronted us either. The boundaries got hazier the older and mouthier we got.

When Dad was away on the road and Mum was on her own with us, it was much worse. She could never get Jamie out of bed in the morning, or into bed at night, not even when he was quite young. Rather than have a fight with him, she let him stay up late watching TV or roaming the streets with his friends. It sounds so silly, but I think that's where Jamie's problems started – bed, and my parents' inability to get him into one. Once they lost control of that, they lost control over other areas, too.

Before he hit puberty, Jamie was a beautiful kid. He was fun and bubbly, and I looked up to him like he was Jesus. He was everyone's favourite – lively, funny and sweet. I was always a serious child and people didn't take to me the way they took to my brother. I never envied him, though, because he didn't seem like a child to me. To me, seven years his junior, he was a grown-up. There are photos of him carrying me on his hip when I was baby. According to Mum, he used to carry me around like that all day. When I was on his hip or in his lap, I was always happy. As early as I can remember, I was caught up in his charisma and had a huge appetite for his attention. He was my world, right up until he started to be a man.

I was flattened by Jamie's death, but I wasn't broken by it the way my parents were. I think it was because I'd already lost him a few years before he died. It's hard to say exactly when it happened. I think that the rock incident made me realise that he was making fun of me all the time. I've always hated being laughed at and I think that's where it comes from. At the beginning I did my best to laugh along with him and make out that the horrible pranks he played didn't hurt my feelings, but eventually I gave up. He became a first-class dickhead, and I say that not because of the thieving or the vandalism, but because he treated me like dirt.

In the end Jamie had no respect for my feelings or belongings. On the night of his death, he'd just stolen my computer after returning from a two-month stint in juvenile detention for burglary. Dad refused to confront him about it, but I had the nous to do it. Jamie called me a bitch and a slut and told me to rack off, before retrieving the laptop, throwing it at me, and then driving off in Dad's car. Dad gave him the keys.

Jamie had received counselling in juvy as part of his sentence, so my parents had some faith that he'd return to us in better shape. That's the only explanation I can think of for Dad letting him have the keys. It's a decision he's been punishing himself for ever since. Mum blames him a bit, too, but if it was his fault, then it was as much her fault. I wish they'd been stricter with both of us.

After all that's happened I still love Mum and Dad to bits. I see no point in giving them a hard time because they do a good enough job of that themselves. I try to be kind to them always, even when they drive me up the wall with their feebleness and ignorance. Even if you only have one smile, you've got to give it to the people you love, right?

After I get off the phone, I go back downstairs and look for Jenny. In her upbeat, love-struck mood, I'm hoping to find a different reality. Though she knows all about my brother's death, she doesn't know that today is the anniversary. I'd never burden her with that. I wouldn't even dump it on Lou-Anne's strong shoulders.

The Oakholme minibus hits the road later that afternoon, practically trembling with the anticipation of its occupants.

'It's the nerds' day out,' I joke to Jenny, and we both crack up. One of the science teachers, Miss Pemberton, is chaperoning us, and Mr Tizic, the school groundskeeper and handyman and apparently the only employee with a minibus licence, is driving. I really do feel sorry for him, getting unwanted, behind-the-scenes insights into the behaviour of overexcited teenage girls.

'Crank up the radio, Miss P,' someone shouts from the back of the bus.

Miss Pemberton, who, in spite of her youthful title, is a little old lady, does as she's told and we all sing along to some unspeakably lame chart-topper until we arrive at St Augustine's.

With such a mammoth build-up, there's no way the revision session can be anything but an anticlimax. There's no meet-and-greet, no cordial and Tim Tams, just a bunch of clean-cut boys in blazers sitting on one side of a classroom that has a million-dollar view of the harbour. It's not *that* view we're interested in, though. I can't help stealing a look at Stephen Agliozzo's rower's shoulders as I pass by. Jenny alternates between gaping at his Romanesque curly hair and fiddling with her pencil case.

'There you go,' she whispers, wriggling and squeezing. 'There he is! He *is* smart enough, after all.'

'*Paris*,' I remind her in a whisper.

One of the St Augustine's teachers, who introduces himself as Dr Peters, hands out a roadmap of Introduction to Legal Systems and Methods and a proposed study timetable, then gets right to the point. He talks about the style of assessment at university and how it differs from the HSC.

By the end of the hour, my brain's starting to hurt and Jenny still hasn't stopped looking at Stephen Agliozzo. Miss Pemberton manages to corral us back into the bus, avoiding even minimal fraternisation with the opposite sex.

'I thought you were *wonderful* ambassadors of Oakholme College,' she sighs as she counts heads in the minibus. 'You comported yourselves with grace, dignity and intelligence.'

The phrase 'ambassadors of Oakholme College' is often bandied around, usually during assemblies and by Mrs Green. It used to irk me that I should be an unwilling representative of a school I didn't fit into, a school that felt so sorry for people like me that it waived my fees, but now that I'm a seasoned old biddy of seventeen, I'm beginning to see why it matters. Behaviour matters. Manners matter. Even when people who have no manners seem to rise to the top of the pile, it's about what *you* do.

Actually I think that Miss P is just happy to have all of us back on the bus in one piece. The teachers are always so tense at 'mixed' events like these, and I'm sure it's a contributing factor to the rampant boy craziness. The politeness and etiquette have a tension, an edge of danger.

The excitement in the minibus on the trip back to Oakholme is just as loud and flappy as it was on the trip to St Augustine's. It's hard not to get caught up in it, because the trip to St Augustine's wasn't just about Year 12 boys in blazers, it was also about our future. A future that's becoming wider, further-flung and less fathomable. It's giddy-making.

As we drive along New South Head Road, I look out onto the harbour, shimmering brilliantly under an early autumn sun. The sun usually shines on the anniversary of Jamie's death, or something wonderful happens. It's like the world is mostly cruel, but just kind enough to think of something to stop me losing all faith. If I believed in magic, I'd say that Jamie was trying to cheer me up. Or rub my nose in it.

On this day and many others each year, I want to forget about Jamie's anger. I don't want to think about the three-day benders and the fights in the street and the Children's Court. One of the reasons I try to invoke good memories on this day is to crowd out the bad ones. My brother was a lovely kid who became an angry young man. My parents didn't know what to do with his anger, how to channel it or break it down. There was nowhere for his fury to go except around and around our house and finally into a gum tree.

69

Even some of the happy memories have angry roots. Why fool a little kid with a box of rocks for Christmas unless you're mad at the world? He obviously wanted me to taste the disappointment he felt all the time.

Still, today, the sun is shining. And I will believe that it's Jamie trying to make it up to me.

Then we get back to Oakholme, and just as I'm powering past the reproving eyes of the Reverend Doctor Sterling McBride, Miss Maroney catches me on the staircase. She's in her netball gear and seems to be in a rush.

'Phone call for you this afternoon from someone called Nathan O'Brien.' She can't help but smirk as she says his name. 'Number's on the call register. You can phone him back, but no more than five minutes, okay? The queue's huge.'

At times like these it gets up my nose that the girls who can afford their own phones aren't allowed to use them. I have an important call to make to a cute boy, and I have to wait for everyone else to finish their banal conversations.

I force myself to go upstairs and unpack my bag before running (almost squealing) back down to Miss Maroney's office, my friends trailing and teasing me. Like everyone else in the dorm, they know about Nathan's call.

Today's been quite the shit pie. Very high quality pastry. At Oakholme College there is nothing quite so hallowed as getting a phone call from a Real Live Boy. Especially if you're not around to take it.

7

On Saturday after prep. the powers-that-be at Oakholme College release us boarders from captivity and we're free to hit the mean streets of Sydney in our civvies. All we have to do is sign out and be back by six.

Lou-Anne, Indu, Bindi and I pile into Bindi's brother's Alfa Romeo and hit the road.

Bindi's at the wheel. She has her learner's permit and her brother, James, is helping her notch up some hours. It's not a relaxing experience for anyone concerned. Bindi's not one of those calm drivers, and it doesn't help that James shouts at her while pumping an imaginary brake with his Bruno Magli boot and occasionally grabbing the steering wheel. Lou-Anne, Indu and I sit stiffly in the back seat trying to avoid injury and nausea as the nipple-pink Alfa lurches and swerves, sometimes across more than one lane, around the eastern suburbs of Sydney.

'Why do you keep accelerating to sixty and then braking back down to fifty?' barks James, his forehead popping sweat. 'Why not take your foot off the pedal when you hit fifty?'

'I *never* go past fifty!' Bindi shrieks in reply. 'It just looks like I do because you're seeing the speedo from an angle.'

James whips around to face us. 'Did she go past sixty, girls?'

We all shrug. James rolls his eyes. 'I'd like to get to Bondi Beach in one piece.' He turns to face the front again. '*Bindi!* You just ran a stop sign!'

'I did not!'

'There was a stop sign back there. There's been a stop sign there for the last ten years.'

'Well, they must have moved it,' hisses Bindi.

James pumps the imaginary brake again and sulks. 'Yeah, they must have moved it,' he mutters sarcastically.

James and Bindi are the eldest and the youngest of four Coroneos children. James's a lawyer, and the middle siblings, Anastasia and Nick, are law students. Somehow Bindi's dad, who works on a strawberry farm in southwestern Sydney, has managed to pay for their education. Bindi's mum died of pancreatic cancer a few years ago and her father shacked up with a 'skippy' woman Bindi refers to as The Skank. That's why Bindi's at boarding school. She can't stand to be under the same roof as The Skank. During school holidays she gets passed between her brothers and sisters. Apparently it's very normal in Greek families for children to completely reject a step-parent like that. My uncle Mick, Andrew's father, is Greek, so I understand a bit about their culture.

I don't think I've ever met siblings as close-knit as the Coroneoses. Bindi talks to all of them every day (frustrating for those behind her in the boarding house phone queue) and even though about half their conversations are fights, they absolutely have each other's backs. I suppose one disadvantage of being so close to your family is that sometimes it stops you from needing close friends. With Bindi, I always feel that there's a barrier between us that has less to do with skin colour and more to do with a lack of interest on her part. She prefers, and is more loyal towards, her family, and that's that. But she's still great fun to be around, and no fool either.

We make it to Bondi a little worse for wear. Because there's never any free parking at the beach, we leave the car in the driveway of a colleague of James's. Bindi takes out said colleague's letterbox on the way in, though it's as much James's fault because he grabs the wheel while she's turning.

'That's the most appalling driving I've ever seen!' roars James while examining the scratch on the bonnet mournfully.

Bindi, Lou-Anne, Indu and I grab our satchels and hightail it down to the beach.

'You'd better be back here by five,' James yells after us, 'or I'm leaving without you!'

James would *never* do that.

'And you'd better not be meeting any boys here, or I'll call all your parents!'

He'd never do that either.

'God, how does he know?' I whisper to Bindi.

'He has two sisters and two daughters,' she explains. 'He knows everything. He won't call your parents, Shauna. Don't worry.'

The fact is, this whole girls' day out at the beach is just a big cover for my date with Nathan O'Brien. When I plucked up the courage to call him back earlier in the week, he told me he was coming to Sydney to visit his cousin, who lives in Surry Hills, and suggested that we 'hook up'.

It was very weird speaking to him after all that time. He sounded different on the phone, older but less confident. Maybe it was nerves. I was really jumpy, too. My words spilled out fast and loud. I blathered about the HSC, about Paris next year. I didn't know what else to talk about. All the topics I could think of seemed either too big or too small, considering what we'd already done.

'And what about you?' I asked finally, almost panting, having spent myself on my own soliloquy.

'Next year?' he said in his quiet, soft-edged drawl. 'Next year I'm coming to the city.'

'*This* city? Sydney, you mean?'

'Yeah. I'm going to study agriculture at Sydney Uni. I'm going to flat with some mates from school.'

'I thought you hated Sydney?'

'I do, but you've got to get an education somewhere.'

'And you're going to go back to your parents' farm after that?'

'Well, maybe...see, Shauna, I want to work in agriculture, but I don't want to work on a farm all my life. I see the way my parents work, and it's not what I want.'

Even though I was so jittery that the receiver was slipping in the sweat from my palm, it was nice to hear a slow country voice. Try as I might, though, I couldn't moderate my own voice. Afterwards, I thought I'd sounded clipped and snotty. Obviously Nathan didn't mind too much because he made a date to meet me at the beach. Little does he know that all three of my dorm buddies are coming with me for moral support. I don't know that I would have had the stones

74

to show up by myself. I mean, Nathan's a Wrangler-wearing country boy, maybe not of Keli Street-Hughes's calibre, but he's reasonably well-off. His type and my type don't mix. Not often, anyway.

Whenever I think about the last time I saw him, in his swag, my cheeks get hot. I can't picture him exactly, but I do remember his light blue eyes and the way his eyelashes and eyebrows matched the sand blondeness of his untidy hair. I remember how big his shoulders seemed when his shirt came off, compared with his waist.

It's a beautiful afternoon, maybe one of the last hot afternoons before the weather turns, and the crescent-shaped shoreline is sparkling. Every tourist and their dog are out today, but the girls and I find a patch of hot white sand to lay our beach towels on. As usual, we all spend a moment taking stock of the thin, blonde, bikini-clad women around us before stripping down to our bathers. Of the four of us, Bindi is the only one who can get away with a bikini, mostly because what's up top comprehensively distracts the eye from any imperfections below. She's blessed and she knows it.

'How do they do it?' Lou-Anne demands of no one in particular as a pair of two blonde beach babes saunter past without an ounce of fat to jiggle. 'I could starve myself for weeks and still not look like that.'

'Don't worry,' says Indu. 'Black don't crack. In another twenty years we'll still look like we do now and they'll be walking melanomas.'

We all laugh, but we're a bit envious, too. Feminine beauty in the eastern suburbs of Sydney has startlingly narrow parameters, and all of us, except maybe Bindi, fall well outside them. It seems like every girl who has managed to squeeze herself into conformity is on this very beach right now. After a few minutes of checking out the overwhelming competition, Indu decides it's snack time and goes off in search of the waffle stand we saw on the beach a couple of weeks ago. Lou-Anne and I decide to brave the cool, busy waves. Bindi stays on the beach to police our satchels.

Both Lou-Anne and I are strong swimmers. We go out deep and float in the swell, with just our heads bobbing between the waterline and the sunshine.

'I don't even like the beach that much,' says Lou-Anne.

'Neither do I. Too much sand.'

'I just like the sea.'

'Me too.'

Lou-Anne brings her knees to the surface and then stretches out, floating on her back, her full, brown limbs slick with seawater, glinting in the sun like sealskin. She's the kind of person you have to look at from different angles and in different moods to appreciate. When she's uptight or defensive she could be mistaken for a Kings Cross bouncer, but when she's relaxed and unselfconscious she looks like an island princess.

We float on our backs for a while and then swim all the way out to the shark net, where there aren't many people. It's not rough, but there's still a swell, and by the time we swim the length of the net and then back into the breakers, we're both breathing hard.

'Oh my God,' puffs Lou-Anne.

'I know. I'm really unfit, too.'

'No, I mean, oh my God, there's your boyfriend, next to Indu!'

I look up to the shoreline, and oh my God, there he is. Standing next to Indu in his khaki shorts, a button-down shirt and boat shoes, looking white-legged and aggy and shy. Farmer's day at the beach. It's kind of cute.

I texted Nathan on Bindi's phone in the car on the way, suggesting we meet at the Bondi Pavilion, but if there was a reply I didn't see it. Now here he is, in the flesh, and so am I.

It's not easy to emerge from Australian breakers with grace, and I am living proof of this. I rise from the shallows like some sea monster, my coral one-piece askew, my long, black hair twisted and bunched with sand and seaweed.

'Hi, Nathan!'

'Shauna.'

It turns out that Nathan, having arrived early, decided to buy a waffle and met Indu in the queue at the waffle stand. They got talking – one of Indu's many talents is striking up conversations with strangers – and they worked out they were both here to hang out with the same girl. Me.

He tells me all this, oozing politeness and kindness, as we walk together to the pavilion steps where we sit side-by-side at a respectable distance.

It's weird. The last time I saw Nathan I wasn't wearing any pants. Now I'm the picture of beachside modesty, with a towel pulled up to my armpits. Nathan looks into the surf and bites into his waffle.

'I forgot what the beach smelled like,' I tell him, sniffing the salt on my own shoulders. 'I haven't been here for ages.'

'Why did you want to meet here?' he asks.

I shrug. 'I haven't been here for ages.'

He laughs and offers me some of his waffle. I lean over and take a bite. My wet shoulder leaves a print on his t-shirt.

'It's good.'

'So why did you bring your friends?' he asks. 'Safety in numbers?'

'Well, I don't have a car. My friend drove us.'

'I could have picked you up from school.'

I shrug, smiling stupidly.

We both look out over the water. I don't know what to say to him, and he probably doesn't know what to say to me either. If only we'd gotten to know each other before sleeping together, things would be flowing a lot more smoothly, I'm sure of it. Where do you go from sex on the first night? Anything you say after that will probably just sound like phony small talk. I'm beginning to think that, in spite of all the hype, sex is the easy part. I think about the sex and its aftermath – the morning-after pill and twenty-four hours of gut-wrenching nausea. It wasn't very romantic.

'So Paris next year, Shauna? And studying journalism?'

'Maybe. Hopefully.' I wipe the chocolate sauce from the corners of my mouth self-consciously. 'And agriculture for you?'

'Doesn't sound very glamorous in comparison, does it?'

'I love animals,' I blurt.

'You should really come to the Easter Show and meet my cows.'

This conversation could be among the World's Most Boring. I realise that I'm at least half responsible for its shortcomings.

'Do you want to go for a swim?' I suggest limply.

'I think I'll let the waffle settle.' He turns his head and looks at me. I glance at him, catch his eye briefly, and then look back out to sea. 'Listen...' he begins apprehensively.

'Sorry about my friends, but I—'

'Your friends are fine. I just wanted to apologise for that night.'

'Oh, don't worry about—'

'No, listen. I had a great time with you, but you should know that it was my—'

'Look, you don't need to—'

'*First* time, Shauna. It was my first time. So I hope I didn't disappoint you.'

'You didn't,' I lie. Amazing! I was so afraid that *I* had disappointed *him*.

'So maybe I'll get another chance sometime,' he says, blushing. 'I wanted to talk to you but you did the dawn dash on me.'

He smiles at me, his eyes light and creased at the edges with fun. I grin and cringe.

'I had to go and find my cousin Andrew. I was under strict instructions to stay by his side the whole night.'

'I guess you broke that rule.'

'On the whole I break a lot of rules,' I say sassily. I realise that there's still chemistry between us, that I want to flirt with him.

'Is that right?' he says with a grin, leaning against my arm. I lean into him. 'You go to a pretty fancy school for someone who breaks a lot of rules.'

'Like you didn't go to a private school, Nathan.'

'Whoa, I never said that. But what makes you think so?'

'You're polite. You look kind of...I don't know...' I want to say *sure of yourself*, but he speaks for himself.

'I went to an Anglican boys' school in Tamworth. Not some posh harbourside hotel like Oakholme College. I'm middle class.'

'And you think I'm not?'

'I think you're pretty posh. Going to Paris next year and all.'

'Guess what my dad does for a living?' I challenge him. 'I'll give you a hundred bucks if you guess right.' I don't have a hundred bucks, but that's okay. He'll never guess.

'I dunno,' he says. 'Doctor? Lawyer? Banker?'

'Truckie.'

'So he owns a trucking company.'

'No, he drives a truck that someone else owns.'

'So how does he—'

'Pay for Oakholme College? He doesn't. I'm on a scholarship.'

'So who's paying for you to go to Paris?'

'That's a good question. Haven't figured it out yet. Maybe I'll get a job at the Barraba servo for a month. They're always looking for staff.'

We're both starting to relax now. I tell him about the challenges of getting to Paris on a shoestring. Then Nathan suggests we take a stroll on the boardwalk.

'Your friends have been staring at us this whole time,' he remarks with a chuckle. 'I can't take it anymore.'

Nathan clasps my hand as we walk.

'So your friend, the one I met at the waffle stand,' he says, 'she's Indian or Sri Lankan or something?'

'Her parents are Indian. They live in India but they want her to go to an Australian school.'

'And your parents?'

I wondered when we'd get to this. Nathan's from Kootingal, not far from Tamworth, where a lot of the blacks look more or less like me. Tall and lanky, but plump and luscious in the face. Now that he knows I'm not rich, he suspects that I'm Aboriginal, which was probably his initial impression, but now he's too afraid to ask. Maybe he's hoping that I'm half Sri Lankan. Boong girls and aggy boys don't go around together in Tamworth. Too late in our case, though.

I feel sudden terror at answering the question, truthfully or not.

'My parents met at a bar in Cairns. Mum was working behind the bar. Dad was a drummer in a band that was touring Queensland. Dad's people are from Barraba so when Mum got pregnant with my brother, they moved there so my grandmother could help with the baby. Dad gave up the drums and started driving trucks so they'd have a steady income. They were both really young.'

'Is the guy you were with at the music festival your brother?'

'No, that was my cousin, like I said.'

I still haven't answered his question, and now I kind of have an aversion to doing so. Why is it always a confession and never a claim to glory?

'You didn't have to get in touch if you didn't want to,' I tell him indignantly. 'I never expected you to.'

Nathan seems taken aback, but his tone remains polite. He's like my father in that way.

'Is that the kind of guy you think I am?'

'I don't know you very well.'

'That could change.' He squeezes my hand.

I don't say anything and he lets go of my hand. We keep walking. I feel hot in the face. Embarrassed when I know I shouldn't be.

'Did I say the wrong thing, Shauna?'

'Well, why don't you just come out and ask?'

'Ask what?'

'Whether I'm a coon. I suppose you already know the answer?' I'm suddenly fired up. 'Most racists do.' I regret the words even as they're coming out of my mouth.

Nathan stops in his tracks and turns to face me. He's angry. I can see his chest rising under his t-shirt. His cheeks go pink, but he doesn't raise his voice.

'I knew you were Aboriginal before I even asked you to dance on New Year's Eve. And I would never use that word. I can't believe you did.'

'I'm sorry.' He's shamed me! I've let him shame me! Now I'm breathing hard, too.

'I asked you to dance because I thought you were tall and pretty, and I like tall, pretty girls. When I kissed you, I could hardly believe someone as brainy and funny as you would kiss me back. And that's why I took you to bed, even though I didn't know what I was doing.'

I'm staggered by his words. I'm shocked that he likes me. Or liked – past tense, maybe. He turns around suddenly and starts walking back to where we came from. I follow him, beach towel billowing behind.

'I'm sorry, Nathan!' There I go apologising again. 'I thought you were asking about my parents because you wanted to know whether I was Aboriginal.'

'I just wanted to know about you in general. I'm not a racist and I don't like being called one. What are you going to do next? Get your big brother to bash me up?'

I stop suddenly on the boardwalk. 'My brother's dead.'

Nathan stops and swivels around. 'I'm sorry, Shauna.'

'Well, don't be.'

He stares at me for a few seconds, takes me in. Then his face softens. He gulps and then smiles.

'Why don't we start again?'

'Okay.'

'Come and see me at the Easter Show. Come to the cattle pavilion and meet my cows.'

That's quite an invitation. 'Can I bring my friends?'

'I'm sure they'll follow you even if you don't plan to bring them.'

He's probably right.

'I'll try,' I say.

He kisses me on the cheek.

'I have to go and meet my cousin on the other side of town now,' he says, looking at his watch.

I'm sure it's an excuse, but I don't blame him. Why did I let myself get so upset? He obviously likes me. Like, a *lot*. Why did I make it so hard for him?

By the time I make it back to my friends near the flags, Bindi's sunburnt and Lou-Anne's bathers are full of sand. No one's in a good mood.

'We ate your waffle,' says Indu sulkily.

'How long was I gone? It felt like five minutes.'

'It was an hour and a half!' they shout in unison.

8

I NEED TO be Olivia Pike's mentor like I need a hole in the head.

This afternoon we're meeting in the withdrawing room again. Reverend Ferguson delivers her personally and we sit like dining aristocrats at opposite ends of the long table. Our last meeting was mercifully cancelled due to Olivia's ill health, but that's not going to get me anywhere in the longer term.

Olivia hates my guts now. She hates me because I nearly scuttled her little friendship with Keli Street-Hughes. She hates me because I dobbed on her to Reverend Ferguson for not showing up yesterday. She hates me because I'm pieces of her.

'How was your day, Olivia?'

She sighs. 'Fine.'

'Fine?'

'Yep.'

'So how come you piked out yesterday? No pun intended.'

'Forgot.'

'Forgot?'

'Yep.'

'Anything you'd like to talk about?'

'Nup.'

'Come on, Olivia. Throw me a bone.'

'Why? Cos you're a dog?' She scoffs at her own nasty joke. The mouth on this thing! She sounds rough, too. I was rough at her age, but not this rough.

I wonder what has happened to Olivia to make her so spiky? I don't think I have a right to ask at this point, though. We're so far from being friends.

'Any plans for the weekend?'

'No.'

'Did you do anything last weekend?'

'No.'

I slap both my palms on the table hard enough to make Olivia flinch. She's embarrassed by her reaction and looks out the window.

'I went out on a date last weekend with a cattle farmer from Kootingal.'

She looks kind of intrigued. She shifts forward. I think I might be getting somewhere when—

'Do his parents know he's dating a boong?' she asks, grinning falsely.

'I don't want to hear you say that word again.'

'Boong. *Boong. Boong. Boong. Boong. Boong.*'

'Where'd you learn that word? Keli Street-Hughes? She coughs it onto my neck every second day.'

'Keli's nice to me.'

'You wait till she finds out you're acting.'

'You won't tell her. I know you won't.'

'You're right. I'm not going to tell her. But she'll find out anyway, believe me.'

I've hooked her now. Her eyes narrow. 'How?'

'It's written all over your lily white face.'

'What is?'

'*My name's Olivia Pike and I hate myself.*'

She shakes her head and folds her arms tightly across her chest.

'*I hate myself so much that I'm not going to give myself or anyone else a chance.*'

She titters through her nose.

'I've never seen anyone with self-esteem as low as yours,' I say.

'What about your friend with the man hands and the moustache?'

'Don't bring Lou-Anne into this. She's happy. She's going to be an opera singer. What are you going to be?'

'Nothing.'

'That's what I thought. Good luck with that.'

She sets her jaw and looks around the room. Only her eyeballs move.

'Is that it?'

'No, that's not it, unfortunately. Self-Raising Flour said we have to be here for not a moment less than half an hour.' I look at my watch. 'Only twenty-seven minutes to go.'

'I can sit here for twenty-seven minutes.'

I'd really like nothing more than to let this kid have it and walk out. But I know I'll have to see her again. And again. And another time after that. Reverend Ferguson will expect me to keep trying.

'Look, Olivia, while we're waiting, let's work out a way of making you pass for white.'

'I'm already doing a good job on my own.'

'Oh yeah? How many of the girls in your dorm room answer "nothing" when they're asked what they're going to be? "Nothing" is a dead giveaway, if you ask me. You've got to come up with *something*. There must be something you want to do. Me, for example, I want to study journalism and languages. Maybe even become a journalist.'

'Name one Aboriginal journalist.'

'Stan Grant.'

'Name two.'

I can't.

'So what are you saying, Olivia? That I shouldn't try?'

'I'm not saying anything. You do what you want and I'll do what I want.'

'So tell me what you want to do.'

'I don't know!' she shouts. This is as big of a rise as I've ever gotten out of her. 'I don't know what I want to do, okay? I'm not good at anything. I'm not smart. I don't even know what I'm doing here.'

'It's better than being in foster care, though, isn't it?'

Her face falls so hard that I want to take her in my arms. But quite quickly she seems to recompose herself, to gather herself around that tough knot of anger and get quiet and still.

Something has happened to her, I know it now. Something very bad. Maybe even worse than losing a brother.

'Guaranteed, Olivia, that every white girl in this school knows what they're doing here and feels entitled to be here.

If you want to keep passing for white, you'd better work it out. Or else the likes of Keli Street-Hughes are going to be on you like stink on poo.'

Olivia says nothing. She's back to her stiff little self.

'You're entitled to be here too, Olivia. You're entitled to get an education and get into uni and get a good job.'

'Fine.'

'I want to hear you say it.'

'I thought you didn't have a boyfriend?'

'What?'

She glares at me, challenging me.

'In the common room, you said you didn't want a boyfriend because you're going to flippin' France. Now you're going on dates?'

'I changed my mind,' I say. 'A girl's allowed to change her mind, isn't she?'

Olivia shrugs. Shakes her head. Looks away again.

I get up and her eyes follow me around the room. I go to the bookshelf and pull out a copy of the school yearbook. I sit back down and start reading. The yearbook's three years old. I flip to my class photo and find myself. I'm standing up the back because I'm one of the tallest in the class. I look more or less the same as I do now. Thin body, chubby baby face, black hair pulled into a long, loose plait. I'm not half as pretty as Olivia, though.

'What are you doing?' she asks after about five minutes.

'Reading. It's more interesting than talking to you.'

'Thanks a lot.'

'Anger's very boring, you know. It's also very black. You're going to have to find another emotion if you want to pass for white.'

We stay there for the full half hour without another word. When Reverend Ferguson knocks on the door, I tell her to come in.

'How are you girls going?'

'We're having a great time,' I reply.

She lets Olivia leave and closes the door behind her.

'How are you going really?' Reverend Ferguson asks softly.

'She's angry.'

'I know.'

'What happened to her?'

'I can't tell you, Shauna. It's confidential. Obviously the school psychologist knows, but even she can't get a word out of Olivia.'

'Give her some time,' I say. 'She'll probably come good.'

I'm not sure I believe this, though. I think Olivia's going to scarper sooner rather than later. I hate to say it, but I'm rather hoping it's sooner. I'm literally sick at the sight of Olivia Pike. *Literally*. Ever since she arrived at Oakholme I've been feeling sick and exhausted. It must be an allergic reaction. Or maybe it's from the coal dust from that damn fireplace in the withdrawing room.

9

I WAKE IN the dead of night to a blood-curdling scream.

There's a trill to it, a certain high-pitched vibrato that could only be produced by the specific anatomy of a coloratura soprano's throat.

I sit up and stare terrified into the blackness.

'Lou-Anne!'

She screams again and the windows vibrate.

I see a ghost-like flash of white hair at the dorm room door before it slams shut.

Indu turns on her lamp and Bindi and I get out of bed and rush to Lou-Anne's bedside. She's crying and has her hand clamped over her nose.

'Something just bit my lip!' she sobs. 'A spider!'

'Omigawd! A spider!' Bindi echoes hysterically.

Indu pulls Lou-Anne's hand away from her lip as I turn on Lou-Anne's lamp.

'Your whole upper lip's covered in tiny red dots,' proclaims Indu. 'It's some kind of rash!'

'Yeah, from a spider bite,' says Lou-Anne. 'A bloody funnel web!'

I look down at the floor to see whether there's a rogue spider crawling around and that's when I realise that there's a rectangular piece of plastic stuck to the sole of my foot. I rip it off and hold it to the lamplight.

'That was no spider!' I announce. 'This is a wax strip with Lou-Anne's hair stuck to it!'

Everyone leans in for a closer look at Lou-Anne's bow of short, black hairs that were, a minute ago, attached to her upper lip.

'Omigawd!' shrieks Bindi. 'They took your moustache!'

'I don't *have* a moustache,' sobs Lou-Anne.

'Not anymore,' I mutter.

'But who?' cries Indu. 'Who would do such a thing?'

'I know who,' I say, scowling as I recall the whitish blonde hair that whipped around the corner in the second after Lou-Anne's scream rent the air.

I storm into the hallway, ready to rip someone into pieces. That someone is standing across the landing right in front of Keli's room. She looks back at me over her shoulder and then disappears into the dimly lit room. The lights go off. Raucous giggles ensue.

'*Did you do it? Did you do it?*'

Now I understand. Olivia just tore off Lou-Anne's moustache to impress Keli Street-Hughes and her cabal of scrubchooks.

'*Where's the moustache? What did you do with it? We could stuff a doona!*'

More giggles. How dare they! As my hand, trembling with rage, reaches for the doorknob, a larger, more solid hand descends on my shoulder.

'Shauna, don't do it.'

It's Lou-Anne, with tears in her eyes. I can see her ravaged upper lip glowing red in the dim light of the hallway.

'I can't let them get away with that!'

'You'll be the one who gets into trouble. So just leave it.'

'It was that little shit, Olivia Pike,' I tell her, loudly enough to be heard on the other side of Keli Street-Hughes's door.

'Leave it, Shauna.'

I want so badly to stomp into that room, throw on the lights and bawl those girls out until I'm hoarse, but Lou-Anne takes me by the elbow. I have to respect her wishes, I know.

We all get back into bed, and after a few minutes of whispered outrage and the application of some vitamin E oil, the room falls silent. But my mind is far from silent. I stew so badly that Lou-Anne tells me to stop stewing.

'I can't fall asleep to the sound of angry sighing, Shauna.'

'How's your lip?'

'Bald.' A few seconds later she adds, 'Sore.' Then I hear some sniffles that could be crying, but I know when and when not to make a fuss of Lou-Anne. She's embarrassed, so I leave her alone.

Eventually everyone else falls asleep, but I remain very much awake. I am so angry that I could burn down the scrub-chooks' henhouse. How could Olivia do that to Lou-Anne? Lou-Anne, who's never hurt a fly. Lou-Anne, who never says anything nasty about anyone. Lou-Anne, who *defends* Olivia when I say mean things about her.

I toss and turn, ruminating. Then, at around three in the morning I get out of bed, open my pencil case and withdraw my scissors. They are in fact my mother's former sewing scissors and they can make it through just about anything. Diamonds, probably.

Silently, I slide like a serpent from beneath my doona, out of the dorm room and into the hallway. I cross the foyer and sneak into the darkness. I go all the way down the end to the bad real estate, where the younger girls sleep, and with ever-so-quiet tippy-toed steps, slip into her room. It's obvious Mr Tizic keeps the hinges very well oiled, because not the slightest scritch disturbs the air as I push the door open. All the Year 8 boarders are asleep. Two of them are snoring loudly. I go to Olivia's bed. She's lying on her back with her blonde hair fanned out on her pillow. Ever so gently, I lift a thick lock of hair – about a third of it – from the crown of her head and swiftly lop it off, close to the scalp. She puts her hand to her forehead, mutters something and rolls over, without waking up.

It's revenge enough that Olivia will look in the mirror in the morning and see Friar Tuck, but I decide that some finishing touches are necessary. So I also sneak into Keli's room and sprinkle Olivia's fine hair all over her bed. It's like the horse's head in the bed in the *Godfather* movie. Keli's going to wake up screaming. They both will.

'Some pretty strange things happened in the boarding house overnight,' snaps Miss Maroney the next morning. She's called a special meeting in the dining room after breakfast. 'If the girls responsible for this nonsense don't come forward before the first bell rings, I'm giving every single one of you a Red Mark.'

There's a flurry of furtive glances. I look at Olivia. Olivia looks at Keli. Keli looks at Lou-Anne. Lou-Anne looks at me. Whether four pairs of darting eyes attract Miss Maroney's attention or not is unclear. The bell rings.

'One Red Mark to each of you!' she roars.

One of the Year 7 girls bursts into tears.

Welcome to justice, Oakholme-style.

10

NATHAN HAS ONLY called me twice since our 'date' at the beach, but somehow everyone knows we're 'dating'. Having a boyfriend at Oakholme is kind of a big deal, especially for those who live in the boarding house. Not that many boarders have boyfriends. I mean, Lou-Anne's got a hunk up in Eumundi named Isaac, but he'd probably prefer to chew off his own face than call her at the boarding house.

One boarder who definitely doesn't have a boyfriend and wants one is our beloved scrubchook Keli. She talks about her neighbour, Matt Adler, so often that an outsider would think he *was* her boyfriend. However, during my time at Oakholme Master Adler has called Keli a total of zero times. To my knowledge, anyway. Which is not to say that she doesn't speak to him on Miss Maroney's phone. In these times of fourth-wave feminism, Keli feels completely free to stall the phone queue by calling Matt and talking about herself in this saccharine little voice that she never otherwise uses.

Jenny Bean gave me some interesting insights into Matt Adler's feelings for Keli after going to the second fortnightly Introduction to Legal Systems and Methods support class at St Augustine's last week without me. I'd been sick and dizzy that afternoon and Miss Pemberton wouldn't let me go. I really should have gone. I'm already way behind on the online reading and haven't even started the first assignment, but I've been feeling so rotten that I just can't do it on top of everything else.

Anyway, I assumed that Jenny would be lost *sans moi* in that St Augustine's testosterone pit, but apparently she struck up a conversation with one of Stephen Agliozzo's less attractive friends, Tom Something-or-Other. Stephen had told Tom, who told Jenny, who told me that Matt Adler wishes Keli would stop 'stalking' him. Apparently the last time she called the St Augustine's boarding house, Matt pretended to have a broken leg and said he couldn't get to the phone, because he'd already used the 'out at rowing practice' excuse too often.

Of course I relay this juicy piece of intelligence to my other friends during prep. late one afternoon. It's almost dinner-time. Keli's coven is in the back corner discussing something dreary in tones of great hilarity.

'How is that even *possible*?' shrieks Annabel Saxon.

The usual suspects and I are all huddled around our table discussing the undesirability of Keli Street-Hughes in hushed tones.

'Imagine waking up next to *that* every morning,' says Indu.

'You'd wake up orange,' chimes in Bindi.

We all break apart laughing, and Keli's group looks over at us. We don't care. We keep cutting up in barely whispering voices.

Then in walk some Year 7 and 8 boarders, including Olivia Pike. I hoped that she'd even out her hairstyle with some sheep clippers, but she's opted instead to pull the hair either side of her baldpate into a topknot. It's 'passable', to fire her own words back against her, but to me she looks like some denounced detractor from the Chinese Cultural Revolution with half their head shaved. What a traitor! I was right about her from the beginning. Anyway, I feel like she's been justly served and that our frosty relationship can resume as normal during our next meeting.

'So how's it going with Nathan?' Bindi asks at regular volume. She knows full well how it's going with Nathan, but this is prep. and it's a public conversation.

'I might go and pay him a visit at the Easter Show,' I answer casually.

'I'm in,' says Indu.

'Me too,' says Bindi. 'Is he entering the wood chopping competition?'

We, and all the girls around us who've been eavesdropping, burst into uproarious laughter, even though no one quite gets the joke.

'Nathan's handsome,' says Indu. 'I don't know about those boat shoes, though.'

'You should have seen him at the music festival in his cowboy boots and Akubra.'

'That's weird, Shauna,' says Bindi.

'Not when everyone's dressed the same way.'

'Or undressed the same way,' murmurs Lou-Anne.

I've been thinking about Nathan quite a lot since the day at the beach. It's hard to avoid it with my friends analysing every moment of our date. We've entertained every possible theory as to why he didn't want to go into the water, from shrinkage to an inability to swim. I know that we're *over*-analysing, but I do enjoy talking about him. There are certain details, however, that only Lou-Anne will ever hear.

I like Nathan and that scares me a bit. I have to watch what I say to him. I know I put my foot in it at the beach by accusing him of racism, but sometimes it's like I see it everywhere. And a lot of the time it really is there. When I was in Year 9, I had a boyfriend who I met at a science camp. His name was David and it was about as serious as it gets for a Year 9 camp romance, featuring exchanges of 'I love you', passionate sessions that involved tongue kissing and underclothes groping, and promises of staying together forever.

One weekend, David invited me to his house for lunch. I met his family and everything seemed to be going well. Then his mother asked me flat-out, 'And what's your ethnic background, Shauna?'

I didn't know what she meant.

'My ethnic background?'

'Where do your parents come from?'

'Barraba,' I answered.

'And where's that?'

'Have you heard of Tamworth?'

'Of course,' she said, 'but what I mean is, what country is your family from?'

I told her Australia. Then I told her that my dad's Kamilaroi and I've got Irukandji blood on my mum's side.

'You're Aboriginal,' gulped David's dad.

I swear, you could have heard an ant fart. David's parents looked at each other in shock. They didn't even try to hide their horror.

'And do you consider yourself Australian or Aboriginal?' his dad asked awkwardly.

How was I supposed to answer that? I muttered something about being both, knowing that it was the beginning of the end.

David never called me again. In fact, I never spoke to him again because whenever I called his house he wasn't there. Eventually I stopped calling. And I decided to avoid city boys forever. I call them 'city' boys and it makes them sound worldly, but they're really just flat-lawn suburban boys, whose parents' jar is just as small as my parents' jar, and with the lid screwed on just as tightly.

I'm glad that Nathan's from the country. It's one of many things I like about him.

The clock strikes six-thirty and, like a herd of hungry cows, everyone rises and thunders down the hall into the dining room. We've got this dumb system for working out who gets fed first. We each take a glass from the service bar and on the bottom of each of the IKEA glasses is a number. The lower the number, the further up in the queue you go. It's a clunky system, and I have no idea who started it or when, but it does work. It stops younger and less popular girls from being pushed around, and scoring the number three glass (numbers one and two were smashed before my time) is like finding the golden ticket in a Wonka chocolate bar. It's very democratic.

Tonight I pull a lousy number and I have to wait around for ages for some kind of stringy chicken dish. We always complain that the boarding house food is disgusting, and at the same time that the portions are too small! For some reason the dining room is a great place to whinge. Prep. hall is a forum for gossip and the dining room is the complaints centre.

At the back of the dinner queue, with my nose full of the smell of bad chicken, I'm jolted by a wave of nausea that makes me weak at the knees. Stuff comes up and I have to make a huge effort to send it back down.

'Shauna! Where are you going?'

'Bathroom,' I mutter to Lou-Anne on the way out of the room. 'I'm sick. I can't stand the smell.'

I hightail it up to our bathroom and this time I really throw up. I feel awful. I sway to my bed and flop down. When I look at the ceiling it spins, so I close my eyes.

I sleep for hours. Literally hours. It's after eight-thirty when I wake up. The first person I see when I open my eyes is Lou-Anne, who's pushed her bed closer to mine. She does that sometimes, if one or both of us are feeling fragile.

She's flat out on her belly copying word-for-word an *Othello* essay I wrote last year.

'How was your nap?' she asks flatly.

'Fine. I don't know what happened.'

'Nathan rang while you were asleep.'

'I'll call him back.'

'Don't forget to tell him you're pregnant.'

I nearly choke on my own nonchalant chuckle.

11

A MINUTE LATER, Lou-Anne and I are locked in the bathroom, arguing loudly.

'Who the hell do you think you are, keeping track of my periods?' I demand. Lou-Anne doesn't take a backwards step.

'I wasn't keeping track. We're usually in synch, Shauna. I didn't even notice it the first month, but last month I noticed you hadn't used any pads.'

'So you went rifling through the sanitary bin counting pads, did you?'

'I know when you're having your period, okay? You're always short of pads and you usually take a few of mine. And you have breakouts on your chin. There's been none of that since we got back to school. Think about it. It's nearly April.'

I don't want to think about it. But I pause. I lower my voice, knowing that Indu and Bindi could be gasping and palpitating with their ears pressed against the door.

'I'm not pregnant. I can't be. I took the morning-after pill.'

'Doesn't always work.'

'But I was sick for twenty-four hours.'

'So what? That doesn't mean it's worked.' She sounds uncertain. 'Does it?'

I actually don't know. I bought the pill at a pharmacy in Tamworth. That was three months ago. Easter holidays are coming up. The last time I had my period was over Christmas. I remember going Christmas shopping with Mum in Armidale and sloping off to the chemist to buy pads.

Lou-Anne is right. I've missed two periods. Which doesn't *necessarily* mean I'm pregnant.

'I've just been sick. My body's all out of whack since Olivia Pike got here.'

Lou-Anne shook her head. 'It's got nothing to do with Olivia Pike. It's called morning sickness.'

'But I'm sick all bloody day!'

'It's *called* morning sickness,' points out Lou-Anne, 'but it should be called all-day sickness. My sister was sick all day every day for the whole nine months.'

I burst into tears. How am I going to do the HSC feeling the way I do now? What if I have the baby in the middle of the exams?

I quickly do the maths. Suppose I am pregnant. My last period was around Christmas. That means the baby would be born at the end of September, maybe the beginning of October, which is right around the time of my exams.

Lou-Anne hugs me hard from behind.

'I can't have a baby,' I sob.

'Yes, you can,' she says calmly. 'You don't have to do anything. They cook themselves, and when they're ready to come out, they come out themselves.'

'But I can't do it at school. Not at *this* school. Can you imagine? The teachers...Keli Street-Hughes...'

I'm really crying hard now, tears rolling down my cheeks.

There's a loud knock at the door.

'Piss off!' snaps Lou-Anne.

'There's absolutely no call to use language like that,' comes Miss Maroney's voice. 'This door should never be locked. Now, is everything all right in there?'

'Fine,' says Lou-Anne tetchily. 'We'll be out in a minute.'

'You're getting two Red Marks, Lou-Anne, which makes three for you altogether,' says Miss Maroney. 'You'll be on Wednesday afternoon detention.'

Lou-Anne opens the door slightly

'Bloody cow!' she whispers. 'I should tell Mrs Green about her little pool parties.'

I walk to the sink, with Lou-Anne still clamped to my back, and look in the mirror at my puffy, tear-streaked face. I start to shake my head.

'I have no choice,' I say. 'No choice. I have to leave the school. Or have an abortion.'

'No, you don't, Shauna.' Lou-Anne lets go of me and turns to stand beside me, so that I can see her in profile in the mirror. 'What goes on under your uniform is no one's business but yours. No one will even know you're pregnant for a few more months.'

'And when they do?'

'Still none of their business.'

'But everyone will *talk*. I'll lose the scholarship. I'll probably get expelled. And my parents...'

'Let's just keep it quiet for now. Take it one step at a time.'

Lou-Anne takes my hand. I can't believe how level-headed she's being, but I sure do appreciate it. It makes me feel calmer.

'I'll get a test and make sure I'm really pregnant. I mean, maybe I'm not. Maybe I *am* just having an allergic reaction to Olivia Pike.'

We meet each other's eyes in the mirror and smile sadly. Lou-Anne really is the best of best friends. I know I don't have to tell her to keep the secret. She would never betray me, not in a million years. Not even to Bindi or Indu.

There is no easy way of going out and buying a pregnancy test during the week. No easy way of paying for one either, not unless I can bum ten bucks off someone under false pretences. I won't steal, though, and I won't let Lou-Anne steal for me, though she does offer. I know what stealing does to you.

By Saturday afternoon we've managed to scrape together a few bucks by emptying our backpacks of coins and selling Lou-Anne's amethyst pendant for a steal at Cash Converters in Bondi.

'But Isaac gave that to you, Lou-Anne!' I plead miserably as she lays it on the counter.

'I don't care about Isaac.'

'But I've heard you tell him you love him on the phone.'

She dismisses me with a wave of her hand. 'That's just to keep him sweet.'

We go to a nearby chemist, blush ferociously when we make the humiliating transaction, and then rush to the nearest McDonald's toilet. Lou-Anne stands just outside the stall door with the instructions.

'Do you need a cup of water?'

'No, it's...I'm fine...'

In spite of my best efforts, I soak the whole testing stick in wee.

'Now, it could take a few minutes,' says Lou-Anne, 'but are there two bars or just one in the plastic window?'

The two bars light up at the same time.

'There are two, Lou-Anne.'

'That means you're pregnant.'

The bottom falls out of my stomach. I feel black. Quivering and immobile at the same time. *Shit*.

'Shauna?'

I flush the toilet and come out of the stall. Lou-Anne follows me to the sinks and watches me silently as I wash my hands.

'Well, congratulations,' she says eventually. I meet her eyes in the mirror and raise my eyebrows.

'Over-the-counter tests can be wrong,' I say shakily. 'I should really have a blood test. That's what Dr Google said.'

Lou-Anne and I have already done some frantic googling on the prep. hall computers. I've got all the information. I just want someone to tell me that I'm not pregnant. Pregnancy, however, is a fact that's difficult to rebut.

Getting to see the doctor as an Oakholme girl with an embarrassing little condition can be a tricky business. The school's obliged to tell the student's parents when she's seeing the doctor. We are allowed off school grounds in the afternoons to go to appointments with parental permission, as long as we're back by a given time. I have to make up a story about 'girly problems', which covers a lot of territory but kind of sounds like thrush. I get Miss Maroney to make an appointment for me at Dr Baker's surgery in Double Bay the next week.

Miss Maroney hands me my Medicare card and on Wednesday after school I walk to Dr Baker's surgery on my own (Lou-Anne being on detention).

Dr Baker's a lady doctor who treats most of the boarders at Oakholme College. Being an old hippy, she's very kind and approachable and I've never felt particularly awkward telling her about my medical problems. I feel nervous now, though.

'What can I do for you today, Shauna?'

'I think I'm pregnant.'

Dr Baker's face doesn't even change. She must have had this conversation a hundred times before.

'When did your last period start?'

'The day before Christmas.'

'That's over three months ago. Did you have sex?'

I nod. 'The condom broke. I took the morning-after pill, but I don't think it worked.'

'Have you done a urine test?'

'Yeah.'

Dr Baker waits a few beats. 'And?'

'Well, it *seemed* to be positive.'

'False positives are possible, but very rare.'

'I think I need a blood test.'

'If you're still in doubt, let's do another urine test.'

She rummages through one of the drawers in her desk and pulls out a plastic jar.

'Go to the bathroom and get me a wee sample. That'll give us a result in a few minutes.'

I go to the bathroom and pee into the jar, clutching it to my chest as I walk back through the waiting room to Dr Baker's office.

She unscrews the lid from the jar like it's nothing more disgusting than a cup of coffee and dips a plastic stick into it. She leaves the stick on her desk and smiles at me.

'If you're sexually active, we should really talk about contraception.'

'I'm not *that* active, you know. It was my first time.'

'But your contraceptive method didn't work. You might want to consider a hormonal method like an implant as well as using condoms. You need to keep using condoms because they're still the best protection against sexually transmitted diseases.'

'Is an implant expensive?'

'No. It costs about thirty dollars.'

And that's not expensive…

'I probably won't have sex again for a while,' I say lamely.

In the time that it's taken to have this short conversation, the pregnancy test has come up positive. Dr Baker picks up the stick and holds it across the table. There's a big red plus sign in the little window.

'It seems that you're pregnant,' she says. 'What would you like to do?'

I get that black, bottomless feeling again. My face heats up and I feel my eyes fill with tears.

'I just wish I wasn't pregnant. I mean…how unlucky can I be, getting pregnant the first time.'

Dr Baker reaches for my hand. 'You've got options. A pregnancy doesn't mean the end of the world.'

'I can't have a baby. I just can't.'

'It's not a big deal, Shauna,' she says in a gentle, matter-of-fact way. 'It's probably too late to take the abortion pill, but you're still well within the time for a surgical abortion. It's a simple procedure and very safe. I can make an appointment for you at The Choice Foundation.'

'The Choice Foundation? Is that an abortion clinic?'

'It's a women's health clinic, yes. It's on Macquarie Street.'

'You won't tell the school about it, will you?'

'Of course not. You're almost eighteen years old. I have to respect patient-doctor confidentiality. You're old enough to have sexual privacy.'

This comes as a huge relief. I know if I want to, I can make this all go away and the only person who'd ever know is Lou-Anne. Even she wouldn't have to know if I didn't want her to. I could tell her that I wasn't pregnant after all and then quietly have the abortion.

'How much does it cost?' I ask, my heart full of shame.

'It costs about five hundred dollars.'

I start to cry. 'I don't have five hundred dollars.'

'I think it would be better if you talked to your parents about this, Shauna.'

I just shake my head, keep shaking it. I don't want to tell them. I don't want to admit to them that I've failed like this. But where to get the five hundred dollars? The only person who has it *and* will give it to me with a minimum number of questions is my cousin, Andrew. I'll tell him it's a loan for the ticket to Paris.

'Do you want me to give you the clinic's details?' Dr Baker asks kindly.

I nod, desolate.

12

I'M IN THE withdrawing room with Olivia Pike. Reverend Ferguson had to deliver her here personally again. She's putting a fierce effort into staring me down, but I only glance up at her intermittently. I haven't said a single word to her since Self-Raising Flour left the room.

Let's face it, I've got problems bigger than Olivia.

For one thing, I'm lying to my best friend. When I got back from my appointment with Dr Baker yesterday, I told Lou-Anne that my pregnancy test results were 'inconclusive', and that I have to go back for a blood test in a few days. In fact my appointment at The Choice Foundation is in a few days. After that, I'm planning to tell her that I'm not pregnant, which by then will probably be the truth.

I didn't make a clear-cut decision to lie to Lou-Anne. It just happened. She confronted me as soon as I walked into the dorm.

'So?'

Her dark eyes were on me, burning with compassion. I couldn't tell her that I was booked in for an abortion. I just couldn't, not when her own sister delivered twins at fifteen. So I lied my arse off. I didn't feel very good about it and I still don't.

Now I'm opposite Olivia, not really caring about what happened in her past or whether she says anything. I examine my fingernails, and then the knots in the smooth surface of the mahogany boardroom table. We've been here for about ten minutes.

At the other end of the table, Olivia has begun to fidget. Her legs are swinging under the table. She's tapping her fingernails, one hand after another, like she's playing a scale on a piano. Eventually, her mouth opens.

'Is this some kind of reverse psychology?'

'What?'

'This silence. Are you trying to trick me into talking?'

'No,' I say simply. 'I don't care whether you talk or not. Actually, I don't care what you do.'

'I know it's a trick.'

'It's not a trick.'

'It's a trick.'

'Okay, it's a trick. How's your ponytail? Has it lost weight? It seems thinner than the last time I saw it.'

Olivia looks bowled over. The sneer leaves her face for a good two seconds while she considers her next move.

'You're supposed to be my mentor,' she observes. 'You're not doing a very good job. You're a bully.'

'*You're* the bully and you got what you deserved.'

'Maybe I'll tell Self-Raising Flour that you're not doing a good job. Maybe I'll tell her a few other things, too.'

I don't respond and it drives Olivia crazy.

I shrug. I look at my watch. There's another long pause.

'How's your boyfriend?' she asks.

The question makes me physically lurch. I've hardly thought about Nathan since I found out I was pregnant. Now I don't know how to think about him. I'm not even sure I want to see him again.

For Olivia's benefit, I sit up straight and fix my face.

'Fine.'

'When's your next date?'

I lurch again. I straighten up again.

'Um...Easter show.'

'Which day?'

'That's really none of your business.'

I look at my watch. Only twelve minutes to go. Another minute or so passes in silence.

'Are you going home for Easter?' she asks me.

I nod. 'What about you?'

'I'm going to a Sport & Rec. camp and the rest of the time I'll stay at school.' Olivia looks vulnerable for a moment before asking, 'Do you live with your parents or foster parents?'

'My parents.'

'Both of them?'

'Yeah. You?' This is the most pleasant she's ever been towards me, and even though I don't feel like talking to her, I should take advantage.

'I've been in foster care my whole life,' she says in a quavering voice.

'That's a shame.'

'Depends on who your parents are, I suppose.'

I press her. 'What happened to your parents?'

113

Her eyes glisten with tears. I can see them watering from the other end of the table. Her face twists suddenly and savagely.

'I knew this was a trick.'

'Fine. Have it your way. I don't want to talk to you, either. You're a poisonous little serpent.'

We both cross our arms and turn side-on.

When the thirty minutes is up, I let her leave first and wait a few minutes before walking out.

Reverend Ferguson intercepts me in the hallway.

'Shauna! Can I keep you for a moment?'

'Look, I'm trying, Reverend Ferguson, but she's craz—'

'She's making progress,' Reverend Ferguson says firmly. 'She's teamed up with Keli Street-Hughes and some of the other girls in that room to raise money for charity during the holidays. You've heard of Wish Upon A Star? It's a foundation that grants the wishes of kids with cancer.'

'Okay. Good.'

'Did she tell you about it?'

'She mentioned she was hanging around over Easter.'

'I think it's so wonderful that she's participating in the community life of the school. Don't you?'

'It's great.'

Reverend Ferguson grabs my upper arm enthusiastically.

'You're doing fantastic work with this young lady, Shauna.'

I have to force my face into a serious expression.

'Well, thanks, Reverend Ferguson.'

Somehow I know that Olivia's fundraising efforts will be doomed to failure, but I keep my thoughts to myself.

I'm supposed to be her mentor after all, albeit not a very good one.

It's lunchtime and I've promised to meet Jenny in the common room. She's already sitting at a table looking at her laptop when I arrive, deeply absorbed by whatever she's reading. I sit next to her. There are flight details on the screen.

'We've got to move quickly on these plane tickets to Paris,' she says in panicky excitement. 'If we leave it much longer it might cost a thousand more per ticket return.'

'Can we wait for a few more weeks?' I ask, wondering how I'm going to ask my cousin for even more dough. He's already sent me five crisp hundred dollars. He was more than happy to front it, but how can I ask for more money for the same thing?

Jenny figures out that the root of all evil is on my mind.

'If you haven't got the cash, I can buy your ticket now and you can pay me back later.'

In my woozy, lethargic, guilt-ridden state, I find it hard to summon any eagerness, even in support of Jenny's.

'Just give me a few more weeks' is all I can think to say.

'I'm going to buy my tickets tomorrow night, after we get back from the revision course at St Augustine's.' She turns to me and grins, so single-minded that my lack of enthusiasm doesn't seem to make an impact on her. 'Let's hope Stephen hasn't got rowing practice tomorrow!'

The HSC University Pathways and St Augustine's and Stephen Agliozzo's back muscles seem a million miles away now. I realise that I can't even go to the course tomorrow afternoon because I have an abortion to attend. I hadn't even thought about the extra schoolwork when Dr Baker and I were organising the appointment.

'I won't be there tomorrow,' I tell Jenny. 'I've got a doctor's appointment.'

'What for?'

The lie should come out easily. It came out easily enough with Lou-Anne. But there is something in the frankness and intelligence of Jenny's eyes that makes my lying tongue seize up. I start stammering.

'Well...I've been sick lately and...'

'I know.'

'And I think...I'm pretty sure...it's morning sickness.'

'You're *pregnant*?' whispers Jenny, her eyes calculating but never leaving mine.

'Yeah.'

'That night with Nathan O'Brien?'

'Yep.'

'Oh, Shauna.' She sounds so disappointed for me. 'What are you going to do?'

'Where do you think I'm going tomorrow afternoon?'

'I'll go with you.'

'No, you should go to the class at St Augustine's. Take notes for me.'

'You're not planning to go by yourself, are you?'

I nod.

'I think I should come with you. How can you afford an abortion anyway? Don't they cost a bomb?'

'I've borrowed some money from my cousin.'

'Why didn't you ask me?'

'I wasn't planning to tell you. I just wanted to get it over and done with without anyone knowing.'

Jenny looks cheated, almost outraged, that I've kept this from her.

'You have to let me come with you, Shauna.'

'I'd rather just do it on my own. Please don't tell anyone.'

Jenny sighs deeply. 'I wouldn't do that.' She turns back to the computer. 'Should we check out accommodation?'

'Accommodation?'

'In *Paris*, Shauna.'

'Oh, sure.'

Jenny gives me a sidelong look. I shrug. I can't wait to feel normal again.

Later that afternoon, just when my energy levels and general outlook on life have hit an all-time low, who should come knocking on my dorm room door but Olivia Pike? This is the first time she has *ever* solicited my company, and her timing couldn't be worse.

'Come in!' shrieks Lou-Anne. I do a huge double take when Olivia shuffles into the room with her arms folded across her chest.

'What is it?' grunts Lou-Anne.

'I'm sorry about the other night,' says Olivia at a volume barely audible to the human ear.

'So you should be. And if I ever catch you in this room again, I'll finish the haircut that Shauna started.' I have never heard Lou-Anne sound so mean. She was obviously very attached to that moustache.

Olivia turns on her heel.

'Olivia. Wait.' I prop myself up on my pillows.

'I won't bother you if you're busy,' she says, turning side-on.

I give Lou-Anne a 'beat it' look and she rolls her eyes.

'Fine, I'll go to prep. hall.'

She stalks off, muttering under her breath, leaving Olivia and me alone in the room.

'What is it?' I really don't have an ounce of patience left in my body. I'm not feeling well and I'm dreading what's in store for me in the coming days. What do I have to give to anyone else, and of all people, Olivia?

'You said that if I ever wanted to talk…'

'You've been refusing to talk to me for weeks.'

She's still turned sidelong, not looking at me, slouched over her folded arms.

'But we talked today.'

'Yep.'

'About my foster family.'

She turns to face me. Without an invitation she walks to my bed and sits on the end. I'm so shocked by this voluntary closeness that I scoot away up my bed and pull my knees to my chest.

'Don't you ever miss your family?' she asks.

'Sort of. Sometimes they drive me crazy. Sometimes I'm so happy to see them that I just want to stay in Barraba and never come back to Sydney. You?'

'I miss my foster parents, Auntie Marilyn and Uncle Frank. They're the nicest foster parents I've ever had. Their kids are grown up, so I'm like their only child.'

Her voice is trembling and it's obvious that her guard is down. I'm not expecting any barbs, but you never know with Olivia. She's a storm cloud on a summer's day.

'Have you had foster parents who weren't nice?'

She nods. Then she turns her head away and I see the tears shining in her eyes.

'Sure have.'

'Maybe we could talk about it sometime, Olivia, but I'm really sick at the moment. And I've got a huge day tomorrow. Could we take a raincheck on this conversation?'

Olivia blinks away her tears. She's a tough little thing.

'Sure.'

I feel like a moll for sending her packing, but what use am I to her at the moment? Soon enough I'll feel normal and able to talk. Soon enough the problem will be solved.

It takes hours to get to sleep that night. Though my mind's more or less made up about the abortion, it keeps ticking over and over. This is the natural outcome for pregnant teenagers, I tell myself. This is the responsible thing to do. It's what's expected. I'm not the first girl to terminate a pregnancy and I won't be the last. (Didn't I hear a statistic once that one in three Australian women has had an abortion?) No one ever has to know about it, if that's the way I want it. I might forget about it in six months, and then it will be as if it never happened. Only Jenny will know.

To take the other option would be so hard. I'd have to leave school. I'd have to scrap all my plans and expectations. I wouldn't be able to finish Introduction to Legal Systems and Methods.

Most importantly, I wouldn't go to Paris with Jenny. I'd be stuck in Barraba with my disappointed parents. Nathan would dump me, or maybe I'd dump him. In short, I'd lose everything I've got. I'd be destroyed.

Destroy or be destroyed. Those are the options, it seems. And I feel like I've come too far to let myself be destroyed. This time tomorrow, the inconvenient tissue will be gone and I'll have my life back.

Why, then, do I wish there was someone – someone other than silly Lou-Anne – who loved me enough to bloody well talk me out of it?

13

DR BAKER WARNED me that there might be pro-life protesters outside The Choice Foundation clinic on Macquarie Street, but when I arrive at 10 a.m. in casual clothes, the coast is clear. I check over my shoulder to make sure no one's followed me and then enter the building. The clinic is on the third floor. I can hardly believe how easy it's been to get this far.

Not that I haven't had to sneak around. I left school without signing out this morning, naughty me. I have two free study periods before lunch, and I'm hoping to slip back through the school gates by the end of lunch. I've left Jenny with instructions in the event that I'm late for French (fib: I'm in sick bay) and I've lied to Lou-Anne that I'm going to the clinic for a blood test. As long as the procedure doesn't take more than a few hours, I should be able to get away with it.

I'm opting for light sedation rather than a general anaesthetic, so that I'll be out sooner. Apparently the operation itself only takes about ten minutes. It's the checking in, preparation and after care that chews up all the time. Though I'm supposed to have someone waiting to help me back to school after the procedure, I haven't arranged anything like that. I have a feeling that if I do it all by myself, it'll be like it never happened. After a morning of fasting (so that I don't spew during the procedure) I'm not quite present anyway.

My heart begins to pound in the elevator and is still pounding when I reach the front desk. The receptionist who greets me is very friendly and kind. She takes my Medicare card and gives me a clipboard with a form to fill out. The questions are easy to answer, except for the last one: *Why are you seeking an abortion?* I think about it and I write: *Because I feel sick and I'm afraid I won't be able to do the HSC. Also, I plan to travel to Europe next year and I won't be able to do that with a baby.*

The doctor, who's about forty-five and introduces himself as Dr Phillip Goldsmith, comes into the waiting room and leads me into his office. When I walk past the front desk, there's a woman of about thirty opening her wallet to pay for her abortion. I don't know where it comes from, but I feel a surge of hostility towards her.

Her hair is blonde-streaked and blow-dried. Her skin is so stained with fake tan that she'd be perfectly camouflaged on a dish of Tandoori chicken. Her nails and lips are painted the same Hollywood red. She looks well groomed and perfectly nice, but she disgusts me. Maybe it's because I assume (and how dare I!) that someone who has the time and money to preen herself so vainly has the resources to look after a baby. Even the sound of her zipping up her wallet repels me. Your transaction has come to a close, lady, I think. And mine is about to open.

This is the moment when I begin to think that what I'm about to do is not as routine, casual and natural as it seemed when I was sitting opposite Dr Baker and the only thing on my mind was relief from great mortification.

My heart's drumming crazily when I join Dr Goldsmith at his desk. He takes the clipboard from me and reads through it. Then he starts to read what I've written aloud.

'Because I feel sick and I'm afraid I won't be able to do the HSC,' he says. His tone isn't sarcastic, but there's something feeble about my excuses when they're read back to me. He continues: 'Also, I plan to travel to Europe next year and I won't be able to do that with a baby.'

He looks at me through black square-framed glasses. He puts the clipboard down and picks up a pen.

'So you're pretty busy at the moment, err, Shauna?'

'Yes.'

'Having a baby's a huge commitment.'

'I know that.'

He looks down at another piece of paper on his desk. I watch him write on it: *Patient believes she is too young to cope emotionally with the pregnancy.*

I'm shocked. 'I didn't say that.'

'Look, this is *my* paperwork,' he explains. 'You don't need to worry about it, but I'm legally required to come to a view that continuing the pregnancy would pose a serious threat to your mental or physical health.'

'That's fine,' I tell him, feeling my cheeks burn with shame. I feel so uncomfortable standing up to someone as important as a doctor, but I feel even more uncomfortable letting him stuff words into my mouth. 'But I never said anything about being too young or not coping emotionally.'

He shrugs at me and then puts a line through the comment with his pen.

'I said that I feel sick, and that I want to do the HSC and go overseas.'

Dr Goldsmith starts writing again. I watch him like a hawk. He writes: *Patient finds physical stress of pregnancy too great to continue.*

'I didn't say that either.'

Incredibly, Dr Goldsmith attacks me with his furrowed brow, as if I'm the one acting out of turn. He lays down the pen. Is he annoyed with me? Now I'm beginning to wish I'd taken advantage of the free telephone counselling service. The receptionist told me about it when I made the appointment, but I was sure I didn't need it. I wasn't expecting the doctor to be as enthusiastic as Dr Goldsmith.

'This is *my* paperwork,' he says again. 'I can form a view about what effects the pregnancy might have on you based on many factors, not just what you tell me.'

'What factors?'

He shrugs and at the same time throws his hands in the air, as if I'm being completely unreasonable and tiresome.

'You're a seventeen-year-old girl from an Indigenous background. How are you going to cope with a baby?'

'I haven't told you anything about my background!'

'As I said, I can draw my own conclusions, and before I can legally perform an abortion...' He sighs, as if he's sick of explaining it to me. As if he's been talking to me for the whole afternoon and not just five minutes. His eyelids flutter in exasperation. 'Do you want an abortion or not? Because feeling sick and wanting to study overseas are not legal justifications for the procedure you're asking me to perform.'

I know I've gone completely beetroot and I can feel sweat dripping from my hair over my temples and down the sides of my neck. My pulse is slamming in my ears and I can hear myself panting like an overheated dog.

'Maybe you need to give more thought to it,' says the doctor. 'I think we should at least do an ultrasound, though, to make sure you're really pregnant and find out how far along you are. Once you're at twenty weeks, you'll be hard pressed to find a doctor who'll give you an abortion.'

Give me an abortion? Like a Christmas present?

'Okay,' I grunt. All I can do is grunt.

'Okay, you want the ultrasound, or okay, you want the abortion?'

'Ultrasound.'

Dr Goldsmith points to the examination table.

I lie down and undo my jeans as instructed. The doctor squirts some goop onto my belly and then runs the ultrasound probe right down on the line of my pubic hair. He pushes so hard that I have to try not to wet my pants.

The ultrasound screen is turned towards him, so that he can see it and I can't.

'I'd say you're at twelve to thirteen weeks,' he says.

'Can I have a look?'

'Sorry?'

'Can I have a look at the screen?'

He shakes his head. 'We prefer to keep the images out of patients' sight because some women do find it upsetting to see the pregnancy.'

'I want to see the screen.'

'This is *my* equipment.'

'And it's *my* baby.'

As soon as I say that, I know I'm not going to have an abortion. Even though this baby could destroy me, I will not destroy it.

With a roll of his eyes, the doctor swivels the screen around so I can see it. Right away I see the human features. A head, body, arms and legs. It's got fingers, for Heaven's sake. And there's something flashing at the edge of the screen.

'Is that the baby's heartbeat?'

'Yes.'

Dr Goldsmith points gingerly to the screen.

'There's the sac. The foetus is about eight centimetres long.'

I start crying because I realise I've just met someone who's going to be with me for the rest of my life. Someone who might be with me when my heart stops beating. The doctor puts his hand on my shoulder.

'It's a stressful time, I know.'

'It's not that,' I tell him through sobs. 'I'm *happy*. That's my *baby*. I'm its *mum*. How could I...How could you...'

I do up my pants and swiftly sit up. A huge swell of anger rises from my heart into my throat. It's so strong that I can barely get the words out.

'You should be ashamed of yourself!' My voice is pressured and coarse. 'Every girl who comes into this place should look at that screen!'

'If you're still struggling with the decision...' he chips in as I rush past him out of the room.

I don't even look at the woman behind the front desk as I leave. I stand with my back to her and wait for the elevator.

While I'm waiting, I overhear a snippet of Dr Phillip Goldsmith's telephone conversation in his office.

'...*she went apeshit at me*...'

I know he's talking about me, and I'm kind of proud of myself. People like me do not usually stand up to people like Phillip Goldsmith. It makes me wonder what kind of other undoable things I'm capable of.

Instead of catching the bus, I walk all the way back to school, my mind rolling at the speed of sound. It makes me shiver – *literally* shiver – to think how close I came to ending the life inside me over a bit of nausea and a trip to Paris. Why did the two doctors involved let me glide through the process so easily?

By the time I get to school, I've already made a few decisions. First, I'm going to do the HSC no matter what. I cannot remember *ever* thinking or making a decision so clearly. Or loving someone as much as I love the eight-centimetre person living inside my belly.

I feel happy. Tired and frightened, but happy.

14

'PEOPLE ARE GOING to think we're lesbians if you keep holding my hand like this.'

'I don't care if they do, Shauna.'

Lou-Anne has not been able to stop hugging me since I told her the news. Apart from the doctors and Jenny, she's the only person who knows I'm pregnant. I didn't tell her about my visit to The Choice Foundation, only that the pregnancy test had been positive. She doesn't know anything about my little death dance with Dr Goldsmith and I hope she never finds out.

Jenny knows, and she knows I'm still pregnant.

The day after the abortion appointment I tell Miss Pemberton that I need to pull out of the HSC University Pathways. Reverend Ferguson somehow found out and told Jenny before I got the chance, and Jenny figured out why and got seriously pissed off with me. She confronted me in a rage outside our lockers.

'So all our plans for Paris are shot to hell? Just like that?' Her voice is flinty with fury.

'You can still go.'

'You can still have an abortion, can't you? Why *don't* you?' Her voice cracks with every inflection.

'I don't want one.'

'Why *not*?'

'Jenny!'

'I'm sorry, Shauna, but if you had an abortion, then life would just go on as usual. We could go to Paris together like we've been dreaming about.'

'I'm not going to kill my baby so we can go to Paris.'

'A foetus is not a baby. It doesn't know anything or feel anything. It's just goo.'

'I've seen it on the ultrasound machine and it's not just goo. Imagine what I would have felt like afterwards!'

'My cousin had an abortion and she told me that all she felt was happiness and relief.'

'Well, good for her. I'm not your cousin.'

'You're already giving up so much and it hasn't even been born. Do you think Mrs Green's going to let you stay at school with a big, fat pregnant stomach?'

I shrug. 'I don't know.'

'I do.'

Jenny looks at me with gritted teeth, both hands clamped into fists and jammed against her thighs.

'This is incredibly selfish of you,' she hisses. 'Does Lou-Anne know?'

'Lou-Anne *diagnosed* me.'

Jenny nods, her lips pursed tightly. I don't know what right she thinks she has to take it all so badly. I'm the one who's got to deal with the pregnancy. She can still go to Paris.

'And what about pulling out of Introduction to Legal Systems and Methods? Now you'll have a big, fat fail on your university record before you've even started!'

'I…I…'

I hadn't really thought about that. A failure on my record?

'You don't seriously think you can study at university next year *and* have a baby, do you, Shauna?'

I mouth and stammer. 'I…I don't know.'

'I do.'

'Jenny, I'm sorry.'

'You should really think about this over the holidays,' she says. 'There's still time.'

She turns and walks off without saying goodbye or promising to call me.

'Don't tell anyone, Jenny!' I call after her, feeling rotten for having let her down so badly. And for the failure on my uni record.

I'm so worried about the blot on my academic record that I go to see Reverend Ferguson in her office. My hands are glistening with nervous sweat.

'I've just got too much on my plate,' I say when she asks me to explain my decision.

She nods slowly, sympathetically. 'I thought that might be the case. Miss Pemberton said you missed the last session at St Augustine's.'

'It's just too much,' I say feebly.

She reaches across the table and squeezes my hand.

'I understand.'

But for once, she doesn't understand at all. She doesn't have a clue.

'Will I have a failure on my record, Reverend Ferguson?'

She grimaces. 'I'm honestly not sure. Let me call the university. See what we can do.'

Just before dinner, Lou-Anne and I go for a walk around the school. The weather's cooling down and we're both shivering in our short shirtsleeves. There are only two more days of school left.

'I can't wait to see the twins,' says Lou-Anne, linking her arm through mine and pulling me close to her side. 'I can't wait to have them in my arms!'

Lou-Anne's nieces, Charlotte and Chelsea, are criminally cute. They've got bouncing black curls, deep dimples and skin like cocoa butter. They're crazy about Lou-Anne. She's the cool auntie who spoils them rotten. When she's with them, from the time they get up to the time they go to bed, they have her undivided attention. Whenever I stay with Lou-Anne for the holidays, I'm in awe at her patience, and the way she can just play with them for a whole day without a break. She even gets in the bath with them.

When I'm with little kids, I get bored after about fifteen minutes, no matter how cute they are. I guess it'll be different with my own baby. It'll have to be.

'What was it like for your sister?' I ask her. 'Being pregnant, I mean.'

'Oh, it was hell for Beth with the morning sickness, but other than that...'

'Did she get a hard time? Did people stare?'

Lou-Anne shakes her head. 'The only thing she was embarrassed about was that the boy didn't stand by her. She was hoping he'd stay in Eumundi to help her raise the girls.

He was only sixteen, though. What can you expect from a sixteen-year-old boy?'

'But Beth was only fifteen and she did the right thing.'

'Didn't have a choice, did she?'

'She could have had an abortion or put them up for adoption.'

'That's not what I mean by a *choice*, Shauna. I mean that they're *our* girls and we could never let them go.'

When Lou-Anne talks this way, it's hard to believe that she's only sixteen. In spite of her spectacular vocal talents, Lou-Anne doesn't get good marks, not even in music. But she has this rock-solid emotional intelligence that people at Oakholme don't appreciate. I appreciate her, though. I know that when she becomes a rich and famous opera singer, she won't be one of those celebrities who gets photographed stepping out of their limo without underwear. She's got it together.

We walk arm-in-arm down the side of the grassy oval, where some senior boarders, including Keli Street-Hughes and Annabel Saxon, are kicking a soccer ball around barefoot. They're still in their long uniforms, with the skirts tucked into their undies. They're whooping and catcalling. Someone yells, 'You're the boss, Ollie!' and then I see a flash of white-blonde hair as Olivia Pike breaks away from the pack.

'That kid's thirsty,' says Lou-Anne casually.

'I know exactly what you mean. Just wait until they find out.'

Then I think, just wait until they find out what's going on inside me, and an icy shiver runs up my spine. I don't want to think about it.

We do a full loop of the oval and the boarders ignore us as usual. Keli does a pretty impressive job of head-butting the ball and it comes bouncing towards Lou-Anne and me. Lou-Anne kicks it back and everyone in the group just stands there and watches as it rolls back to them. No one says thanks. Except Lou-Anne and me.

'Say thanks to your dad for me!' we both call out, just one last time for the term.

I try to imagine what Keli Street-Hughes will do at home in Coleambally these holidays. Ride her horse in the dam? Zoom up and down rows of cotton on a four-wheel motor-bike? Maybe the Street-Hugheses will go to Tuscany for a couple of weeks and Keli will get fat on truffle linguine. I have no idea what she'll really do. Isn't that incredible? We've been living in the same building for over four years and we barely know one another. (Apart from my cyber-stalking, that is.) We know we don't like each other and that's about it.

15

IS THERE AN easy way for a seventeen year old to break it to people that she's pregnant? It was difficult enough with Lou-Anne and Jenny. What the hell am I going to say to my parents? And Nathan? I haven't even worked out how to tell Indu and Bindi.

The Easter holidays have arrived. I'm always tired and sometimes sick, and I don't know how much longer I can keep 'the news' from people who count. There will come a point – there *has* to, though I can't really imagine what it will feel like – when everyone will know. But how do I come out with it now?

'You've got to tell Nathan,' says Lou-Anne. 'Like, *today*.' We're in the bathroom, getting ready to meet Bindi and Indu at the Easter Show. They've already packed up and left the dormitory for the holidays. Lou-Anne and I aren't leaving Sydney for home until tomorrow.

'I can tell him anytime,' I say, trying to sound detached.

'What are you afraid of, Shauna?'

What am I *not* afraid of?

'I don't know. His reaction, I guess. He'll probably run a mile.'

'Then he's a bastard and you don't want him anyway.'

'I could *not* tell him. You know, if I wanted. Save everyone the trouble.'

'But then your baby won't know its dad. That's not cool.'

'Charlotte and Chelsea don't know their dad.'

'Their dad's a dropkick and not worth knowing,' replies Lou-Anne assuredly. 'You've got to give this guy a chance. Even if you think he's going to run. You must still like him or else we wouldn't be going to see him.'

'I do like him, but the stakes are really high now.'

'Maybe he'll rise to the occasion.'

'Maybe.'

We catch the train out to Sydney Olympic Park, dressed as aggy as good taste will allow. We're both wearing white linen shirts, and luckily jeans and ankle boots are in at the moment.

Bindi and Indu are waiting for us at the gates.

'Omigawd,' Bindi scoffs when she sees us. She's wearing a mini-dress and wedge heels.

'You're going to get cow poo between your toes,' I taunt her.

Getting into the Easter Show costs a bomb, even when you're a student. Luckily Nathan's mum is on some committee of the Royal Agricultural Society and has access to a certain number of complimentary passes. He's sent me four, which means we're all getting a free ride.

We go through the turnstiles and dive into the overwhelming crowds and noise.

'Look!' cries Indu suddenly, and all eyes shoot to the direction she's pointing. It's a kebab stand. We raid it, even though it's only ten o'clock in the morning. Everyone buys one except me. I'm too nervous to eat.

We park ourselves in the midst of the thronging crowd, getting shoved and squashed. We look at each other and stifle laughs. This is the way it is with us when we fly the Oakholme coop. We look forward to outings, talk about them and prepare for them, twist ourselves inside out over them, and only when we arrive at the much-coveted venue do we realise that we were much happier belly-down in our beds in the dorm in our uniforms. All of a sudden I realise that this feeling is a relic, a phenomenon of the past. Everything is about to change.

'So where's this cow shed?' asks Indu.

'Just follow the cowboy hats,' says Bindi.

This is more or less what we do.

I get so nervous that I start to have this feeling of not being attached to my legs. I'm just floating along above, carried by the crowd. I have an inkling that something major is about to unfold.

The incidence of cowboy hats spikes as we enter the cattle pavilion, and the hot, sweet, shitty barn smell hits us like a slap.

Bindi pulls a face. 'At moments like these, I sometimes wonder whether I'll ever eat meat again,' she says, pushing the last piece of her kebab into her mouth.

'Really?' says Lou-Anne. 'Looking at cows makes me hungry for steak.'

'What colour are Nathan's cows?' asks Indu.

'I think…' I begin, trailing off into nothing, taking a few seconds to realise that I don't know. 'The breed is called Santa something-or-other…'

Then I see him in one of the wash bays at the front of the pavilion, standing side-on to a huge, chestnut-coloured cow, a brush in one hand and a rubber mitt over the other. I see him before he sees me and I begin to wave as our eyes meet. Nathan's pale blue eyes soften and crinkle at the edges.

'Shauna!'

I break away from my friends and plunge into the wash bay.

'Well, here we are,' I say awkwardly.

'Yeah,' he says, 'here you all are. Thanks for coming.'

My friends gather around cautiously, oohing and aahing about the cow, a two-year-old heifer called Gemma. I don't know how any creature could get so big in just two short years.

'Our first class is in about an hour,' Nathan explains. 'I'm just doing her hair.'

We giggle at this, and I feel a huge gush of affection for him. This is the first time I've laid eyes on him knowing what's inside me and that, one way or another, I'm going to be joined to him for the rest of my life. As he moves confidently and gently around a beast that must literally weigh a ton, I notice little things about him that I haven't given much attention until now. The leanness of his body and the light- ness of his movements. The way he looks down when he's listening to someone. Perhaps it's because he's in an envi- ronment he feels comfortable in, but he seems manlier. Or maybe I just need him to be.

'Nathan!' a woman's voice calls out. I don't want to seem too eager to catch a glimpse of Nathan's mum, but I can't help turning and glancing over my shoulder. A short woman with a stubby, blonde ponytail bustles over. She's about fifty, overheated and smudged in her all-denim outfit. She looks like a scrubchook. I know that she's his mother before he calls her 'mum' because they have the same pale, down-turned eyes.

'Is she dry yet?'

She arrives with a pump pack of hair gloss in her hand, not seeming to notice us.

'Almost,' says Nathan, glancing quickly to me. 'Just a bit damp around the legs. Mum, this is Shauna.'

Nathan's mother looks around at us.

'Hi.' I smile at her, but there is something about the shuddering way her gaze settles on me that knocks all the confidence out of me. It's an unmistakable double take and of course I know what it's about. Her eyes pan briefly over my friends and flutter back to me.

'How are you?' she says without meeting my eye, and she walks to the other side of the cow before I can answer.

I turn to Lou-Anne. 'Let's go.'

'What? I thought we were going to…'

I scowl at her and she stops dead.

'Okay,' she says quickly.

'We might see you later, Nathan,' I say in a shaky voice.

Nathan's blonde brows gather in confusion.

'Are you coming back to watch the classes?' asks Nathan, still brushing the cow.

I don't smile or even nod. 'I guess.'

'There's something I wanted to talk to you about,' he says. 'Could we talk in private later?'

'Maybe,' I answer coldly.

We leave the stifling pavilion, with Bindi whining about how bad it smells.

'Yeah, the smell really was starting to get to me too,' I mutter, feeling as limp as a wet sail on a windless day.

Lou-Anne gives me a wide-eyed, reproachful stare as we sink back into the crowds outside.

'I want to go,' I tell her.

'You want to leave the show?'

'Yeah.'

'But he gave us the tickets. We can't just leave.'

We stop to let Bindi and Indu catch up.

'I think I'm going to go back to school,' I say. 'I'm feeling pretty dodgy.'

'What's wrong?'

'I'm dizzy. I need to sit down.'

'I guess you don't feel like going on the rides then?' says Bindi.

'No, Bindi, I don't,' I snap, not meaning to. I apologise straight away.

'Don't worry about it,' says Bindi, folding her arms over her chest. 'It's just that you were the one who wanted to come.'

In the end, Bindi and Indu decide to stay at the show and make the most of it. Lou-Anne can't be talked out of coming back to school with me.

'What happened just now?' Lou-Anne demands as we head towards the train station.

'Did you see the way his mother looked at us?'

'How?'

'Oh, *come* on, Lou-Anne!'

'If she didn't want to stop and chat, so what? She was busy.'

'I just don't like being looked at like I'm a piece of dog shit.'

'Did she really do that?'

'Yes!'

'Well, she doesn't know that you're pregnant with her grandchild.'

'And she's never going to. Buggered if I let that family have anything to do with my baby.'

'Shauna, I think you're choosing to take it the wrong way. Was she really throwing shade?'

'Yes, she was.'

'But that's not Nathan's fault.'

'Like mother, like son. I think he was about to dump me anyway. He said he wanted to talk to me in private. What else could that have meant?'

'Well...' Lou-Anne trails off.

She lets me simmer for a while, which is probably the right thing to do. When I'm in one of these states, no one can talk to me without getting their head bitten off. And that's exactly what I'm going to do if she tells me I'm jumping to conclusions because I know I'm not. Jumping to conclusions is something that people like Nathan's mother do.

On the train back to the city I fume. Every racist experience I've ever had whooshes through the floodgates. The open, barefaced name-calling. The smaller, pettier slights. The nasty looks and the standoffishness. The pity and the overniceness. I hate it all. I hate them all. And now I'm bringing a child into the whole fetid mess.

When we get back to school I ask Miss Maroney whether there are any messages for me. There aren't. I want to call Nathan and tell him about the baby but I just can't. I decide that I'm never calling him again.

I just want to run to a place where people already love me.

16

THE COUNTRYLINK TRAIN service is a peculiar beast. I'm used
to catching the train to Tamworth, so I'm comfortable with
the kind of rabble you find on a country train on a weekday.

The weirdest thing is that all the poor people and boarding
school students (such as *moi*) can travel in the first-class cabin.
This leads to an interesting cross-section of society, from
tourists and wealthy older people, to poor people visiting
family, to skid-row drug addicts who come to Central Station
to buy cheaper gear than they can get in the country. There
are always Aboriginal people in the first-class carriage when
I'm travelling on the Tamworth train. We nod and smile at
each other and the older women ask 'where you from?' That's
how Aboriginal strangers start conversations with one another.
Those words, when uttered in a soft, sweet, slow voice, are like
music to my ears.

People generally behave themselves on the country
lines, even the junkies, but every now and then something
terrible happens. On the Tamworth train, for example, I've
witnessed some fairly harrowing scenes, caused mostly by
drug or alcohol addiction. Once I saw an old man stagger-
ing out of the bathroom with a tourniquet still tied and a

needle hanging out of his arm. Another time I saw a woman who'd overdosed on heroin being brought back to life on the platform next to my window. I remember her sitting up and abusing the paramedic because he'd given her Narcan and wrecked her high. The worst thing I ever saw was an ice-addicted mother with green foam at the edges of her mouth swinging an unresponsive newborn baby by its little bootied foot. The green-foam woman upset me the most because, apart from the unconscious baby, she was Aboriginal.

I don't know why I, Shauna Harding, seventeen-year-old high school student, feel the need to take on the sins of other Aboriginal people, but I do. And I don't think I'm alone. Aboriginal people behaving badly scare and embarrass other Aboriginal people behaving well. Watch the black passengers in the first-class carriage when another black person's making an ass of themselves. Watch the cringing and headshaking and downcast eyes. Watch the relief on their faces when the black behaving badly gets booted off the train at the next station.

Sometimes I think it's a survival mechanism, acting good and quiet and smiling while silently eating shit. It hasn't got much to do with being good people, though I swear we are. It's more serious and more basic than that. It's got to do with keeping our race alive. The older folk, the aunties and uncles, are more awake to it than the young. That's why they're still alive while the other people of their generation, far too many of them, have died and turned to dust. If you want to stay alive you shut your mouth, smile and remain in a seated position. Those of us who don't do that end up biting it in the back of a police wagon, hanging in bedsheets from the door of a jail cell, crucified on a bottle or needle, or tied to a dialysis machine. Or wrapped around a tree, like my big brother.

So people sit down and stay alive. If you want to stand up and stay alive you'd better have a good education, a quick mind and a lot of white friends backing you up. And most Aboriginal people don't have all those advantages. I intend to have all those advantages, and when the time is right, I intend to stand up.

I've been racking my brains for solutions to the problem of going to university next year. I know I'm going to have to live at home in Barraba with the baby. There's no way I'll be able to afford to live in a big city and pay for rent *and* childcare, so I've been investigating online university courses. There are plenty of universities that offer Bachelor of Languages and Bachelor of Arts degrees online. It's do-able, *if* I stay at home.

The upsetting thing is, I don't want to stay at home. I've been looking forward to leaving Barraba and Oakholme for ages. Recently I've been looking forward to leaving Australia for a while too. The arrival of the baby slams most doors in my face, for the foreseeable future anyway. While I know that I will still be able to get a university degree and study the subjects that interest me, it makes me sick to think that my dreams of living in a big city, going out with my friends and travelling to Europe will remain just that – dreams. I already really, really regret getting pregnant so young. The only way I can deal with the heartbreak is to tell myself that I will end up where I want to be eventually. I will be a journalist or work in communications. I will find a platform to say the things I have to say, but I'll do it with a baby. The people who judge me and want me to fail will be bitterly disappointed.

And so will the people who love me.

Dad's waiting for me when I walk out onto the platform at Tamworth station. The first thing I notice is that he's let his beard grow bushy, all the way down to his chest. It makes me hesitate for a second or two before I dive into his open arms and trampoline off his belly before settling into the cuddle.

'My little scholar!'

'Hey, Dad. Did Mum come?'

'No, I came straight from Brisbane. I'll take you back home and then head on down to Newcastle.'

'You got the truck?'

'Nah. Walked.'

He roars with laughter, so loudly that everyone around us on the platform stares. Obviously we have the same sense of humour. And a healthy appreciation for our own jokes.

It's a warm autumn afternoon in Tamworth. Even though I had lunch on the train, Dad insists on taking me out for a pub meal. We walk down the main street looking for a joint with its lunch board still out, Dad in his stubbies and singlet, me with my prim Oakholme College backpack slung over my shoulder.

We settle on the Standard Hotel because it doesn't look too rough and there's a twelve-dollar deal on steak and chips.

I feel so comfortable in a country pub, it's crazy. All the old drunks slumped at the bar turn as we walk in, and I know exactly how to handle them.

'Good afternoon,' I say, gazing casually straight at them.

They all nod and say 'Good afternoon' in unison.

Dad orders himself a schooner of beer and me a glass of Coke, and we move along the tatty red carpet to the brasserie area.

'So how's the university subject going?' Dad asks after we order our steaks.

That is about the all-time pinnacle of Dad's understanding of my academic life. It might be the most insightful thing he's ever said about my education. And I'm not even pursuing it anymore.

'Ah, I decided not to do it. It seemed like too much.'

Dad nods slowly like he understands everything.

'Focus on the important things,' he says, stroking his beard.

'That's right.'

I'm planning to tell my parents about the pregnancy sometime in the next two weeks. I know they won't be happy about it, not because they don't love babies, but because they'll be worried about school and uni. And those are reasonable worries. Even I don't know exactly how I'll manage it. I just know that I will.

Mum's not well enough to look after a baby. I wouldn't expect her to care for mine while I went off to uni. Anyway, I don't want to be separated from my child. I've seen what Lou-Anne's like during those first days of separation from Charlotte and Chelsea, and they're just her nieces.

I ask Dad who's coming to stay with us over Easter. We always have Easter and Christmas at our place because we've got the biggest house. If we're having a big shindig, then I won't tell my parents that I'm pregnant until after everyone's left.

'Just Julie and family.'

Just Julie and family add up to ten people if everyone comes. Dad's sister, Julie, her husband, Mick, and my cousins, Stephanie, Andrew, Jody and James, plus my cousins' boyfriends and girlfriends if they've got any.

'Does Mum want me to cook?'

'Oh, I don't think she's expecting that.'

'I'll do the pavlova at least.'

'What about the Toblerone cheesecake?'

'Won't be a problem.'

After Jamie died and my parents went crazy, I learned to cook. I got sick of pasta and jar sauce and frozen pizza, so I taught myself. The secret to cooking, I swear, is nothing trickier than reading a recipe and practising it over and over again. Whenever someone says to me, 'I don't know how to cook', I say, 'Well, do you know how to read?' Maybe I've got tickets on myself, but I'm prepared to say that I've become a fairly handy cook by just reading and practising. Dad says that Mum's not expecting me to cook, but I bet she is. The first thing she'll ask me to do when I get home is to write her a shopping list.

I enjoy every second of the trip to Barraba in Dad's truck. Riding up high in the cab with a steak in my belly and my hand on the radio dial reminds me of being a little kid, when all I wanted to do in life was become a truck driver like my father. Jamie and I would both sit in the front seat fighting over the music and whether one of us had spent more time than the other in the middle seat. We both wanted to be next to Dad, because when he was in a good mood, he'd let us change the truck's gears. I don't care about changing gears anymore, but I still like sitting next to Dad.

He drops me out the front of our house without getting out of the truck.

'I'm already running three hours behind, love, but I'll be back early tomorrow. Be nice to your mum, okay?'

'I'm always nice to her, Dad.'

When I get inside, Mum's in the kitchen chopping onions. She seems to become aware of me slowly, looking up from the chopping block as if I've caught her in a daydream she's reluctant to break from. I'm so relieved to walk in and see her doing something as normal as cooking that I feel like I could cry.

'Hey!'

She keeps on chopping as I go to her to kiss her cheek.

I look a lot like my mum in the face. Chubby, with a wide, turned-up nose and a fleshy mouth shaped like a bow. Jamie used to say that we look like black versions of Miss Piggy. That's the kind of backhanded compliment he used to give before resorting to flat-out insults.

Mum's put on a lot of weight over the last few years because of the anti-depressants she takes. She gets the munchies at night and pigs out on chips and biscuits. She sleeps a lot, too, often passing out on the lounge in front of the TV and not getting up until eleven or even midday the next day.

'Julie and the family are arriving on Saturday,' she says. 'You'd better give me a shopping list. If you want fancy ingredients, I'll have to drive into Tamworth.'

Ha! I knew it.

'What are you making now?'

'Spag bol. But I'm just getting started. You can finish it, if you like. I'm sure you know better.'

'I like your spag bol.'

'The last time I made it you said it didn't taste like anything.'

'Aw, Mum. C'mon…'

Mum's got it in her head that I don't think she's good enough for me anymore. It doesn't matter what I say or do, that's the conclusion she always comes to. Mostly it's because I'm away in Sydney getting an education at a fancypants school, and the other side is this idea that I blame her for Jamie's death. She's edgy and defensive before I even open my mouth.

'How's the painting going?'

She puts her hand in the air and motions so-so.

'We sold one to the bank a few weeks ago. Dad's been talking to an art gallery in Tamworth about putting on an exhibition – you know, a show with my work only. Maybe it'll happen. Probably not.'

'I bet it'll happen.'

Mum stops chopping. 'Well, how would you know, Shauna?'

'I know how great your paintings are, Mum.'

'Nothing compared with what you see in Sydney, I'm sure.'

'I don't know. I don't know anything about art. That's your department.'

'So your opinion that my paintings are great…' She starts firmly and then trails off. Even when it comes to putting her own daughter in her place, her confidence fails her.

I start helping her in the kitchen, even though I know she'll do her best to take it the wrong way. I heat up some oil in a saucepan on the stove. Mum throws in some chopped onions.

'Beef mince is in the fridge,' she says, 'and before you ask, let me tell you that I didn't look at the fat content.'

I pull the plastic container of mince out of the fridge and lay it on the bench. The general whiff of the fridge is enough to start a small wave of nausea, but the sickness I feel when I peel the plastic off the mince knocks me off my feet. I haven't handled raw meat since the morning sickness started. I over-balance and fall backwards against the bench, dropping the mince on the tiles.

'Oops,' says Mum, as if nothing serious has happened.

'Mum, I need help,' I say.

'The dishcloth's in the sink.'

Faint, dizzy and exhausted, I sink to the floor.

Finally Mum twigs that there's something wrong. She shrieks and skids heavily to her knees by my side.

She asks me if I'm okay and I say no.

She asks me why not and I just can't keep up the charade until after Easter.

I tell her.

150

It's been a long time since I've seen my mother mad. Not since Jamie was walking these halls. In the last few years I've seen her sad and grouchy and nutty, but never angry.

'You little *idiot!*' she screams, leaping to her feet. Her hands are clenched into fists at her sides, as if she might finally break her stance against corporal punishment. 'How could you let that *happen*?'

I grab the edge of the kitchen bench and hoist myself to a standing position.

'We used a condom,' I scramble to explain, 'but it didn't work. I took the morning-after pill, but that didn't work either.'

'When did this happen?'

'New Year's Eve.'

'I should never have let you go to that music festival! Where was your cousin while all this nonsense was going on? He was supposed to be supervising you!'

'It wasn't Andrew's fault, Mum. I got carried away.'

'It certainly sounds like it!' My mother's voice is high-pitched and hysterical, like I haven't heard it in ages. She's practically squealing at me and her eyes are burning. I can't remember the last time I saw her quite so awake. 'This is a disaster, Shauna!'

'I know!'

'You've got no business having sex. You're a child. How are you going to look after a baby? How are you going to finish school?'

'Don't you think I've considered all that, Mum?'

'I don't know *what* you've *considered!*'

She asks me if I'm sure I'm pregnant, and whether I've been to see a doctor, and I tell her about Dr Baker and the awful Dr Goldsmith.

'You were planning to have an abortion without discussing it with us first?' she gasps. 'When were you going to tell us?'

I shake my head. 'I don't know.' I start to cry and so does Mum.

'I can't believe it,' she sobs. 'I can't believe that a smart girl like you could be so stupid. You're throwing your life away.'

'Is that what you did, Mum? You had Jamie when you were nineteen. Did you throw away your life on us? Was it all a big waste?'

Mum looks at me with dark, blazing eyes.

'My opportunities were nothing like yours. There's no comparison. I had terrible parents, and so did your father. They didn't care what we did. But I care about you. I didn't raise you to have one-night stands.'

'You didn't *raise* me to do anything, Mum. Half the time you left me to raise myself.'

'Shauna!'

'It's true, Mum. Kids grow up whether you raise them or not. Look at Jamie. Did you raise him to become a thief and a liar and a drunk?'

'*Stop* it, Shauna!' She grabs at her chest as if I've just stabbed her in the heart. 'Please don't use your brother against me. I can't take it. I just can't take it.'

She staggers into the lounge room and collapses on the couch. I follow her in there and stand over her with my hands on my hips. I'm suddenly furious with her and I'm not even sure why. Is it because she's criticising me? Or has it got more to do with Jamie? I've never had it out with her like this, not once. I've never felt so free to hurt her feelings.

'Jamie should never have been allowed to drive that night,' I tell her. 'You and Dad should have stopped him.'

Mum's face breaks and she holds her palms out in surrender. '*Please...*'

'He had no respect for either of you. You did nothing to make him respect you. You did nothing to make him respect himself.'

'I *loved* that child!'

'Of course you did. And he probably loved you too, but love just isn't enough.'

'Please don't blame me, Shauna. I already blame myself. I already beat myself up every day.' She curls her fists, clutches them against her body, which is tense and bent forwards. 'But if I'm such a terrible mother, how do you explain the way *you* turned out?'

'The way *I* turned out? Look at me! I'm seventeen and pregnant!'

'And that's *my* fault? You didn't have to carry on the way you did. You know that sex leads to pregnancy. You came second in biology last year, if I remember your report card correctly. You got ninety-three.'

Jesus, she remembers my individual marks from last year. That takes me down a notch. The fact that she's standing up for herself is a surprise. She is right, though. I didn't have to sleep with Nathan on New Year's Eve. I knew I was evading

Andrew and having too much fun, but I did it anyway. Mum seems to know what I'm thinking just by looking at me. Her face and body soften. She sinks back into the couch and sighs, exhausted.

'We all make mistakes, love. Especially when we're young. Some of them have tougher consequences than others.'

'I'm sorry, Mum.'

'We're so proud of you,' she says, her voice faltering. 'Because of you, we're respected around here.'

'Oh, for God's sake, that's rubbish. You and Dad were always popular in Barraba. You've been here forever. Look how many people came to Jamie's funeral. The whole bloody town. Nothing to do with me.'

'Your father's been invited to run for Tamworth Regional Council next year. That's because Reg Daley's niece went to that fancy school of yours. When he found out that you were there he encouraged Jim to run as the first black councillor. Now we're the kind of black family that even white people like.'

'Who cares what white people think?'

'*You* do. Or else you wouldn't bother with all those airs and graces and big words.'

'Well, I'm going to have this baby, and I don't care what anyone thinks. Bugger anyone who looks down on me. They can go to hell.'

'Of course you'll have the baby. Of course you will.'

'You don't want me to have an abortion?'

'Abortions are for white middle-class princesses. I would *never* let you have an abortion. Not on my watch.'

I sit on the arm of the couch and reach for Mum's hand. She lets me take it. We say nothing for about thirty seconds. We're both thinking, thinking.

'Do you know the father?'

'Of course I do!'

'Well, who is he?'

I give Mum a minimum of details about Nathan.

'And what does he think?'

'I haven't told him yet.'

'Aren't you gonna tell him?'

I shrug.

'We need to talk about this, Shauna. So you're three months gone, at least.' Mum shakes her head. 'You're still so young.'

'I know. I'm sorry. I knew you and Dad would be disappointed.'

'We have such high hopes for you.'

I slot in next to her on the couch and lean against her.

'I'm still going to go to uni. I don't know how, but I'm going. See if I don't.'

Mum goes quiet next to me, but straightens up and rests her elbows on her knees. I can tell she's thinking hard. She burns and buzzes against my side.

'Do the teachers at school know?'

'Of course not!'

'Don't say anything about it. If they can find some way of snatching that scholarship back, they'll do it, you know. There's nothing people love more than to watch a privileged Aboriginal person fail. There's probably people there who are already hoping for it.'

I think about Keli Street-Hughes and Annabel Saxon. 'There are, Mum.'

Mum covers her face with her hands. 'I knew this would happen,' comes her muffled voice.

'The pregnancy? How could you have known?'

She lifts her face out of her hands. 'Not about the pregnancy. I mean I knew that they'd find a way to tear you down eventually. After building you up so high, of course they'll try.'

We both smell smoke at the same time and she jumps up and runs to the kitchen.

'I'll be doing the cooking from now on, Shauna!' she calls out. I stretch out on the couch with a pillow clutched to my chest, swallowing desperately as the smell of browning onions, which smells like dog food to me now, wafts from the kitchen. I'm desperately hungry, but I also feel like I could never eat another bite. It's a weird and sickening contradiction.

Talking to Mum has worn me out. Though confessing has been a relief, I feel like there are new things to be afraid of. I've never heard my mother speak about Oakholme College in anything but glowing terms and I wonder whether her theory could be true. Are they really waiting for me to fail? Maybe the likes of Keli Street-Hughes and Annabel Saxon are, but why would the school have started the Indigenous scholarship in the first place if they wanted the recipients to fail? It doesn't make sense. But then you look at the dropout rate of the Indigenous scholarship recipients and it's seventy per cent. There's just me, Lou-Anne and Olivia. I understand why girls get drawn back home, even when home isn't very good. Even when home isn't safe, what *feels* safe is what you're used to. Home is home, and no matter how good the other place is, it isn't home. But do people at the school actually *enjoy* seeing us come and go?

I know that's not the way it is with Reverend Ferguson. She's been my cheerleader from the get-go, since back when I was almost as ragged as Olivia Pike. When she finds out I'm pregnant, she might change her tune. She might have to. I can't see Mrs Green turning a blind eye. I just can't.

When Mum and I sit down for dinner, I feel the same heat and energy come off her as I felt when we were on the lounge. I haven't seen her this sharp for ages. Maybe not ever.

We start to work on the problem, which is not something I've been able to do with anyone so far. With Dr Baker and Jenny, there was no problem that couldn't be solved with a quick curettage. With Lou-Anne, there was no problem at all. But Mum and I talk about delivery dates and exam dates. If I have the baby before my exams start, she'll come to Sydney and take care of the baby while I study and do the exams.

'If worst comes to worst, you could go back to Barraba High.'

'I'm not going back to Barraba High, Mum. I'd rather be dead. I don't mean to be a snob, but it's a jungle.'

I sleep like the dead that night. Between the train trip, the truck ride, spilling the beans to Mum and the eight-centimetre energy sapper growing inside me, I'm wiped out. After so much stress, it's wonderful waking up in my own lumpy bed. Even if it's to the terrifying sight of my father standing over me.

'Get up!' he spits.

I sit up and see Mum standing in the doorway behind him. It's eight o'clock in the morning and she's up and fully dressed, an anomaly in itself.

'Calm down, Jim,' she says.

'Is it true? You're pregnant?'

Honestly, I thought Mum and I had gone over all this yesterday. Now I have to justify myself to Dad, too?

'Of course it's true. Do you think it's some kind of April Fools' joke?'

'Don't you *dare* talk like a smartarse to me, Shauna. This is disgraceful.'

I get out of bed and face him. He's never spoken to me with an acid tongue before. I didn't feel ashamed when Mum was telling me off, but now I feel heartily ashamed. It's different with dads.

'I'm sorry. It was an accident.'

'How do you plan to go to university now?'

'I don't know, Dad.'

'Is the father going to do the right thing?' he asks.

'The father doesn't know,' Mum pipes in.

'I'm asking Shauna.' He forces me to look him in the eye. 'Will he do the right thing?'

'I don't *know*. I don't even know what the right thing is.'

'Well, let me tell you what it is,' he says in a raised voice.

'Jim...' starts Mum.

'Jackie, let me say my piece!' he snaps. Then he seems to make an effort to calm himself. 'I'm far from happy about this situation, considering your age...'

158

'I know.'

'…but I'd feel a lot more comfortable if the fella stepped forwards and took responsibility. I'm not saying you have to get married – I don't even think that's a good idea – but the man has to pay for raising his own child.'

'I don't want to ask him for money, Dad. I don't want him to think I'm just another Aboriginal teen mother with her hand out.'

'You're the mother of his child.'

'I don't want him to think badly of me. And his mother's a racist pig.'

'If you won't tell this kid, Shauna, I will.'

'He's not a kid,' I say. 'He's a man.'

'So let him stand up and be one.'

I sway and topple back onto my bed. I can't stand it when Dad's pissed off with me.

'I'm so sorry. I'm really sick. I just can't do anything at the moment.'

Dad gives me one last, long look of total disappointment before tears fill his eyes and he leaves the room. Mum leaves too, but returns a short time later wielding a glass filled with evil-smelling orange liquid. She holds it in my direction.

'Carrot and ginger juice,' she says, proudly. 'It's meant to help with the morning sickness.'

I take the juice to be gracious, and when I've finished it I go out to the kitchen table. As Mum fusses around me with butter toast and eggs, I realise that she must have already been shopping this morning. There were no eggs in the fridge last night, and Mum's just not the type to have a fresh piece of ginger hanging around the house. I know it can only be my baby news that has given her this shot of energy. She's happy. It's a catastrophe, but it's made her happy.

I'm not particularly happy, though I assure Mum that I will both see a doctor when I get back to Sydney and let Nathan in on the news. The truth is that I'm swinging between never talking to Nathan again, because I'm frightened of what he'll think, and wanting to fall into his arms. I know his family will think that I'm just a lazy, greedy boong who's trying to hitch a free ride on a white man. They'll think I've trapped him deliberately. I'm sure that's what they'll think. And I'm afraid that's what he'll think, too.

I say I don't care what white people think, and sometimes I really believe it, but when it comes to white people I care about, it's simply not true.

17

WITH THE BABY news off my chest, I'm hoping we'll have a pretty good Easter.

Julie, Mick and their family are going to arrive on Easter Saturday and stay for two nights. Mum and Dad decide that it's best not to tell them about my pregnancy until later on. At first I don't really understand the reason for the secrecy, but Mum explains.

'Julie's always had an opinion about you going to Oakholme College. It upsets her. She says that we're disrespecting our culture by sending you there, trying to turn you into something you're not – blah, blah, blah. But I think Julie's jealous of you.'

'Oh, Mum, she's *not*...'

'No, listen. I think she is. I think she wishes she could do something better than bake bread at the back of Coles, and she's ticked off that you are on your way. I don't want to give her the satisfaction of knowing that there's been a bump in the road.'

'But who cares, Mum?'

'I do. She might call your school and tell them, just to spoil things for you.'

'She wouldn't do that. Would she?'

'Julie's a great person to have around when things are going badly. When your life's going to hell in a hand basket, she loves to help out. But when your life's going well, it's much harder for her to take.'

'But she seems like such a nice person.'

'And she *is*. Don't get me wrong. At least she cares enough about you to have an opinion. But not everyone who loves you wants the best for you. Some people want to keep you in your place so that they can stay in theirs.'

I don't really get where Mum's coming from, but I agree to keep things quiet. This applies to my friends around Barraba, too. Not that I have that many left – just two out of four I used to go around with at the time Jamie died. Melinda is dead (she died in a car accident) and Kiara is missing (she disappeared with her deadbeat boyfriend). The other two are still in Barraba. Ashley's a young mother who lives with her boyfriend in the same street as her parents. My neighbour Taylor is the only one who's made it to Year 12.

I feel like such a snob when I admit this to myself, but I have a tolerance span of about an hour at a time for both of these girls. Being with them is exhausting because I feel like I have to cut myself in half intellectually to come anywhere near to fitting in with them. They rake over the same small, smelly gossip every time I see them. The most exciting thing that's happened to either of them is Ashley's baby, Bella.

Before I tumbled down the rabbit hole of pregnancy and babies, I had been finding Ashley increasingly hard to take. This holidays, though, when my old friends swing by to visit

(Taylor just has to walk through a gate in our shared fence), I'm full of warmth and conversation, and it's completely genuine. I play with eighteen-month-old Bella, interrogate Ashley about sleeping and feeding, and even congratulate her on the great job she's doing.

'It's the hardest job in the world,' says Ashley. 'And the most important.'

'I'm sure Shauna will find a harder job,' says Taylor, who has a habit of swinging at me every now and then. She could have gotten the Indigenous scholarship, but she refused to want it. 'Splitting the atom or some such crap.'

I pull a fake greaser at her. 'I think you'll find that some-one's already done that Tay-Tay. I'm only interested in breaking new ground. I'm going to split the electron.'

Taylor scrunches up her button nose. 'Is that even possible?'

'I don't do physics. You tell me.'

Taylor's eyes narrow as she considers whether I'm having her on.

'I don't think so. It's a single particle. There's nothing to split.'

There you go, Taylor is better at science than me. But I'm guessing she'll probably take all her intelligence and spark and funnel it into a job at a petrol station and a guy who doesn't appreciate her. Hopefully she'll prove me wrong.

In the end, Mum does almost all the cooking for our Easter Sunday lunch. All I have to offer is inspiration and two desserts that require no cooking. I make a Toblerone cheesecake and a lemon meringue dessert using shop-bought meringues and a jar of lemon curd. Mum roasts three chickens and tray after tray of vegetables. Unaccustomed to the workload, she heaves and sweats around the kitchen all Sunday morning, and collapses on the lounge after lunch. Luckily the Kiprioses (Julie's husband, Mick, is Greek) have brought loads of cold meat and bread with them, and Mum doesn't have to do any more cooking until Monday.

I spend the weekend hanging out with my cousins and their squeezes-du-jour. I'm a little miffed that Andrew's new girlfriend 'Frizz' (who doesn't even have frizzy hair but whose name is Caitlin Frismond) is in attendance. She shows me a furry Easter bunny toy he gave her, which has *RED HOT LOVERS* sewn across its chest in shiny red thread.

'It's true!' she says with a sleazy lurch of her eyebrows.

This dumb present provokes a shamefully sharp stab of jealousy in me. It's not just that I'd prefer to have Andrew to myself. It's that Nathan isn't around to give me cringe-worthy gifts, which I'd dearly love to receive.

I shoot Andrew a withering look, which he blushingly shrugs off. He still hasn't lost his hallowed status as My Favourite Cousin. I can't help but adore him, silly girlfriend or not. He's an acquired taste – old fashioned and masculine. Not everyone takes to him, but I love him because he's smart and he doesn't suffer fools. Not unless he's sleeping with them.

At lunch on Monday, Julie tells us that Andrew's been offered another promotion, but it depends on whether he'll do a business degree, which his employer's offered to pay for. It's obvious that Julie's proud of Andrew, but she's also dead-against him doing the degree.

'People in our family don't go to university,' she says.

'If the company's paying for you, why not?' says Dad.

'I was really bad at maths at school,' says Andrew. 'How am I going to do all the maths involved in accounting and finance?'

'I'm good at maths,' I tell him. 'I could help you.'

'You've got enough on your plate, Shauna,' Dad says softly.

Julie throws her head back and laughs, high and loud. 'Oh, Shauna, you're funny,' she titters.

'What's so hilarious?' I ask, more confused than offended.

'Do you really think…' she scoffs, shaking her head, but she doesn't finish the question. Instead she turns to Andrew. 'It's just a piece of paper. It's not worth anything. Your skills and experience are the important thing.'

I start watching Mum, finally having some insight into her warning about Julie. Mum's looking between Julie and Mick. Mick's a soft-spoken, hardworking man who often gets steam-rolled by Julie's brassy personality.

'What do you think, Mick?' Mum asks.

'I don't see the harm,' he says cautiously.

'The harm is that he *fails*,' says Julie, gesturing wildly. She's still smiling, but she's almost shouting now. 'Why fail if you don't have to? Especially if you're on the kind of salary Andrew's on.' She looks at Mum as she mock-whispers, 'Six figures and he's only twenty-three.' Then she continues at normal volume. 'There are plenty of successful people who didn't waste years of their life pushing pencils around at university.'

'I'm going to university next year,' I say, aware that I'm stirring the pot.

'Well, I hope that works out well for you, Shauna,' says Julie. 'I hope they treat you the way you deserve.'

Though my aunt's tone isn't taunting or even all that insincere, I think I finally have a perspective on what Mum was saying about her earlier. A part of Julie is hopeful that I'll fail. And not just me, but anyone who breaks the mould that has held her in shape since she started making decisions for herself. It's the mould that she's forced her own children to fit.

After lunch, I manage to prise the dreaded Frizz from Andrew's side and get him alone on the back porch. I want to encourage him to do the business degree. It's impossible to turn him around, though.

'I've made up my mind. I'm not going to do it. I don't know why Mum keeps rattling on about it.'

'Because she's proud of you.'

He shrugs.

'Maybe she doesn't want you to do it because she's afraid you'll do *too* well?' I suggest.

Andrew shakes his head. 'She's just looking out for me, and I think she's right. You stick your head too far out and there's always someone with a machete waiting to hack it right off.'

'But who's got the machete, Andrew?'

'The bosses. White men.'

This is not the way Andrew usually talks. Generally he's reluctant to blame white people for anything.

'So why don't you become one of the bosses?'

Andrew takes a long time to answer. All the while he's shaking his head. 'Life is not like boarding school, Shauna,' he says eventually.

'I'm not an idiot, you know. I realise that. And thank God it's not like boarding school.'

'Wait till you get out into the real world. Then you'll understand. Everything is stacked against us. They'll let us come only so far. And anyway, who wants to be like them?'

'And you've come as far as you're ever going to? At age twenty-three?'

He pauses for even longer this time.

'I reckon I've done pretty well,' he says finally.

'Well, there's no doubt about that,' I agree. I know that I've pushed him as far as I should. Any further and it will be none of my bloody business. I drop it for another subject. With a sheepish smile, I hand him the envelope he sent me with the five hundred bucks in it. Andrew looks confused.

'What? You're not going to Paris anymore?'

'I'm gonna leave it to another year.'

He pushes the envelope back in my direction. 'Keep it. Go and buy something you want. A phone.'

'I don't need a phone.'

'Then keep it for uni next year.'

'I don't want it, Andrew. I really don't. Why can't you just respect my wishes?'

Andrew laughs bitterly, stuffing the envelope into his jacket pocket. 'Why can't you just respect mine?' he retorts.

We exchange fed-up smiles and settle on the porch as the sun sets over the back fence.

'Hey,' I say eventually, looking down at the grass, 'I'm not as perfect as I seem.'

Andrew smiles wryly.

'Oh, you don't seem that perfect to me, Shauna,' he teases. 'There are plenty of things I could point out, but I'm much too polite.'

'And I suppose Frizz is perfect?'

'She's pretty great.'

'So is it serious between you guys?'

He gives me a sidelong look.

'I'd say so, yeah.'

I take a moment to summon the courage for my next question.

'What would you do if she got pregnant?'

'Shauna! I don't wanna have this conversation with you!'

'I'm not talking about sex. I'm talking about pregnancy. What would you do?'

'Well, we've worked out that one leads to the other. And we're careful. So I don't have to ask myself that question.' He elbows my arm. 'Next topic, please.'

I'd like to confide in him, but his prudish, brotherly attitude just knocks all the will out of me. If I can't tell someone apart from my parents who I love and trust at home, who will I be able to tell at school? Dread of the new term at Oakholme seeps in and soaks me to the bone.

While the Kiprioses are still staying with us, I sneak onto Mum's phone and plunge to the hilt into Keli Street-Hughes's gloriously unprotected social media accounts. She's in Margaret River, Western Australia, staying on a vineyard with her extended family. There are lots of gastro-porn shots of fancy food on huge, white plates, and people huddled with their arms around each other on a background of endless rows of grapevines running up green hills. I envy the girls and women in the photos their empty wombs and squeaky-clean consciences. For once it's not their wealth and impressive friends and followers lists that bother me.

I get so wretched that I even look up Andrew's girlfriend, and when I find a photo of her in an embrace with another man, I take it straight to my cousin, pulling him into the kitchen by his shirtsleeve.

'She's two-timing you!' I shout-whisper.

Andrew combines a deep sigh with a soaring eye roll. I shrink.

'Is that her ex-boyfriend?' I whisper, mortified.

'Her brother,' says Andrew at normal volume. 'What's going on with you, Shauna? Why are you in such a funk?'

He snatches Mum's phone from my hand.

'Jackie!' he calls to the next room, holding the phone out of my reach. 'Your naughty daughter has been caught playing on your phone!' I jump up and down, trying to get it back, laughing uncontrollably, and the sounds of my cousin and then my mother cracking up fill me with joy.

It takes a few days after Julie & Co leave for me to start feeling better physically. There's no explaining it, but the morning sickness goes. I just wake up one day feeling completely normal. After a few months of wanting to vomit myself inside out, normal is better than great. It's ecstasy, and it makes me feel more positive in general.

On the train trip back to Sydney, I spend a long time thinking about the person inside me, whether it's a boy or a girl, and what it will look like. I'm about four months gone now, but you wouldn't know it. My belly has always stuck out a little and it doesn't seem to protrude any further than usual. The only part of my anatomy that's exploding out of its garments is my boobs, but that's hardly something to complain about. No one's going to call me out for having too much cleavage.

Now that I feel so good and I can imagine my foetus as a real person, I can't believe that I ever considered having an abortion, let alone made it all the way into a clinic. I wonder how many other girls like me let their morning sickness and crazy hormones tip them into the well-greased abortion pipeline.

And I imagine how hard it would have been to say no if my parents had been real dicks about it or my best friend hadn't been so supportive. It would have been impossible. For all the wretched cant about women's choices, there would have been no choice.

18

ON THE WALK from Central Station back to school, who should I bump into but my best buddy Olivia Pike? There she is, in full uniform, standing on a street corner selling badges and teddy bears to raise money for Wish Upon A Star. I feel a pang of guilt about the scene in my room, just before the end of last term, when she wanted to talk to me. I haven't spoken to her since. Between schoolwork, stress and morning sickness, I just never found the right moment to follow up.

Initially I spot her in profile, but then I cross the road and come up behind her. When I'm close enough that I can see the mole on the back of her ear, I lean over her shoulder and yell the black slang, 'Give it up, sista girl!'

I soon regret my little prank. Olivia squeals and throws all her merchandise, notes and coins in the air.

'Fuckin *hell*, Shauna!'

It's the first time she's ever called me Shauna.

'Shit, I'm sorry.'

We both get down on our hands and knees and start cleaning up the mess. Two twenty-dollar notes flitter onto the road and I dive for them, only just making it out of the path of a furiously honking bus.

Olivia abuses me non-stop as she scoops up the badges, bears and pens.

'You've really got shit for brains.'

'I'm sorry.'

'You're a fucking mental case.'

'I'm *sorry*, Olivia.'

It takes a few minutes to get everything back in its box. When I hand her the last two gold coins, she goes nuts at me, right in front of the small crowd that has gathered around us.

'I told you *not* to come up to me at school! That goes double when we're in public! Leave me alone, you *psycho*!'

'What's going on here?'

I can't believe it, but two young police officers – one male, one female – have stumbled upon our scuffle.

'Are you bothering this young lady?'

'That Aboriginal girl was grabbing her money,' someone in the crowd says.

As I turn around to see who said it, the lady police officer shoves me to the other side of the footpath. Instinctively I put my hands in the air.

'I didn't do anything,' I say. 'She's a friend of mine. I was just joking around with her.'

The lady police officer asks Olivia, 'Do you know her?'

Quick as a flash that little psychopath yells back, 'Never seen her before in my life!'

'You wait, Olivia. I'm gonna get you, you little *shit*!' I shriek, and the police officer hauls me further down the footpath. She points her finger right in my face.

'You've just threatened a child and used offensive language in public. Do you want me to write you up now or would you prefer to move on?'

I want to snap off this cop's accusing finger and stick it up her arse. It takes all my self-control not to get physical with her. I know that I won't win if I do.

I take off across the road and manage to keep the tears at bay until my face is turned away from the crowd.

It kills me that in this age of stifling political correctness, I can still end up on the wrong side of the law for nothing more than having Aboriginal facial features and brown skin. As I walk through Rushcutters Bay, bawling my eyes out, I think about all the things I could have said to those cops. I could have explained that Olivia and I go to the same school. I could have shown them my student card. I could have told them that I've been appointed Olivia's mentor. I could have calmly stood up for myself and cleared up the misunderstanding.

Why did I run off? Why didn't I stand my ground?

I've been in some trouble with the police before. It was during the months I wasn't going to school back in Barraba. I was lonely and I fell in with a crowd of older kids. We talked tough but, apart from binge drinking and occasionally shop-lifting, we never did anything really bad. The police had it in for us though, and it got to the stage where we couldn't hang out together at the park or pool, or anywhere in public, no matter what we were doing.

Back then, I had no confidence. I was insecure and surly and rude, and whenever an adult criticised me, I had the feeling that I deserved it. Now that I'm older and surer of myself, I know that I didn't deserve to be moved on or called 'black dross' or accused of vandalism that I had nothing to do with. I know that I was entitled to be out in public with a mob of other kids like me. Sometimes when I think back to those days, I get so angry I could kill someone.

So why have I let it happen again? And in front of Olivia Pike!

I wipe my eyes and clear my throat, determined to be out of this state when I get to school. By the time I walk through the front gates, I've pulled myself together and I've decided that I will never, ever allow myself to be stood over by the powers that be again. I'm done with that damper.

Up in the dorms, Lou-Anne's lying face down on her bed with her backpack still looped over her shoulders. She's in the throes of her usual post-holiday depression. I lie down beside her and lay my arm over her shoulders. I can see that the side of her face is all scrunched up against the pillow.

I whisper in her ear, 'You wouldn't believe what happened to me on the way here.'

'Shauna,' she grunts without really moving her mouth, 'I'm in no mood for your crap this afternoon.'

Lou-Anne's often like this after she's been with her family. It's the only time she's ever in bad humour. I know she'll get over her sullenness in a few days, but it's always difficult in the meantime.

'Olivia Pike almost got me arrested!' I throw it out there but Lou-Anne doesn't blink.

'*Seriously,*' I add.

Lou-Anne still doesn't blink.

'I could be in the lockup *right now!*'

Lou-Anne finally moves, shifting onto her side.

'Well, obviously you didn't get arrested,' she drones, 'because here you are, driving me up the wall as usual.'

I know she doesn't mean it. I try a different tack. 'Guess what?'

Lou-Anne sighs heavily. 'What?'

'My morning sickness has disappeared.'

'I'm so happy for you. I'm *so* glad you feel like a hundred dollars.'

'You mean a million dollars.'

'What did I say?'

'You said a hundred dollars. Maybe you feel like a hundred dollars, but I feel like a million dollars.'

'You know I'm no good at maths.'

I start laughing, but Lou-Anne doesn't join in.

'Laugh away, Shauna. You won't be laughing when that baby gets here.'

'What do you mean?'

Lou-Anne sits up suddenly. Her eyes narrow. Her expression curdles.

'Well, let's see. First you're going to go through twenty hours of the worst pain you've ever experienced. Think diarrhoea plus period pain to the power of infinity.'

'I thought you sucked at maths, Lou-Anne.'

My joke makes no dent on her whatsoever. She ploughs on as if I never made a peep.

'Then you're going to get ripped from your fanny to your arsehole by a human head. If you're lucky the doctor will make the cut with a scalpel and it won't just tear by itself. After that you won't get more than two hours sleep at a time for at least a few months. Your nipples will bleed. Your fanny will bleed. You won't be able to go anywhere or do anything you want for ages. You'll be so tired that you won't be able to think straight.'

'Jesus, Lou-Anne. You've never told me this before. You're making it sound like hell.'

'I just think you should know,' she says with a tight smile, 'that I watched my sister give girth and it's not a bowl of bloody cherries.'

'But after the first few months, it gets better, right?'

Lou-Anne raises her eyebrows and then slowly shakes her head. Oh God, there's more.

'Maybe you'll get a little more sleep, but it'll get worse.'

'Worse how?'

She shakes her head and looks to the ceiling, as if the words she's searching for might be written up there. She opens and shuts her mouth a few times before finally speaking.

'Because you'll have to follow them around every second of the day to make sure they're happy and they don't get hurt.' She levels her gaze at me. There are tears in her eyes. 'And they'll break your heart because they're so cute and you love them so much. But they'll drive you crazy, too, and some-times you'll wish they'd never been born and then you'll hate yourself for thinking like that.'

'Is that the way Beth feels?'

Lou-Anne nods.

'It's not something people talk about, is it? But it's true. Sometimes I feel the same way, too, and I'm just their auntie. Most of the time I love being with Chelsea and Charlotte, but sometimes I get sick of the crying and fighting and whining and the bloody running off. Then you realise that the only thing worse than being stuck with them is being stuck without them. God, I miss my family. Sometimes I just want to pack my bags and go home. And *never come back*.'

'Don't you ever do that. I couldn't stand it here without you.'

'You should know, Shauna, that your life from now on is going to be one big worryfest. You're about to become a hostage to good luck. Like my sister.'

'What do you mean?'

'I mean you can be the best mother ever, keep a real tight watch over your kids, and *still* lose them. You have no control over whether your life will be wrecked.'

'Did something happen during the holidays, Lou-Anne?'

She nods and struggles to control her voice. 'Beth picked Chelsea up off the bottom of our neighbour's pool on the weekend.'

'Oh my God! Is she all right?'

'Yeah, she's fine. But it could have been a disaster. She swam into the middle of the pool and took her floaties off. Beth was there, but she didn't notice until Chelsea had sunk right to the bottom. If Beth had been distracted for ten more seconds, Chelsea might have...well...it could have been a lot worse.'

177

Lou-Anne wipes away her tears and shrugs.

'I'm sorry that happened.'

'Beth was beside herself. And that's what you've got to understand about kids. You can lose them and then your life's over. That's the worst thing about them.'

I think about the way my brother ruined my parents' life. I know what Lou-Anne's talking about all too well. Sprinkle some bad luck over a handful of mistakes, and hey presto! – you get a dead kid and a life sentence of grief. All of a sudden the terrible responsibility of what I'm doing crashes down on me. I've taken something the size of a grain of rice and I'll be shepherding it all the way into adulthood. Until it's older than I am now. It's an awesome task, and I don't necessarily mean that in a good way. That's the truth of it, I realise. Even with the right intentions, if you're not careful *and* lucky parenthood can go horribly, horribly wrong. And I'm not just talking about your kid calling you a bitch and stealing your credit card and maybe smoking dope. It's much deeper and more dangerous than that.

Do I have what it takes? Can I be a good mother? Will I get the good luck and the help that I need? It's really a wonder that any girl or woman's prepared to take on motherhood. Anyone who gets as far as Lou-Anne's sister deserves a bravery medal.

'So you were saying that something happened to you on the way here?' Lou-Anne finally smiles at me, but not with teeth.

'Oh yeah. Well, I just got Piked.'

I cheer up Lou-Anne with the tale of Olivia and the cops. Lou-Anne, whose support for Olivia is at a particularly low ebb, is outraged on my behalf.

'That little turd,' she hisses through her teeth. 'After all you've done for her.'

'She is definitely the most ungrateful person I've ever met,' I agree self-righteously.

19

A few weeks later I come first in a French test.

Our teacher, Mademoiselle Larsen, always hands the tests
out in descending order of marks, and it's my test she lays
down before anyone else's.

Jenny elbows me. 'Not again,' she moans. 'How do you
do it, Shauna?'

At the moment I'm beating Jenny in French and 3-unit
maths, and giving her a good nudge in every other subject we
do together. This is no mean feat, considering that Jenny's
parents have hired private tutors for her in every subject
except English. (She doesn't need a tutor in English because
her father's an English professor.) I, on the other hand, only
have my foetus to bounce ideas off, and he doesn't know
much about Albert Camus.

I'll admit it, okay? I'm trying hard. To be a 'try-hard'
in Australia is to be a loser, but how can you be a winner if
you don't try hard? I've been hitting the books and practice
papers every afternoon, even during prep., a marvel in itself.
I study in my bed first thing in the morning. I study in the
Year 12 common room at lunch. Bindi and I often study
together at the same desk in our room until late, snarling at

anyone who makes a peep. The other night, well after ten, Indu was whispering prayers to her spiritual mentor in Hindi when Bindi suddenly yelled, 'Sai Baba, can you tell Indu to *shut the hell up!*'

Indu didn't take it well. 'You're sharing a room with three other people, Bindi!'

'Yeah, and two of them are quiet.'

Indu stewed in her pyjamas for a couple of minutes before unhooking Sai Baba from his place on the wall and stomping out. Miss Maroney intercepted her in the hallway, gave her a Red Mark and sent her back into our room. She ran into the bathroom and slammed the door.

Petty tensions like this keep rearing their heads. The atmosphere is heavy among the Year 12 girls, and how could it not be? The HSC results will have a huge influence on our lives, not just in terms of our options at university, but in the way we see ourselves. Will I consider myself a success if I don't get into journalism at uni? What else can I study? What am I good at? What will I tell my parents and friends if my performance falls short? The pressure is intense and it's driving us crazy.

During chapel, Reverend Ferguson reminds us to keep things in perspective, to remember that God sees each of us as a whole person, not as a mark or rank or even as a prospective career. It's easier for me than most to remember that there are other things in life, like the life of my baby. At the same time, though, all our teachers seem to care about is what questions will be in the HSC exams and what scores we'll get. When you're doing a timed practice paper with a teacher looking over your shoulder, it's hard to remember what Reverend Ferguson said in chapel about not panicking. Luckily, my baby never quite lets me forget its presence or value.

Lou-Anne and I have started calling my foetus by the codename 'Fred'. We figure that talking about a foetus or a baby or pregnancy might arouse suspicion, so now it's 'Fred's wearing me out' or 'Fred ate my lunch and now I'm hungry again' or 'Fred stole my period'.

Jenny hasn't asked me about Fred since we returned to school. She didn't return my one phone call to her during the holidays and she's been cool with me since term began – she and I *never* study together – but at least she's not trying to talk me into an abortion anymore. Though she hasn't asked, I suspect that she knows I'm still pregnant. Probably it's better that we don't discuss it. Given that I'm five months pregnant now and can feel Fred fluttering inside me, I don't think I'd take too kindly to suggestions that Fred should be dead. Also, remembering what Dr Goldsmith said about the twenty-week mark, I think it might be too late to press the delete button now, even if I wanted to.

To the uninformed observer, I probably look like I've put on a little weight. My face is fatter than usual, my boobs have become bazookas, and my stomach looks like I've eaten too much lunch. My uniform still fits – *just* – and to use Olivia Pike's word, I'm 'passable', as long as I'm dressed. Things in the shower have become somewhat outstanding, though. When I'm warm and nude, I look as ripe and juicy as a plump summer plum. My nipples have become huge and dark, and there's a thick, black line leading from my belly button to my pubic hair. I don't know what it's doing there or when it arrived, but there it is.

My skin is better than it's ever been. I don't have a pimple anywhere on my body, not even on my back, where I usually have at least three at any given time. My eyes are bright and my hair is lustrous. The only physical downside is that my gums have been bleeding sometimes when I brush my teeth. Mentally, I'm firing on all cylinders. Studying's easy, my memory's good, and I'm not suffering at all from what Lou-Anne calls 'baby brain'. I'm just a bit tired.

That morning, Mademoiselle Larsen asks me to stay back after class. A tiny splinter of panic jabs me, but I tell myself not to worry. She can't see Fred. She doesn't know he's there.

Miss Larsen, if you remember, used to hate my guts, but I can't really blame her for that. I was not very likeable. I've woken up to myself since then and, like most of the other teachers here at Oakholme College, Miss Larsen has given me chance after chance to redeem myself. Now, after my stellar performance in the French test, it looks like I finally have.

'You're going to take out the French prize this year if you're not careful, Shauna. I haven't handed back the Camus papers yet, but I think you've probably come first in that too.'

I can't help grinning. 'Cool.'

'I don't know what's happened to you this year,' she goes on, 'but you're proving to be quite the dark horse.'

I'm a portrait of modesty. 'There's no big secret. It's just hard work.'

'Well, it's paying off, *ma chérie*, so keep it up.'

I can tell we haven't quite reached the point of our little meeting, so I'm not surprised when she changes the subject.

'Jenny Bean tells me that you two were planning a trip to Paris next year.'

'We were talking about it, yeah.'

'She says that you pulled out for some reason.' She pauses, obviously waiting for me to tell her why, but of course I can't. 'Is it a financial problem, Shauna?'

'Partly.'

'The cost of accommodation in Paris is very high, isn't it?'

'And the flights.'

Mademoiselle Larsen sits daintily on the corner of her desk and crosses her ankles, as if this conversation might take some little time.

'Look, if you still want to go, I might be able to help you out. Especially if you decided to stay there for a while.'

'What do you mean?'

'Well, what if you did a French language course, or even got a job, or both? If you stayed there for six months or a year, it'd make the cost of the flights worthwhile. It'd be more than just an expensive holiday.'

As she continues, I smile, though I really feel like crying.

'I have some friends who own an apartment in the fifth *arrondissement*,' she says, 'and their son's just moved out of home. I've spoken to them about you, and they've told me that you'd be welcome to stay with them. They wouldn't charge you board, though they might expect you to help with housework.'

As she talks, an image opens in my mind. I can see myself in Miss Larsen's friends' apartment. It's on the third floor. We're eating breakfast in the sun-filled kitchen. I'm slurping hot chocolate from a bowl. Monsieur offers me a *pain au chocolat*, and I take it. Madame says that there's chocolate on my lip. I lick it off and we all laugh.

It's tantalising, but with Fred on board, I know it's out of my reach.

'That's such a nice offer,' I tell Miss Larsen, 'but there are other reasons I can't go to France next year. It's not just about the money.'

'Something to consider, though.'

'What about Jenny?' I ask. 'I'm sure she'd love to stay with your friends.'

'Jenny's parents can afford to keep her in Paris,' Miss Larsen replies firmly. 'The offer's only open to you, okay? And it's confidential.'

'I won't tell Jenny,' I say.

Afterwards, I find Jenny waiting for me in the hallway.

'What was that all about?'

'The French prize. As in I'm getting it.'

'She did *not* tell you that you're getting the French prize!'

'Nah. She just wanted to know why I don't want to go to Paris anymore.'

'And what did you say?'

'Can't afford to.'

Jenny gives me this hard, searching look, like she doesn't quite believe me.

'Well, I can't!'

'You still have options, Shauna.'

'I know,' I say coolly.

Frankly, I think Jenny is still miffed because Reverend Ferguson managed to withdraw me from Introduction to Legal Systems and Methods without any consequences for my academic record. Somewhere, deep down, Jenny wanted me to be punished for my decision. Well, tough luck. There's no failure on my record. Not yet, anyway.

She asks me if I want to go to the common room for recess, but I can't. I have a hot date with Olivia Pike.

Ugh, Olivia Pike.

After she almost got me charged with public misdemeanour offences, I honestly felt like cutting her off for good. I had visions of confronting Self-Raising Flour and telling her that I was done being Olivia's mentor. The main reason I decided against it was to deny the little jerk the satisfaction.

This is only our second mentor/mentee meeting since the new term began. The last one went a little like this: twenty-seven minutes of silence.

Olivia: 'Look, are you waiting for me to apologise? I'm sorry, okay?'

Me: 'Apology not accepted.'

Olivia scoffs.

Three further minutes of silence.

Today I plan to continue the silent treatment, with some study thrown in. I've brought my Biology notes with me.

I'm absolutely charming to Reverend Ferguson when she arrives at the withdrawing room with Olivia, but the moment she's gone, so is my smile. I take a seat at my usual end of the boardroom table and start reading.

This time Olivia holds out for fourteen minutes before cracking.

'Keli Street-Hughes's a real vile twat,' she says.

Well, I think, like fucking duh. But this is an interesting turn of events, if it's not a trick. Olivia has my full attention, but my eyes don't move from my notes.

I measure my response carefully. 'I thought you two were friends?'

'Not anymore.'

I glance up at her to see whether I'm being had. Then I look back down. If she's got something to say to me, I'm going to let her say it.

'She's telling everyone I stole from the Wish Upon A Star collection.' Olivia's voice cracks on the word 'Star', so I suspect she's being genuine.

'And?'

'And she says if I don't pay the money back by the end of the week, she's going to report me to Mrs Green.'

'Did you take the money?'

'No.'

'So what's the problem? Tell her you didn't take it. Go to Mrs Green now and tell her you're being falsely accused.'

Olivia looks decidedly dissatisfied with my solution.

'How much has gone missing?'

'Eight hundred bucks.' She gulps. 'That's what Keli says, anyway.'

'Go and tell Mrs Green about it. You don't have to sit on your hands while Keli Street-Hughes shakes you down.'

'Shauna, I can't.'

Whoa! That's the second time Olivia has called me by my name! Then she has the nerve to ask, 'Can you talk to Mrs Green?'

I explode into laughter, sounding much smugger and meaner than I intend to.

'Fine. Don't worry about it.' She folds her arms and slumps.

'I'm not pleading your case with Mrs Green for you. I'd rather gnaw off my own genitals.'

'Okay. You don't have to rub it in.'

Her gaze drifts to the side and I notice that her eyes are shining with tears.

Tant pis pour toi, Olivia. Too bad for you.

It serves her right for bargaining with the Devil, otherwise known as Keli Cailey Street-Hughes.

20

IT'S NOT THE last I hear about those pesky eight hundred bucks. And I know it's serious business when I get a note in roll call:

Please see me and Mrs Green in Mrs G's office. SRF

'Has Olivia mentioned anything to you about eight hundred dollars missing from the Wish Upon A Star fundraising effort?' Mrs Green asks me as soon as I sit down.

'My meetings with Olivia are confidential,' I say cautiously.

'Actually, Shauna,' says Self-Raising Flour, 'they're not. You're not her psychologist. You're just her mentor.'

'Has she told you anything, Shauna?' asks Mrs Green in a way that tells me I'd better stop mucking around.

'She said that Keli Street-Hughes was trying to blackmail her into paying her eight hundred dollars.' I must admit that after years of daily racist remarks, I relish sticking the dagger between Keli's shoulderblades.

'She said Keli's trying to *blackmail* her?' Mrs Green gives Reverend Ferguson a doubtful look.

'That's what she said. I told her to come and see you right away, Mrs Green. That was my advice.'

'Well, it was Keli who came to me, and she sounds very upset and very sincere. Did Olivia sound upset to you?'

'Kind of.'

'Were you inclined to believe her or not?' demands Mrs Green.

'Well, yeah,' I answer.

'As disappointed as we are,' says Reverend Ferguson, 'we don't know why Keli would make up a story like that.'

'Unless *she* took the money?' I suggest maliciously.

'We've considered that,' says Mrs Green, 'and we're as sure as we can be that that's not what's happened. Keli is the beneficiary of a trust fund set up by her grandparents. She also receives an ample amount of pocket money each week from her parents. She has no reason to steal.'

Wow, you wouldn't know it from the way she dresses, I think. Typical country uniform of moleskin poocatchers and flannel shirt that you could buy at Vinnie's.

'Maybe she's trying to frame Olivia to get her expelled?'

'That's quite an allegation, Shauna,' says Reverend Ferguson, puffing up baking-soda-style.

Mrs Green looks interested. 'Why do you think Keli would try to frame Olivia? They seemed like good friends.'

'Because, as I've already pointed out, Keli is a racist pig from way back.'

The two women look at me agape, like I've dropped the biggest bombshell of the century. Oh, *please*... We've been

190

over this, haven't we? The racial slurs, the name-calling, the murmurs, the sign on my door.

Do you know what I do then? I let Keli have it. I take no prisoners. I tell them all about every nasty word that I can remember ever coming out of Keli's freckly mouth, just to jog their faulty memories. Hell, I even exaggerate.

By the end of it, Mrs Green and Self-Raising Flour look like they've been caught in a tornado. Their hair's blown back, their suits are akimbo and their mouths are opening and closing like they're codfish.

I watch the women exchange grave looks. I think maybe they're starting to see it my way. Or at least realise that they can't keep letting it fly.

Mrs Green asks me to bring up the missing money with Olivia again and then report back to her. I leave her office thinking like hell I will.

It's not Olivia I plan to confront, but Keli.

I wait until the late afternoon, because I know Keli's usually out on the oval or in the netball courts until the hour before dinner. At about five-thirty, I take a stroll across the landing to the room that Keli shares with Annabel and two other scrubchooks. I knock on the door. Annabel opens it. She sneers when she sees it's me.

'What?'

God, she's rude. 'Is Keli here?'

'In the shower.'

Annabel begins to shut the door in my face but I jam my foot in it.

'Hey!'

She tries to push it from the other side, but I barge through, shoulder first.

'You can't just come in here!' Annabel roars, spittle flying from the tracks of her braces.

I march into the steamy bathroom. The shower's running in the last cubicle. With Annabel shrieking like a banshee behind me, I make a lunge for the shower curtain and haul it back, revealing Keli Street-Hughes in all her wobbly, dimply, ginger magnificence.

She lets out a blood-curdling scream. 'Get out!'

I reach into the cubicle and grab Keli's wet arm.

'I'm getting Miss Maroney!' cries Annabel, spinning on her heel.

I pull on Keli's arm and she slides across the tiles, thrashing like a fur seal on the deck of a poaching boat.

'Let me go! Let me go!'

Dragging her into the middle of the bathroom, I get up in her face and waggle my finger in front of her eyes, the way that cop did to me.

'You are a lying, racist arsehole,' I say, my voice dangerously low. 'I've just come from Mrs Green's office. I've told her everything about you. She suspects you're trying to frame Olivia because she's Aboriginal, and I wouldn't be surprised if you got expelled this afternoon. You deserve to be.' I'm exaggerating, of course, but I want to put the fear of God into her.

'But I haven't... I didn't...'

Keli's face is red and ravaged by a desperate frown.

'Shut up!' I yell in her face.

192

Keli whimpers and then starts crying.

'Here's what you're going to do. You're going to get dressed and go down to Mrs Green's office right now. You're going to tell her that it was all a big mistake, and that the eight hundred bucks was never missing.'

'But what am I gonna do about the money?' she wails. 'You think that Wish Upon A Star's not going to notice it's gone missing?'

'Why don't you take it out of your trust fund?'

An expression I've never seen before passes over Keli's face. She looks cheated and crushed at the same time. She looks so humiliated that I actually feel sorry for her.

'Okay,' she says, her voice trembling.

I leave her in the bathroom, and as I walk back through the dorm room and into the corridor, I pass Olivia, who must have heard every word. We lock eyes. I expect her to be grateful, but she looks petrified. I see Miss Maroney in the hallway, walking towards me with a squawking Annabel in tow.

'Shauna! What happened in that bathroom?' she demands.

'Nothing.'

'Don't you just walk past me! I want to talk to you.'

I stop and turn to face her. She asks me again what happened.

'Nothing,' comes a voice. It's Keli. She's dressed in a tracksuit and her wet hair is stuck to her face and neck. 'It was a misunderstanding,' she says flatly.

Miss Maroney looks from Keli to me and back again, unconvinced.

'Go and get ready for dinner,' she says coldly.

At dinner, Olivia sits at a table by herself. I keep trying to attract her attention to invite her to sit with us, but she refuses to meet my eye. She curves over her meal like a C, staring vacantly into her food as she turns it with her fork. There is something about her bearing that's familiar to me, and I really don't like it.

In the middle of the night I'm woken by a squeeze of my shoulder. I wake suddenly, gasping, panicking.

'Shh!'

It's Olivia. She crouches at my bedside. I sit up.

'I'm going,' she whispers.

'Where?'

'Home. Don't tell anyone. Don't try to stop me either. If you do, I'll admit that I stole the money and I'll be expelled anyway.'

'Did you really take the money?'

'Yes.'

Words can't express how disappointed I am to hear this. 'Why, Olivia?'

'I don't know.'

It's such a shame it's taken this long for us to speak frankly to each other. I understand how she doesn't know, because I used to steal and I still don't know why. I feel a flood of empathy for her.

'Go back to bed,' I whisper. 'We'll sort it out in the morning.'

'I'm going back to Bourke. I'm catching the six o'clock train.'

'We can keep the money a secret. I won't tell anyone.'

'But they know I'm a boong now. You *told* them, Shauna.'

'I thought they already knew! I thought that was why Keli was accusing you!'

'They didn't.'

'Well, they know I'm a boong, and I'm still here. Stay at school, Olivia. It'll be okay.'

'I don't belong here. I can't stand it, pretending to be something I'm not. I'd rather be a boong in Bourke.'

'I know how you feel.' I take her hand and squeeze it. 'But please don't leave. Things will change, I promise. You'll change, and then your feelings will change, and then people's attitudes will change. *Some* of them, anyway. You have to give school a chance. Give it until the end of the year. You deserve to be here, you know.'

She squeezes my hand back. 'Thanks for trying to help me,' she says.

I want to tell her all kinds of things. That I know what it's like to feel terrified and strange. That I used to hate myself, too. That I did bad things and was dishonest and unlovable. That I've decided that I'm going to make it in spite of my past, and that she can too.

But I let her go.

In the morning I wake up early. My first thought is that I hope Olivia has changed her mind, but then I see the envelope on my bedside table. I open it and count the money. There's seven hundred and eighty bucks in there. Twenty's missing. She's planning a trip to Bourke, a sandwich and a can of Coke. She's gone.

On the front of the envelope there's some childish writing. It says: *Here's to you, Mr Street-Hughes!*

I tiptoe up to the other end of the dorm building and push the envelope under Keli Street-Hughes's door.

Later in the morning there's all strains of mayhem, what with Olivia and most of her stuff missing. The police arrive. Every boarder gets interrogated. I don't give away anything. It's all resolved by the afternoon, of course, because she turns up at her foster parents' place in Bourke.

I get a note from SRF and I meet her in her office. She asks me what happened, and whether it had anything to do with Keli, and I tell her that I don't know.

'I just hope it didn't have anything to do with me,' I say.

'You did your best Shauna,' she says, 'and that's all anyone expects of you.'

The more I think about it, though, the more sure I am that Keli Street-Hughes didn't know that Olivia was Aboriginal – not until I shouted it into her face in the bathroom. And that's what sent Olivia packing. I know that her flight is at least partly my fault. I jumped to conclusions about what had happened, and I was very badly wrong.

After dinner, I catch Keli Street-Hughes alone in the stairwell. When I call her name, she stops dead, turns and her eyes widen in some shape of horror.

'I owe you an apology,' I tell her. 'I made a mistake and I'm sorry.'

Keli looks stunned for a moment before sharpening up smartly.

'Tell your cuz she owes me twenty bucks,' she says gruffly. 'You're lucky I didn't report you both to the police today.'

She shoots off ahead of me, taking two stairs at a time. At the top, she goes her way and I go mine. I know that in her mind, everything she's ever believed about me and Aboriginal people in general has been confirmed today. She was right all along. Of course she was.

It hits me with a great jolt of guilt that Olivia has been let down on my watch. I should have drawn her out that afternoon she came into my room wanting to talk. I shouldn't have brushed her off. The only way to redeem myself, and maybe the only way to redeem Olivia, is to find her and convince her to come back to Oakholme.

21

My PARENTS KNOW that I have better things to do with the July school holidays than travel to Bourke to coddle Olivia Pike, but they're reluctantly letting me go.

'Is it really any of your business, love?' Mum asks me in the car on the way to the coach station at Tamworth.

'Yeah, it is.'

'Seems to me like you've already got enough to worry about. Study and...everything.'

'I'll only be a few days, Mum.'

It's quite the odyssey from Barraba to Bourke, and it's nowhere near any of Dad's truck routes. I have to catch two buses, and between the bus travel and the layovers, the trip's going to take a whole day.

As the second coach leaves Dubbo for Bourke, the woman sitting beside me asks me where I'm from. Then she asks me how far along I am.

'Six months,' I tell her proudly. Babies are good news to a woman like Jeanine from Nyngan, a hugely built, hugely creased grandmother who's probably only in her fifties. 'Most people don't notice.'

'You're not showing much,' says Jeanine. 'It's more the look on your face and the careful way you move, like you're carrying an important secret.'

'I am.'

It's strange how sometimes talking to a stranger can be easier than talking to someone close to you. Or is it just the ties that bind women over pregnancy and childbirth? Whatever the reason, Jeanine and I hit it off. She tells me the stories of her births. She had five babies, but lost one of them when he was a teenager. He got hit by a car while crossing the street drunk. I tell her about Jamie and she knows exactly how to respond. At first she says nothing. She rests in her seat and I rest in mine, and we each imagine the other's loss with tight chests and thick throats.

'That baby's gonna love you,' she says finally.

'I know.'

'Gonna love you like you're God. And there'll be a piece of your brother in that love. You'll see it in your baby's eyes when they open. I found my son in my grandchildren's eyes. He's alive in all of them. I hope your parents are going to be at the birth.'

'They sure will. My friends, too, probably.'

'And the father? Will he be there?'

'I don't know. I really don't know.'

Jeanine doesn't press me. She knows better than to agitate a sad story. I turn away and stay wide-eyed on my seat, thinking about Nathan and the way I left things. The way he left things, too. He hasn't exactly been falling over himself to get in touch. Will he be at the birth? Not if I don't tell him, and at this stage I'm not planning to. I'm not giving his mother another chance to kick me in the teeth. A surge of anger thinking about the look on her face at the show sends a charge of energy – hateful energy – that never quite disperses. I move from anger to sadness and back again in an emotional double helix.

When the coach pulls into Bourke, I feel barely rested enough to face the task ahead of me. It's something that I just don't feel like doing. It frightens me. It makes me feel like my own childhood is far behind me.

I haven't warned Olivia that I'm coming today. I could have. One of her dorm buddies coughed up all her contact details, but I didn't want to give her a chance to pick up her guns. If someone threatened to turn up at my parents' house with their irritating good intentions, that's exactly what I'd do. Get armed.

Olivia's foster parents are called Marilyn and Frank McCrae. They live in a small, well-kept house close to the centre of town.

'You must be Shauna,' says a tall, busty woman with big, blue glasses and a long, grey ponytail. She appears at the door a few seconds after I ring the doorbell. 'I'm Marilyn.'

'I didn't realise you were expecting me,' I tell her, shocked to be recognised, suspicious that Olivia's friend grassed on me.

'We're not, but Olivia's told us so much about you, I could pick you out in a crowd.'

She invites me inside and puts the kettle on. I notice when I get a better look at her that she's got a big, fresh keloid scar on her cheek, near the right corner of her mouth. It's distracting and I have to make an effort not to stare.

'Ol's not here at the moment. She's out at the hardware shop with Frank, but she'll be back soon.'

Marilyn offers me Anzac biscuits, which Fred and I wouldn't knock back in a million years. I tell her that I've come to Bourke to convince Olivia to return to Oakholme. Marilyn doesn't like my chances.

'You'll have your work cut out for you. We've tried, believe me. Everyone has. Her friends. Her psychologist. Her social worker. That nice woman from the school, Reverend Ferguson, has called several times. Olivia won't even discuss it. What happened over there?'

'There was a misunderstanding with one of the girls. Olivia took it really hard.'

Marilyn grimaces. 'She takes it all so hard. Running away and going into herself is the way she deals with hard times. I have to say, though, things did seem to be improving after she started at boarding school. Reverend Ferguson reckons that it had a lot to do with her friendship with you.'

A giant, splintering stake of guilt plunges straight into my heart.

'Actually, I didn't do as much as I should have.' My voice is crackly, like I've been up all night drinking beer and singing karaoke. Not that I've ever done that, but I can imagine. 'I could have been there more for her, I think.'

'Reverend Ferguson says you spent hours with her.'

I shrug, not sure how to explain. 'She told me that you and your husband are the best foster parents she's ever had.'

Marilyn smiles affectionately for a second before a storm cloud passes over her face. 'I'd like to take that as a compliment,

Shauna, but as I'm sure Olivia's told you, some of our predecessors were pretty rotten.'

'She mentioned that.'

'Her mother was a violent alcoholic. Olivia was placed in foster care when she was just a baby. So was her half-brother.'

'She has a half-brother?'

'*Had* a half-brother. He died, unfortunately, a few years ago.'

I nod and the wooden stake in my heart twists with horror and empathy. 'That's awful.'

I don't even want to know how he died because I'm already so upset I can't take another bite of Anzac biscuit. I swallow what's already in my mouth. When Olivia and her foster father, Frank, walk into the kitchen a few minutes later, I stand, half-hoping that Olivia will relent and fall into my arms. Or maybe I need to fall into her arms. I'm not sure.

'What the hell are you doing here?' Though her words are rude, Olivia's tone isn't. Behind the folded arms, I sense a heart that's bursting with pride at the sight of me. 'I thought that was what the Great Dividing Range was for? To keep all the shit in Sydney.'

'Only during term time, Olivia.'

Frank, who's small and bald, throws his head back and laughs. I smile, too.

'Frank,' says Marilyn, 'this is Shauna. Shauna, Frank.'

We shake hands. 'Great to finally meet you, Shauna. Olivia talks about you all the time.'

'No, I don't,' mutters Olivia.

Both Marilyn and Frank are warm and they don't seem to mind Olivia's salty language and sharp-tongued sass. It could be a lot worse, I suppose, considering what some kids her age get up to.

'Come and put your stuff in my room,' says Olivia, pulling me by the wrist. 'You *are* staying the night, aren't you?'

'Of course, she is!' calls Marilyn after us. 'Your parents know you're here don't they, Shauna?'

Actually, I had no idea where I'd be staying. And I don't know how far my budget of about eighteen bucks would've gotten me, even in Bourke. I guess I was banking on being well-received.

Olivia stops in the doorway of her room and then turns to face me sheepishly.

'I need to redecorate it, okay? I haven't changed anything since I was ten.'

'Don't worry.' I smile on the inside. 'I won't judge.' Oh, but I do!

It's like some Disney princess playhouse in there. From floor to ceiling it's pink, white and silver. Her doona's spangled with unicorns. There's a one-eyed, white teddy half-tucked under her pillow. The walls are adorned with posters of ponies and kittens, and Elsa and Anna from *Frozen*. There are animal figurines on every spare inch of shelf and table space. A room less befitting of my little mentee's outward spikiness I can't imagine.

'I know, I know, I'm going to do something about it. I just haven't…had time.'

I dump my backpack on the chair by her desk.

'I've got a trundle bed,' she says excitedly, 'so we don't have to sleep top-to-toe or anything.'

'Thank God for that.'

Almost without thinking about it, I peel off my jumper and my shirt rides up with it. In the time it takes me to pull my clothes back down over my bump, Olivia's slammed two and two together. Her mouth drops open. Her blue eyes bulge.

'You're up the duff!'

'Keep your voice down.'

'You're huge!'

'Shh!'

'Oh my God, Shauna. I didn't think you had it in you! You're so stuck-up!' She clamps her palms to her blushing cheeks. 'You had *sex*?'

'No, it's the immaculate conception. I'm carrying the Messiah.'

'Really?' The word's only halfway out of her mouth before she realises she's being had. 'Bullshit! You had sex with that guy from Kootingal, didn't you?'

I shrug.

'You *did*!' she shout-whispers. 'And you've been pregnant the whole time you've been looking down your nose at me.' Olivia's tone shifts from teasing to accusing in a fraction of a second. 'Haven't you?'

'I've never looked down my nose at you.'

'Like hell you haven't.'

I sit down on the end of her bed. I really don't feel like getting into an argument right now.

'I'm sorry if I wasn't always nice to you,' I say. 'But you weren't always nice to me either.'

'It's got nothing to do with being nice,' she says firmly. In her own space, she's remarkably confident. Frightening, actually. 'And it's got everything to do with you being pissed off that I'm not black enough for you.'

I scoff. I shake my head. I blink rapidly. 'You're wrong.'

'But I'm not wrong. I know it and I think you know it, too.' Her mouth forms a small, hard line. 'Don't you?'

I feel too pregnant to argue with her seriously, but I force myself, out of respect for her, to consider what she's saying. Usually I'd have a snap reaction to deny what's being thrown at me, to reject it and throw something equally horrible back, but this time…

'Yeah, okay. The first time we met, I saw that you were blonde-haired and blue-eyed, and I assumed you weren't like me. I didn't think you'd had the same experiences.'

'And what experiences are those, huh? To have your own parents dote on you your whole life? Is that what you're talking about, you spoilt brat?'

'No, it's not, actually. I'm talking about having no choice about the way other people see me. People take one look at me and they make up their minds. People look at you and they think you're one of them. Like Keli Street-Hughes. I could never be friends with her, not in a million years. Because I'm not *passable*.'

'That's not my problem!'

'No, it's *my* problem. And I suppose that's what I held against you at the beginning. That you thought you were passable.'

205

'But I'm not.'

'And you don't have to be. You really don't. You can succeed in life the way you are.'

She sits down on the bed next to me, but not close enough to touch me.

'Did you out me on purpose?' she asks, without looking at me.

'No! Shit, Olivia. I was happy for you to do your bidding, you know. It was an accident. I thought Keli had already worked it out.'

'It wasn't revenge for that thing at Central Station with the police? Or punking Lou-Anne?'

'No, of course not. And if I'd known more about you, if you'd *told* me more about yourself, things would have been very different.'

I think about that afternoon she came into my dorm room.

'That day you came to see me and Lou-Anne was there...well, what did you want to talk about?'

Turning to face her, I force Olivia to make eye contact with me.

'I...I...' she stammers, struggling to look me in the eye. 'It was Marilyn. She'd just been told she had skin cancer on her face.'

Now I know where the scar on Marilyn's cheek came from.

'You were worried about her.'

Olivia nods and looks away. 'She's going to be fine. It's just that...'

'It's okay to care about people, you know,' I tell her. 'I should have been there for you. I don't know why I wasn't.

206

Maybe it *was* because I didn't think you were black enough to deserve everything that was being done for you. Partly, anyway.' I put my hand on her shoulder and she flinches but she doesn't move away. 'I'm sorry, Olivia.'

'I'm sorry, too.'

'But we don't have to be sorry, you know. It's not too late. Far from it. You could come back to Oakholme now and finish the school year.'

'I can't, Shauna. It's too hard. I'm too embarrassed. And I'd miss my foster parents.'

'You're going to have to leave them one day.'

Olivia sighs. She stares. For a moment it seems like she's wavering, like maybe she'll agree to come back. Then, all at once, the tears stream down her face. She breaks away from my hand and covers her face with her forearms.

'I've got a bad disease,' she splutters. As she explains, I slowly realise what those sick days with the Oakholme nurse were all about. 'It's a sex disease. It's not my fault, but now I've got it and I can never get rid of it. All I can do is take anti-viral tablets, but they don't make it better all the time. Sometimes I get so sick that I can't do anything. My body aches and I get these sores all over. Sometimes I'm so sore I can't even sit down.'

'Doesn't sound like fun.'

Olivia sniggers through her tears. 'No, it's not. I don't even know who gave it to me. I've probably had it since I was a baby. My mum's boyfriend used to do things to me. Other people, too.'

'I'm sorry, Olivia.'

'What the hell do you have to be sorry about? You're one of the only people who gives a shit about me.'

At least she realises.

'I'm sorry you have to go through all that. But if you have to go through it anyway, why not go through it at Oakholme?'

'It's embarrassing. The teachers know when I'm sick and they know what it's about. And now Keli and everyone else know that I'm Aboriginal. How do I come back from that?'

'You show up.'

'Easier said than done.'

'Oh yeah?' I point to my belly.

Olivia wipes her eyes with her sleeves. 'Does anyone even know about that?'

'You. Lou-Anne. Jenny. My parents. That's about it.'

'The school doesn't know?'

'Not yet.'

'Self-Raising's gonna shit!'

'I know.'

'What about the guy?'

'I...I don't know him that well, so I haven't told him.'

Olivia doesn't know what to say and neither do I. I realise that I don't have any more wisdom to impart to her, and that now I'm waiting for her to give something to me. But what would she know? What does either of us have to give?

I end up spending two nights in Olivia's trundle bed. She won't agree to come back to Oakholme straight away, but she's promised to think about it at least. I really get to know the softer side of Olivia while staying with the McCraes. For someone so spiny on the outside, she's very sweet and gooey in the middle. And *young*. I suppose that's what the armour's for.

We go for walks around Bourke, which is flat and brown even by Barraba standards. It's cold in winter, too, which is lucky for me because my big, bump-concealing jumpers and jackets are completely justified. I notice that the important buildings in town, like those in Barraba, are the buildings that were important a hundred years ago – the courthouse, the post office and the bank. Why does nothing change in the country?

We do the same kinds of things I'd do during the holidays at Barraba: meet Olivia's old school friends in the park, have hot chocolate at the only good café in town, and watch videos stretched out in bed. Olivia can't hide her pleasure at having me around. There's obviously no value in being 'passable' in Bourke. I'd say one in three people we see on the street is Aboriginal. No wonder she feels comfortable here. No wonder she feels like an alien at Oakholme.

On my second night in Bourke, I check my social media accounts on Olivia's phone. When two messages from Nathan O'Brien flash, my heart swells. Olivia, who's watching my every e-move, says, 'He's obviously into you, Shauna. Why don't you just tell him?'

'I haven't even read the messages yet!'

I shield the screen from her prying eyes. The first message says:

Coming back to Tamworth tomorrow after a month of shearing in Tassie with Luke. You around?

His friend Luke was at the music festival in Manilla on New Year's Eve. I vaguely remember him and thinking how gorgeous Nathan was by comparison.

The second message was sent a day later – yesterday:

Are you getting these messages? I haven't been able to contact you for a month – no internet access in the shearers' quarters. I wanted to tell you at Easter show I was going to Tassie, but you took off so quickly. (Sad face emoji.)

Got to love a man who uses emojis. Fred the foetus is obviously moved, too, because he gives me a huge kick. The kicks have been getting stronger lately, Fred asserting his existence in case I forgot about him. I write back:

Staying with a friend in Bourke. Back tomorrow. Message tomorrow night?

A smiley face emoji comes shooting back immediately and my mood soars. I guess I really did want to hear from him. I log out and hand Olivia back her phone.

'So?' asks Olivia with raised eyebrows.

'So we might hook up sometime during the holidays.'

Olivia claps her hands together like an excited child. 'I can't wait to meet him.'

'Who says you'll ever get to meet him?'

She shrugs, grinning.

If I didn't know it before, I know it now for sure: Olivia Pike is expecting to remain part of my life. She must be on the brink of coming back to Sydney. My trip to Bourke has been a success.

The next day, when Mum picks me up from the station, she tells me there's a surprise waiting for me at home. I don't ask what it is. However, unable to contain her excitement, she spills the beans about the nursery before we've even reached the outskirts of Tamworth.

'Dad bought a cot on Gumtree and it looks brand new! I've been sewing a quilt since the beginning of last term and now it's finished, and yesterday I made a matching mobile. You should see it, Shauna! It's so cute!'

'Can't wait, Mum.'

'Oh, it was meant to be a surprise…'

I've never met anyone less capable of concealing their emotions than my mum. I'm shocked that she was able to keep the quilt under wraps for all this time.

'Where did you set up the nursery?' I ask her.

'At home, of course.'

'But where?'

Mum pauses and swallows. 'Your brother's room. You don't mind, do you?'

I'm so happy that Mum's cleared out Jamie's old room that I could cry. Since his death it's been a creepy shrine, complete with his unwashed clothes folded on the end of his bed and his sneakers with the laces still knotted in his wardrobe.

'I've put all his stuff away in boxes,' Mum assures me. 'You can take it out and have a look at it whenever you like.'

'I don't want to look at his stuff, Mum.'

When we get home, there's still some surprise factor because the room formerly known as Jamie's room – now the nursery – is so beautifully decorated. The pièce de résistance, Mum's quilt, is a marine-themed marvel. Each square of the quilt has a creature from the ocean sewn onto it. There's a hammerhead shark, a sea turtle, a clown fish, a crab, a sailboat and more – all reproduced in the cardboard mobile dangling from the ceiling above the cot. It's her signature style, with beautiful blues, greens and silvers, an Irukandji homage. It's the ocean transported to dusty old Barraba.

Without meaning to, I run my hands over my belly.

'This is *amazing*,' I tell Mum, who's thrilled that I like it so much. It's a vast improvement on the tribute to a bad past that was in here before. I loved my brother to pieces, but we've been living under the shroud of his memory for too long.

Might my parents set themselves free now? Might we all set each other free?

22

'NATHAN!'

He's sitting alone in the food court in Tamworth Plaza, which at this hour of the day has the same atmosphere as feeding time at the zoo. He wanted to pick me up at home, but I wouldn't let him. I didn't want him to meet my mum without first knowing of Fred the foetus's existence. So we agreed to meet with the rest of the Tamworth lunch crowd.

'Nathan!'

He looks up at me, then looks past me. I realise he hasn't recognised me.

'Hey.' I'm standing next to his table now.

'Shauna!' He stands up and grabs my hand, squeezing it. He can't help giving me 'the elevator'. I suppose my shape has changed a lot since the last time we saw each other at the Easter Show.

'So shearing, eh?'

'It's really well paid. I'm regretting it now, though. I'm fairly bent and broken.'

'Your hands are soft,' I tell him.

'That is one advantage of being elbow deep in wool all day.'

'Should we get something to eat?' I suggest.

We buy sausage rolls and Cokes from a nearby patisserie and settle back into the thronging crowd of the food court. Nathan watches me cautiously as I lay into my lunch with what must seem like frightening gusto. I don't even feel the need to come up with an excuse. He'll understand soon enough.

I'm going to tell him, really I am. I don't feel anywhere near as nervous about breaking the news as I did at the Easter Show. Damn his mother and her prejudices. She can do as she pleases with the information. Nathan and his family's reaction won't change what *I* do.

In the last few days, I've seen two people I love – my mum and Olivia Pike – emerge well and cheerful from the most awful long-term traumas. If they have the strength to do that, then so do I.

'You've probably noticed that I've put on some weight,' I begin.

Nathan shrugs awkwardly. What can he say? *Nah, you haven't...*

'Nathan, I'm pregnant.'

Nathan stops chewing. His soft eyes widen.

I'm not sure exactly why I add, 'Sorry.'

He swallows with difficulty and puts down his sausage roll. 'Is it mine?'

'How many men do you reckon I slept with on New Year's Eve?'

'Are you sure?'

'Aren't you?' I lift up my jumper and shirt to expose my outrageously stretched and swollen brown bump. 'I guess the morning-after pill doesn't always work.'

'You took the morning-after pill?'

'Yeah, and it made me puke my guts up for a whole day.'

'I'm sorry…'

He reaches for my belly and I slam my clothes back down over it.

'Oh, I'm sure you are sorry, Nathan.'

'I…I thought it was all fine…and now…' He grasps for words, breathing hard.

I wish he wouldn't sound so panicky. To be fair, I suppose I've had a long time to get used to the idea.

'Well, you should have told me earlier, Shauna!' he says finally. 'How long have you known?'

'A couple of months.'

'A couple of *months!*' He looks around us wildly without really looking at anything at all.

This is not the reaction I was hoping for. What I was hoping for was a hug.

'So you knew about this when I saw you at the Easter Show?'

'I wanted to tell you, but your mum was such a bitch—'

'A *bitch?*' His mouth hangs open.

He's getting shrill and upset. I suppose I could have used a different word.

'What the hell are you talking about, Shauna? She hardly said a word to you.'

'Exactly.'

'Exactly what?'

The people eating at the tables on either side of us have started to steal glances. I don't give a hoot.

215

'I saw the way she looked at me.'

Nathan blinks at me rapidly, a dozen little blinks in a row. Then he becomes suddenly articulate. 'I told Mum about you before the show. Quite a lot, actually. I was really embarrassed when you left the pavilion and never came back. It was humiliating. Now you tell me you're pregnant, and that you've known for months, and I'm humiliated all over again.'

'*You're* humiliated. Oh, poor you! I'm the one who's gotta *be* in the world. Like *this*.' I stand up awkwardly and the legs of my chair scrape against the hard floor. Our corner of the food court goes silent. No one's pretending not to listen now.

'Goodbye, Nathan,' I say dramatically, turning on my heel.

'Shauna, wait…' he calls half-heartedly after me, but he doesn't follow.

I'd been planning to go shopping for fat clothes after lunch, but I'm just too upset. I go straight to the bus stop and hightail it back to Barraba, barely able to stop myself from bursting into tears.

'How did it go?' Mum asks as soon as I walk in the door. She and Dad have been nagging me about telling Nathan all holidays.

'Just great!' I call sarcastically as I stomp in the direction of my room. I slam the door and roll onto my bed. Mum knocks gently at the door.

'If you're coming in here to harass me, forget it!'

She opens the door. 'Shauna, I just wanted to know when you'd like to go and see Dr Skinner.'

'I don't want to think about it now, Mum!'

'You have to see a doctor. You can't just show up at the hospital when your waters break.'

'I'll see Dr Baker after the holidays.'

'That's what you said last holidays.'

'Jesus Christ, get *off* my case!'

Mum sighs heavily. 'Don't worry about the boy. He has to pay child support. He can't get out of his responsibilities.'

'Mum! Out!'

'Wait until your father speaks to him!'

'Mum, get the bloody hell *out!*'

She sighs again and leaves me be.

I heave onto my back and close my eyes. I can't wait to return to school and get on with my life.

★ ♥ ★

When I do get back to school two weeks later, I find that my life isn't quite so easy to get on with. Disaster strikes when I can't squeeze into my winter uniform. I don't know why I didn't think of it being a problem before the first morning of school. I guess I've been in some denial about my appearance. Lou-Anne cuts the tunic down the back so that it can splay out and give me room up front. I put my blazer over the top to cover her handiwork.

'We should break into the clothing pool,' suggests Lou-Anne.

'Why is crime always your first resort?'

I end up borrowing twenty bucks from Jenny at lunch-time. She hands it over reluctantly enough to make me feel bad.

'Did you end up seeing a doctor during the hols?' she asks, forcing me into eye contact as I fumble around for an answer.

'I just…err…well, I ran out of time. Between seeing Olivia and everything else…'

Her clear eyes hold mine in a disapproving, almost parental gaze that I don't much like. I'd give her back the twenty dollars, except that I need it desperately. Indignities like this just can't be avoided when you have no money.

'I was busy, Jenny.'

She nods as if she understands, but I feel like she's scrutinising me, judging me. Does she think she's better than me? Since I pulled out of HSC University Pathways I don't think she even likes me that much. Paris was the icing on the cake. That was not the way I thought our friendship would roll this year. I thought we'd be much closer. I thought we'd be studying together and sharing everything, but Fred has driven a wedge between us.

I toddle to the clothing pool, manned by some mother from the Oakholme Ladies' Auxiliary who somehow knows my name.

'Don't you want to try it on, Shauna?' she asks as I hand over Jenny's money for the biggest circus tent of a tunic I can find on the rack. 'It looks like it might be a bit big for you.'

She holds the bottle-green monstrosity out in front of me. It's old. It's tatty. It's enormous. It looks like it's been passed from generation to generation of obese (or maybe pregnant) Oakholme teenagers since Reverend McBride was in charge.

'It's perfect!' I lie, bundling it into my arms like a parachute. I take it, along with my five dollars in change, up to the dorms and get changed. I look at myself in the full-length wardrobe mirror and cringe at the sight of the girl looking back at me. There's no nice way of putting it. She's fat. Everything's fat except her wrists and ankles. Something tells me I won't be going to the Year 12 formal. I also realise that the jig could be up before our exams if someone has the guts to confront me about my billowing figure.

After lunch, I cross paths with Mademoiselle Larsen. She tries not to stare at my new threads. I plead with her telepathically not to say anything. *Anyone can put on a little weight…*

'I just wanted to let you know that I'm running some extra *dictée* sessions in the language labs every Friday until stuvac,' she says.

'Cool!' I respond with uncharacteristic enthusiasm.

'So, I'll count you in.' She pauses, seeming to take me in. 'Jenny, too?'

'I don't know. You'll have to talk to Jenny about that.'

Then Mademoiselle asks the question I've never quite been able to stomach.

'Is everything all right, Shauna?'

'Between me and Jenny?'

'Generally. Life.'

'Fine.'

'You know that offer of the apartment in Paris still stands.'

When she says that, I shrink. All my rich dreams and great expectations are withering before they had a chance to ripen. It kills me to be reminded of that reality. The reality of ambition foregone. Best case scenario, I study journalism online from my parents' place in Barraba between breastfeeds. I feel both brittle and ashamed standing before Mademoiselle Larsen in my maternity tunic.

'I just can't go to Europe next year and that's that,' I croak.

'Are you having some kind of personal problem?' she asks gently. 'This is probably the most stressful time of your life.'

I shrug in agreement. She's not wrong.

'If there's anything you want to talk about – anything at all – I'm here for you.'

I nod awkwardly. The bell rings and I waddle off to my next class.

★ ♥ ★

Olivia and I have been keeping in touch since I visited her in Bourke. A couple of weeks into the third term, she hits me with the good news – she's returning to Oakholme! I have a meeting with SRF, during which she congratulates me on convincing Olivia to come back.

'This time, Shauna, you need to keep a closer eye on her, and I don't just mean physically. You need to be aware of what's going on with her emotionally, not just during the mentoring sessions but in general. We can't afford another incident like the last one. It's not good for Olivia or the school or the Indigenous scholarship program.'

'Yes, Reverend Ferguson.'

'The other thing is that Olivia will have to apologise to Keli Street-Hughes.'

'But—'

'There are no buts, Shauna. It's one of the conditions of her return to the school. So you talk to her about it, okay?'

And I do. Olivia has a few choice words to say about Keli. In the end, though, she gives her the most grudging, insincere apology I've ever heard. A single 'sorry' is muttered in the aisle while we're filing into chapel one Sunday, with God as Olivia's witness.

'There, I did it,' she grunts to me. Keli just scoffs.

Other than that, there's very little fanfare around Olivia's return to the fold, except that Lou-Anne, sensing the competition, begins to make some jealous remarks when the third wheel is in our presence. Actually, she has no idea how close Olivia and I are now.

The whole Wish Upon A Star debacle seems to be over. Needless to say, Olivia and Keli are also 'over', and, after the 'apology', they no longer speak. They studiously ignore each other, and for a while Keli ignores me, too.

I begin to toy with the idea that perhaps my grand feud with Keli is over. Perhaps now that she's won and been vindicated in every way, she will leave me to lead my dusty little black life unmolested.

Oh, how wrong I am.

It seems like Keli still has a gigantic chip on her shoulder about the incident in the shower, which must have been – let's face it – pretty humiliating for her. The chances of an event like that being kept quiet in the Oakholme College boarders' dormitory were zilch. All the boarders know about it now and the latest piece of gossip is that I am a lesbian. I was so overcome with desire for Keli that day that I peeped at her in the shower. Yeah, right.

Poor old Lou-Anne gets dragged into it, too. Of course she's my lesbian lover because she and I usually have showers together. Never mind that we shower in separate cubicles with the curtains drawn!

Considering what Lou-Anne and I have been through in our lives, it's not that hard to laugh off this ridiculous nonsense. I've got bigger problems than lesbian rumours, anyway. I'm nearly seven months pregnant and I'm well and truly showing. Fred the foetus is turning into Bob the baby. Even the bottle-green monstrosity begins to tighten up. Still, if anyone suspects anything, they're not willing to accuse me. With my blazer on I just look fat, and according to the grapevine, jokes have been made at my expense on that topic. Luckily, I am far from being the fattest boarder, and it's still cold enough to get around in leggings and big jumpers. It will only be a matter of time, though. Surely I can't get through the entire pregnancy with no one twigging? Or maybe I can.

I've told my parents to stop worrying, and for God's sake *stop calling*. They want to know if I'm having any problems (no) and when I'm going to see a doctor (when I have time). I have consulted Dr Google a few times on the computers in prep. hall. The first time I did it, a couple of Year 8s walked in and I had to slam the tab closed. The next time I looked up 'what to expect when you're expecting', I found a website which said that at this stage of the pregnancy I should be seeing a specialist obstetrician every week! Of course this completely freaked me out because it's impossible. How could I ever get out of school that often without arousing suspicion? Where would my parents or I get the money to pay a specialist? So I've stopped looking up that rubbish, assuring myself that women have been giving birth for thousands of years without the help of doctors. As for the birth itself, I don't want to think about it because it terrifies me.

Recently I've taken to googling 'Nathan O'Brien' and staring for ages at an online photo of him leading a cow at the Tamworth Show. He's so handsome that I long for him, but I'm also angry with him. I need to stop googling him – longing and anger are an unpleasant combination.

It's Nathan I'm stewing about while I'm in the bathroom with Lou-Anne (in separate showers) early one morning before class. I'm replaying my mental tape of that scene at the Easter Show, the sidelong looks of his scrubchook mother. It's all too easy to remember the ugly implications in her gaze. And then Nathan's pouty, out-of-line reaction at Tamworth Plaza. Could he have made me feel any worse?

When those feelings spit and sizzle to the surface, I feel totally justified in enforcing my scorched-earth communications policy against Nathan. After a few unreturned messages and telephone calls, he appears to have given up. I don't care. I want Bob the baby to have a family, but not that family.

I have no idea how long I've been in the shower when I hear someone come into the bathroom.

'Showers are full!' Lou-Anne calls out beside me, but I don't hear the bathroom door shut again.

A few seconds later my shower curtain is ripped open. Keli Street-Hughes is standing inches from me in her school uniform. She has her contraband iPhone in her hand and she's pointing it right at me. Annabel Saxon is beside her. I hear Lou-Anne scream as Annabel pulls her curtain aside.

'Oh. My. God.' Keli gapes at my obscenely rounded belly. She's so shocked that she lets her phone drop to her side. 'Annabel! Look!'

I pull my shower curtain back across before Annabel gets the chance.

'Get out of here, you bloody perverts!' squeals Lou-Anne. 'Bloody lezzos!'

I hear Keli gasp, 'She's lathering up for two!' before they both run giggling out of the bathroom.

'It's none of your business!' I shout after her.

Lou-Anne and I dive out of the showers and grab our towels.

'She's going to tell everyone, you know!' I shriek, realising that the moment I've been dreading is about to arrive. My chest feels tight, my head is spinning, and my fingers are so thick and clumsy that I drop my tunic on the floor three times before managing to pull it on.

'What should I do?' I ask Lou-Anne.

'Put your blazer on.'

'I mean, what should I do about Keli and Annabel?'

'Well, we could kill them, but that's the only way I can think of shutting them up.'

What else can I do but finish dressing and go to roll call? I'm not about to beg them to keep it quiet. I know that within ten minutes, every boarder at the school is going to know about Bob.

'Remember that it's nobody's business but yours,' Lou-Anne says as she walks me to my roll call room. 'Nobody has any right to know or even to ask.'

Keli's not in my roll call class, but Annabel is. I stare daggers into the back of her head, willing her to keel over and die before she can do any more damage. I look around the room, searching for huddles of gleefully gossiping girls, but no one seems to be looking at me.

'Are you okay, Shauna?' Jenny asks. 'You look worried.'

I lean in and whisper into her ear. 'Keli and Annabel know.'

'Know what?' asks Jenny at regular volume.

I widen my eyes at her.

'Oh. Well. No one's said anything to me.'

'Tell me if they do,' I say, though God only knows what I'm going to do with the information. What can I do? Anyone who takes a long, hard look at me is going to know it's true. All I can do is wait. It's torture.

I spend the day slumped over my work, pulling in my blazer to cover the bump. I meet Lou-Anne in our dorm room at recess and then again at lunch.

'No one's said anything to me, Shauna. Maybe Keli and Annabel are going to do the right thing and keep their big mouths shut?'

'When have they *ever* done the right thing?' I reply shrilly. 'If they're holding out, it's only to torture me!'

Lou-Anne slings an arm around my shoulder. 'You stay strong, Shauna. They're not gonna get anything out of me, not even if they waterboard me.'

'Maybe I should just go ahead and admit the truth to stop the suspense.'

Anne says as she walks me to my roll call room.

'You don't have to do that. Just keep quiet.'

Nothing unusual happens for the rest of the school day.

The hopeful side of me, the part of me that could believe that Keli Street-Hughes has a shred of compassion or decency in her soul, thinks that maybe she won't tell. Maybe no one will find out. Maybe I'll have the baby during stuvac and no one will be any the wiser.

But then Miss Maroney's waiting for me in my dorm room after the final bell.

'Shauna,' she says soberly, 'we need to talk.'

Fucking Keli Street-Hughes. She's Satan, Lucifer and Jezebel rolled into one giant ranga super bitch demon.

I grit my teeth, suck in my gut, and follow Miss Maroney into her quarters. I remind myself that I've gotten through my brother's death and many anniversaries since, and I can get through this, too.

She comes right out with it. 'A little birdie told me you're pregnant.'

I shake my head. 'Little birdie doesn't know what little birdie's talking about.'

'Come on, Shauna. You've put on so much weight over the last few months. I thought you'd been overeating due to the stress.'

I shrug. Miss Maroney crosses and uncrosses her long, athletic legs. Because she's so young and nice, and she's been a confidante to me in the past, I have an urge to unload on her. But I know I mustn't.

'Can I go now?'

'No, you can't. This is not a problem that's going to go away. How far along are you, anyway?'

I set my jaw and shake my head.

'There's simply no point in denying it. You should look into getting appropriate pre-natal care. You can't just go to a hospital when you start having contractions. You need to have scans and tests first. For your baby's good as well as your own.'

I say nothing.

'Have you been to see a doctor about it? I know you went to see Dr Baker a while back.'

She's trying to hook me, but I won't bite.

'Can I go now?'

'You'll probably be asked to leave the school, you know. You can't stay at a school like Oakholme College when you're pregnant. It's a religious school. Sex before marriage is a good reason to expel you. They won't let such an embarrassing situation continue out in the open. Especially not in your case, when the school has been so generous to you. You'll bring the whole Indigenous scholarship program into disrepute.'

I meet her eye. 'I'm staying here.'

'Well, that might not be your decision to make.'

'Oh, I'm staying here, no matter what. I'm finishing the HSC. I don't care what you try to do to me.' I glare at her. 'If you think you can get rid of me as easily as you got rid of the other scholarship recipients, you've got another thing coming.'

'Do you really think we tried to get rid of the others?' Miss Maroney frowns deeply at me. 'You're so mixed up, Shauna. You are such a disturbed young person.'

'Can I go now?' I ask again.

She nods. I go back to my room and pick up some books to take to prep. hall. The battle I've been dreading has begun. Let them try to get rid of me. I've toughed out this gig for the last five years. I've had it in my head ever since Elodie bailed out that I was going to be Oakholme College's first Indigenous graduate. I'm not giving up that honour without a fight.

My pride in what I have and the fear of losing it sit boulder-like on my chest as I go through the motions of study and going to bed.

'Can I feel your belly?' asks Bindi just before lights-out. She takes a seat on the edge of my bed.

I expose the belly in question and she prods it as if it might nip her.

'You did such a stellar job of hiding it,' she whispers.

'The breasts were a giveaway,' Indu says casually.

'You *knew*?' Lou-Anne and I shriek in unison.

'No one's bazookas get that big that quickly without surgical intervention or pregnancy.'

The way she says 'bazookas' is just so funny that we fall apart with laughter. Then, suddenly, we start frantically shushing each other.

'Guys,' announces Lou-Anne. 'Lights out. This is serious.'

After lights-out Bindi whispers 'bazookas' in Indu's accent and it starts all over again.

23

A NOTE ARRIVES at roll call the next day:

Shauna, see me. SRF.

The message's brevity bothers me. It's got to be about Bob.
Jenny reads the note over my shoulder. 'Is it...?' She
grimaces.

'I'll deal with it.'

'Good luck.'

I don't know whether it's my hormones or the stress of my
situation, but I don't like the way she wishes me luck. Still, in
the scheme of things, Jenny's tone isn't important. I excuse
myself from class and head to Reverend Ferguson's office.

Self-Raising Flour takes me in deeply when I appear in her
doorway, especially around the midsection. I pull my blazer
closed.

'Do your parents know?' she asks softly.

'Know what?'

Reverend Ferguson purses her lips and closes her eyes,
sighing. I can tell that she's trying to be calm about this, but
it's not easy for her.

'You were my special project.'

'I haven't ceased to exist, you know.'

'Mrs Green knows about your circumstances. She's giving you a chance to leave willingly so that you don't have an expulsion on your school record. Otherwise your next stop is her office. She'll hand you your expulsion papers. Your parents will be called to come and pick you up.'

'I'm not leaving.'

Reverend Ferguson leans back in her leather chair, arms folded over her gigantic jugs, head hanging, as though she's examining something in her lap. She speaks slowly, as if each word is causing her pain.

'You've worked so hard to get where you are both academically and personally. I don't know why you didn't tell someone sooner. I thought you would have had more self-respect than that. And to be in the situation in the first place...'

She opens the notepad on her desk and writes something on it.

'I'm giving you the number of a colleague of mine who works in TAFE. You can complete your HSC there. I think you should at least try to do that much.' She rests her elbows on her desk and then her head in her hands. 'You'd come so far and now *this*. It just makes me want to scream.'

With another huge, sad sigh, she rips the page out of the notepad and pushes it across her desk. I don't take it.

It's not easy to resist Self-Raising Flour's will like this. Every cell in my body wants to please her. It's in my culture to go with the flow, to speak sweetly and to agree. Even though I have a strong personality, I'm not immune to the temptation to assume that white people know better. I want to let go. I want to give in. I want to get along.

But I'm not going to get along.

'I want to see a lawyer.'

'A lawyer? You're not on trial.'

'But I have rights.'

'What rights are those?'

'You said that Olivia Pike had a right to privacy. Well, so do I.' I'm unsure if what I'm saying is true, but I try to channel Lou-Anne. 'What goes on inside my body is my private business. Mrs Green's got no grounds for expelling me.'

'The school board met last night. It's been decided. I'm sorry, Shauna. You are the last person I would wish this situation on.'

I get up. Self-Raising Flour rises, too, hot and dishevelled, busting out of her baking tin.

'I'll take you to Mrs Green's office,' she says.

'Can I call my parents?'

'You can call them from her office.'

'I'd rather call them from the phone in Miss Maroney's office.'

Reverend Ferguson looks uncertain, but she lets me go.

On the way to the dormitory building, I realise that I've been preparing for this crunch for a while. I had a plan about how I'd handle myself and I've managed to stick to it. I know that I have to keep going.

But then I get my mum on the phone and I break into tears at the sound of her voice. I tell her that they've found out and that they are about to expel me.

'Oh, Shauna, please come home, love. Just come back.'

How much would I love to do that! To wake up in the same house as my parents. To have the comforting knowledge that everyone living under my roof loves me.

'I want to, Mum, but I can't.'

'Of course you can. Dad could pick you up tomorrow morning. He's driving the truck back from Melbourne.'

The idea of going home is so seductive. I think about my predecessors in the Indigenous scholarship program, who all got a taste of privileged white life and then went skidding back to their families. Talking to Mum, I have this feeling that I was never meant to be at Oakholme College in the first place, that I was cockeyed and naïve to believe I could ever have fitted in here. It would be so easy to just go home and complete the HSC either through TAFE or at Barraba High. It probably wouldn't even make a difference to my marks. So why don't I do it?

Because it would make a difference to *me*.

I remember what I said to Olivia. *You deserve to be here, you know.* I can't let her down. I have to follow my own advice.

I know that I deserve to be here too. And I know that I'm going to fulfil my rights and merits and potential by trying to stay here, as tricky and uncomfortable and embarrassing as that might be.

'Mum, I need to speak to a lawyer.'

'We don't have the money for that. What can a lawyer do, anyway?'

'Well, I don't know. That's why I need to speak to one.'

'A lawyer never did people like us any good, Shauna.'

232

The moment she says that is the moment I know that I *must* speak to a lawyer, and that I'm going to find one today, right now, even if it means wandering around the city from law firm to law firm. Something else occurs to me. In fact, it's something I've suspected for a while. Now I know it, though. I know it like I know I'm alive. The hand on the door that slams in every Aboriginal person's face at some stage – the hand on the machete that my cousin Andrew says is poised to chop off the heads of high achievers – is sometimes a black hand.

If I listen to my mother, I'm going to lose my dignity. If I listen to my own sense of what's right and what's mine for the taking in this life, then I will keep my dignity, even if I turn out to be wrong.

I tell Mum that the school's going to try to call her and Dad. I tell her they can't answer their phones. She agrees they'll stay under the radar, but she begs me one last time to come home. I tell her no, even though I know she doesn't understand. 'This is something I have to do, Mum.'

From Miss Maroney's office, I head for prep. hall, passing the giant portrait of the Reverend Doctor Sterling McBride in the foyer. His expression of tight-lipped, beady disapproval seems magnified today. I stop in my tracks and turn to face him head-on, something I've never done before because he's just so creepy. I look at the small cross around his neck. I notice the way his robes fall around his shoulders. I see how straight he is sitting. Daring to look into his eyes, I notice for the first time that they're green, and that while they are narrowed, they are more watchful than reproachful.

'Please don't let her get rid of me,' I say softly, and of course I'm talking about Mrs Green (to a painting). 'I know I've been rude to you in the past, but please don't let her throw me out.'

Then I skip to prep. hall, log on to one of the computers and google the words 'free lawyer' and 'Sydney' and, reluctantly, 'Aboriginal'. The website for an Aboriginal legal centre in Redfern comes up. I call the number from Miss Maroney's office and try to make an appointment. The receptionist tells me that there are no free slots until next week, but they have a duty legal officer who sees people 'off the street'. If I'm willing to hang around and wait, I'll probably get seen this afternoon.

Before I leave, though, I have to face whatever music is playing for me in Mrs Green's office. I head back to the admin. building, and by cruel coincidence, I run into Keli Street-Hughes. She changes her direction across the quadrangle and loops around to avoid me, eyes to the ground, but I lunge right in front of her.

'What?' Her mean, yellowy eyes settle on my face.

'You're a cesspit,' I hiss.

'I beg your pardon. I'm a *what*?'

'A cesspit. A hole in the ground, full of shitty sludge.'

'You'd better get out of my face. And get that baby out of my face, too, while you're at it. Skank.'

'You told Miss Maroney, didn't you? You're the one who told her that I'm pregnant.'

A flash of confusion passes over Keli's face. She looks disoriented for just a fraction of a second before smiling tightly, but it's long enough to make me wonder whether or not she is the one who told on me. Or maybe no one told? Maybe Miss Maroney just worked it out.

'I don't care what you think I did or didn't do,' she says, 'but do I really strike you as the suck arse type?'

'Yes, you do.'

Keli rolls her eyes and steps around me. She only walks a few paces before turning and calling, 'Green's going to serve your arse up to you on a platter. You know that, don't you?' Her tone is matter-of-fact, not smug for once, which makes me doubt again that she's the one who got me pinched.

'What the hell do you care, Keli?'

'I just don't think you deserve it, that's all. What country girl hasn't had a wild night at a B & S or a race day or a music festival? Most girls would have gone to the doctor and gotten rid of the problem.'

'But I didn't.'

'No, you didn't.'

She nods at me seriously, and I think it must be the first time she's ever related to me. Over a one-night stand at a country music festival. Shit. Maybe she had a close call once?

I go to the admin. building and pause outside Mrs Green's office. The door's ever so slightly ajar and I can hear her talking to Reverend Ferguson.

SRF:... *go quietly. There are certainly no signs so far she's going to cooperate. Surely we can find a way of allowing her to continue with some conditions—*
Mrs Green: *It's out of the question. The board won't have it. It would be a scandal.*

235

SRF: *It's going to be a scandal anyway, Libby!*

Mrs Green: *As long as she didn't fall pregnant while at school, I think we can contain the damage. But if this incident doesn't convince the board that we should discontinue the Indigenous scholarship, I don't know what will. It's been a disaster from the outset, and now this... We went into it with the best of intentions, but it's the same old story. No good deed goes unpunished. These people can't be helped.*

SRF: *I couldn't disagree more. Shauna has been transformed. Don't you remember what she was like when she arrived?*

Mrs Green: *She wasn't pregnant. I remember that much. Now she'll probably be on welfare for the rest of her life like the rest of her family.*

SRF: *Libby!*

Mrs Green: *I'm sorry. That was inappropriate. I didn't sleep at all last night...*

SRF: *We're only six weeks from stuvac. Even if she didn't attend classes, we could...*

Mrs Green: *Sally, it is out of the question. I know you are very fond of this girl, but she's brought this on herself. She's had so many chances. She's had every opportunity.*

SRF: *I just don't see how expelling her is going to help her or the school.*

Mrs Green: *What are we supposed to do? Turn sick bay into a maternity ward? She has to go. Has someone called her parents?*

SRF: *I just tried all their numbers and there's no answer. They haven't responded to my email.*

Mrs Green: *Where's Shauna?*

236

With shaking hands and legs, I push the door open and walk in.

'I'm here.'

Mrs Green smiles thinly. In spite of not having slept a wink – oh, the poor duck! – she's cool and controlled in a way that SRF could never be. Probably because she hasn't got a heart, but a cold little stone where her heart should be.

'Have a seat,' she says, but I don't.

'Reverend Ferguson's right. I'm not going to cooperate. And my parents aren't going to pick me up. I've already spoken to them.'

'Shauna, the board's decided to revoke your scholarship,' replies Mrs Green.

'I know that. And you're inviting me to leave, too, and if I don't accept the invitation, you'll expel me, right?'

'That's right.'

'Well, go ahead.'

'Sorry, I—'

'Go ahead and expel me.'

She blinks at me as she pushes a letter across the table with the embossed Oakholme College letterhead. In big, bold letters at the top, it says: *NOTICE OF TERMINATION OF ENROLMENT.*

I pick it up off the edge of her desk.

'I'll see what my lawyer has to say about this.' I feel like I'm acting, but the words seem to have some effect on Mrs Green. She doesn't know how to respond. She looks at Reverend Ferguson, who shrugs, and then back to me.

'Reverend Ferguson will take you to the dormitory and help you pack your bags. You're to wait there until your parents can be contacted.'

'If I'm expelled, then you have no say about what I do. So I'll do as I please.'

I turn on my heel and stalk out.

Reverend Ferguson comes trotting out a few seconds later. 'Shauna! Shauna!'

I break into an ungainly run, but even at seven months pregnant, I'm like a Kenyan compared with a fat, seventy-year-old pastor in high heels. By the time I've reached the school's front gates, I've lost her.

24

The DUTY LEGAL officer at the Aboriginal legal centre isn't even a lawyer. She assures me that she's a law student, but she looks and sounds like she's in Year 8. She's a tiny, mousy thing with blue-framed glasses and a red nose that won't stop dripping.

'I've got allergies,' she explains.

Her name is Sarah Hogan-Doran. I'm sitting in her 'office', which is a table and two chairs pushed into the corner of a room full of filing cabinets. So far she hasn't exactly filled me with confidence.

'I've never come across a case like this before,' she said after I'd explained my situation, 'but I think there are laws that stop institutions like schools discriminating against pregnant women.'

Now she's doing research on her laptop while I sit opposite her, wondering where I might find myself a real lawyer who can give me a real answer.

Finally, after about fifteen minutes of clicking and frowning at her screen, she closes her laptop.

'So…' she begins.

'So?'

'The Sex Discrimination Act forbids educational institutions from denying enrolment to pregnant students.'

'Great!'

'There's a catch, though. If the school is a religious school, then it can discriminate to its heart's content, *if* it does so to avoid offending the people who are part of that religion.'

'So where does that leave me?'

Sarah looks down at my expulsion letter. 'Well, it's a church school, isn't it?'

I nod. It's certainly a religious school.

'So they can do whatever they like?'

'That's what the legislation seems to say. I can try to find a court case about it, but I don't think that there have been any.'

'So mine would be the first.'

'I wouldn't recommend going to court,' she says, shaking her head gravely.

We talk about other options for finishing the HSC, but I tell her I'm not interested in going quietly.

'Have you got a bone to pick with the school for some other reason?'

That's a question I have to think about before answering.

'Well, they've been pretty good to me, but there have been some problems...'

Then we get into the whole Olivia Pike affair and the other scholarship recipients who've left the school.

'Do you think the Indigenous girls get discriminated against?'

'It's not always deliberate, but yeah, I do. I overheard the principal Mrs Green say that they're gonna scrap the scholarship because we cause too much trouble.'

Sarah nods. 'Interesting.'

'She said I'm going to be on welfare for the rest of my life.'

'She said *that* to you!'

'Not *to* me. I overheard her.'

Sarah opens her laptop. She launches into her furious clicking and typing again.

'A religious school might be able to discriminate against you for your pregnancy,' she says after a few minutes, 'but it can't discriminate against you because of your race. Or vilify you. Saying that you're going to be on welfare for the rest of your life – well, that sounds like racial vilification to me.'

'So I can sue them for racism?'

'Well…yes. But I'm not recommending that. The way the discrimination law works, you have to make a complaint first. You can't bring a case to court until the complaint's been dealt with.'

She explains more about the process, reading from a government website. It seems like she doesn't really know that much about it, but at least she knows where to go looking.

I spend another two hours in the dank corner of that filing closet, writing a statement of everything bad that's ever happened to me at Oakholme College. I feel like a first-class ingrate complaining about a place that has overall been very good to me, but what other option is there? Slink off home so they can pretend I never existed, so the Indigenous scholarship program can just be an unfortunate historical blot on

Oakholme's otherwise unsullied copybook? Forget that! I'm complaining. It doesn't come naturally to me, but so what?

Sarah goes online and files a complaint on my behalf, based on my statement. She prints out a copy of the complaint and hands it to me.

'I'm not saying that you should go to court, Shauna, but I think you've really got something here. Something that might make them think twice about what they've done. I wouldn't be surprised if they revoke your expulsion letter once they get wind of this.'

'Why would they, though?'

'Embarrassment. The possibility of the complaint being leaked to the media. Which you're quite within your rights to do, by the way. In fact, if they don't revoke the termination of enrolment, you call me, okay? And I'll talk to them. Tell them about my journalist friend who works at *The Australian*.'

I really can't see someone like Mrs Green being intimidated by someone like mousy Sarah Hogan-Doran, but maybe she has some tricks up her sleeve I don't know about. Appearances can be deceptive. I, of all people, know that to be true.

I catch the bus back to school with Mrs Green's expulsion letter and my complaint in my hot little hand.

When I get back to the dorm, all hell has broken loose. Everyone had assumed I'd gone back to Barraba in a Pike-style walkabout incident. A large group of boarders crowd around me.

By now everyone knows I'm pregnant. I have nothing to lose by standing on my bed and reading aloud Mrs Green's expulsion letter. As I read pompous-arse phrases like 'inconsistent with the moral and religious ethos of Oakholme College', the girls all shake their hands in the air and shriek, 'Oooooh!'

Then I start reading the complaint. I'm only about halfway through the paragraph entitled 'Nature of the Complaint' when Miss Maroney and Reverend Ferguson burst into our already packed-like-sardines dorm.

'Go back to your rooms!' barks Miss Maroney.

Olivia starts a chant, 'Shau-na! Shau-na! Shau-na!' Within a few repetitions, about twenty girls have joined in. The sound is deafening in a room with such fine acoustics.

Miss Maroney puts her whistle (still hanging there from netball training) to her mouth, and blows it to full effect.

'Back to your rooms now or you're all on Wednesday detention!' she growls.

The crowd gradually falls quiet and begins to file out.

'Shauna, get off that bed,' says Reverend Ferguson calmly. 'If you fall, you'll do yourself a mischief. Not to mention what you've got on board there.'

When there's no one but my dorm buddies left in the room, Reverend Ferguson asks them to leave, too. Miss Maroney escorts them down to the prep. hall.

SRF sits on the bed in an unprecedented state of puffed-up upset. Her face is flushed, her blouse is untucked, and her grey bob has kinked the wrong way. She looks like she's been crying.

'We called the police, you know! We thought you might have done yourself some kind of harm.'

I get down from the bed and stand in front of her.

'Wouldn't Mrs Green have been happy then!'

'That's a terrible thing to say!'

'I'm going to cause her a lot more trouble alive,' I tell her confidently. 'I've been with my lawyer, writing this.' I hand her my copy of the complaint. 'If Mrs Green doesn't retract that expulsion letter by dinnertime, I'm going public!'

Reverend Ferguson reads the complaint, taking her time, in spite of my threat.

With a frown that could kill butterflies in Tasmania, she folds the letter and puts it under her arm.

'I'll pass this on, but please, Shauna, if you're going to leave the school grounds, let us know. You took years off my life this afternoon.'

When she leaves, I take a shower, which I desperately need, and spend a good twenty minutes stroking and talking gently to Bob the baby. I feel like he's been with me the whole time, and that we're going to stand up to the powers that be together and for the benefit of both of us. Everything I'm doing now is for him, and that thought gives me strength.

Dinner in the dining hall is raw and raucous, which totally beats the crap out of silent and ashamed. Everyone wants to pat my belly and congratulate me. Indu asks me whether I'm going to name the baby after her. Bindi ribs me for hiding my pregnancy.

'You deserve an Oscar, Shauna.'

Olivia asks quietly if I'm scared to give birth.

'I'm trying not to think that far ahead,' I say.

'Don't worry, Shauna,' says Lou-Anne, 'it's just like doing a big poo!'

We all fall about in disgusted laughter.

'My sister had two at the same time,' replies Lou-Anne.

'They came out at the same time?' I joke.

'Yeah,' adds Lou-Anne. 'Sideways.'

Olivia's eyes get wider and wider.

'It'll happen to you, too, someday, Olivia,' I say.

After dinner, Miss Maroney corners me in the staircase and tells me that Mrs Green wants to see me in her office.

'She's still here?'

'Under the circumstances, yes,' replies Miss Maroney stiffly. 'You're not making life easy for her.'

Normally a comment like that would make me feel bad about myself. But today I won't allow it.

'Mrs Green could do the right thing,' I say, 'and then everyone's life would be easy.'

'Yes, Shauna, we could all do the right thing, couldn't we?' she replies in a bitchy tone that I just can't let fly.

'I *have* done the right thing. I did the best thing I could ever have done when I said no to an abortion.'

With that, I take off in the direction of the admin. building, full of righteous indignation about the hypocrisy of this school and its staff. If I'd had an abortion, which must be at least as offensive to the religious teachings of the school as out-of-marriage sex, I'd be Oakholme College's irreproachable star student. Some pious little speech in this vein forms in my mind as I make my way to Mrs Green's office. I want to argue with her, to give her a good telling-off.

But the reality of our meeting is pretty banal.

'Please sit, Shauna,' says the exhausted-looking woman seated on the other side of the room. Her hands are clasped together and I notice that they're trembling.

'No thanks.'

'Suit yourself.' She sighs heavily. 'I've had a chance to read your complaint. I want to let you know that while you're still formally expelled, I've decided to let you stay on as a guest of the school until the school board meets and the matter has been resolved.'

'That's not good enough.'

'That's as much as I can offer for the time being,' she says. 'I can't do anything else until the board's met.'

I nod curtly. 'I'll call my lawyer tomorrow.' I turn to leave, but Mrs Green asks me to stay.

'Please understand that our decision to expel you has nothing to do with your ethnic background. Our reaction would have been the same no matter who the student was.'

'I don't believe you.'

'If one of our non-Indigenous girls was in the same boat, we'd make the same decision. Of course we would.'

'I'll bet there are at least five girls at this school who've been pregnant at some stage. Only they don't get punished for it because a dead foetus doesn't embarrass you.'

Mrs Green grinds her jaw. She looks like she's aged about fifteen years since the last time I saw her, which was this morning.

'I resent that' is all she can think to say.

'You resent it because it's true.'

'You can leave now, Shauna.'

I go back to the dorms, thinking what a good job Oakholme College has done on me. When I arrived four and a half years ago, I couldn't look Mrs Green in the eye, let alone stand up to her, let alone stand *over* her.

Look at me now.

25

Life goes on as if I'm watching it through a fish tank. Routines unfold apparently as normal, but everything's deformed, larger, blurry.

I get out of bed and squeeze into my uniform. I eat cornflakes sprinkled with sugar in the dining hall. Boarders swell and smile around me, radiating attention, catcalls and well wishes. Lou-Anne looks on, silent and worried. Olivia, in spite of Lou-Anne's not-too-subtle hints that it would be better if she got lost, hovers. I get the impression that she's waiting for me to do something, but that she's also afraid of what I might do.

The bell rings and I walk as if mired in jelly to my roll call room. Jenny's there. She double takes when I enter the room.

'*Shauna!*' she sings, her voice ringing with tones of surprise and false cheer. Why is she so shocked to see me? I realise before I've even sat down that she's the little birdie who cheeped to Miss Maroney. She's the mole who got me expelled!

I hesitate near the front row where Jenny's seated but then continue to the back of the room. Jenny swivels around in her chair and sends a dramatic shrug in my direction.

'I know it was you,' I say.

Jenny turns back to face the board. I watch her ears go red. She doesn't move.

Why, I wonder, would Jenny have done such a thing? How, I wonder, could she have proven to sink lower than Keli Street-Hughes, that's to say, lower than a snake's belly?

'Bean, Jenny?' calls out our roll call teacher, Mrs Doyle.

'Present,' croaks Jenny.

Soon Mrs Doyle arrives at 'Harding, Shauna?'

'Yes, Mrs Doyle,' I bray, 'I'm present, no thanks to certain people in this room.'

Mrs Doyle looks at me quizzically over her reading glasses and then continues her clinical reading of the roll.

Jenny's ears go purple.

French is my first class of the day. Miss Larsen eyes me carefully as I walk into the language lab. Jenny sits behind me.

'*Bonjour, la classe,*' says Miss Larsen.

'*Bonjour Mademoiselle Larsen,*' says the class.

'I'm going to hand out your papers of Camus's *L'Étranger* now. Congratulations, Jenny.'

She lays down Jenny's paper first. I try not to gasp. Jenny turns it over and I sneak a peek. Nineteen point five out of twenty. At least she lost half a mark.

I wait in poker-faced agony as three more papers are given out before mine hits the desk. Sixteen point five out of twenty. A crap mark for me. The comment in the margin says: *Not your normal lucid standard, Shauna. Careful not to paraphrase other commentators' analyses.* She's written a large question mark at the end of the essay, where I see that I've repeated the same word three times.

Tears sting my eyes. I hate to make mistakes. Is this the way it's going to be from now on, I wonder? Will I keep sliding backwards until I'm just average and I have to get a job somewhere like the post office in Barraba?

Disappointment must be splashed across my face, because Mademoiselle Larsen addresses me directly, right in front of the class.

'It's one essay, Shauna, and you've got legitimate distractions. Don't worry.'

A humiliating silence falls. Jenny's completely still. I feel like she's enjoying this, like she'd be happy to get rid of me because she's been afraid I'll take out the French prize. Maybe the maths prize, too. She wants them for herself. She was happy to be my friend while I was coming eighth or ninth in those subjects, but once there was a danger that I'd overtake her, she decided to rub me out any way she can.

After French, I accost Jenny in the quadrangle.

I put on my widest poo-eating grin. It seems to terrify her.

'Shauna, let me explain...'

'Oh, let me take a wild guess. You're trying to get rid of me because I'm a contender for the French prize! Or *was*.'

'That is *ridiculous*.'

'Then why?'

'Look, I did tell Miss Maroney. Only because I thought you were being irresponsible.'

'What's it to you if I'm irresponsible or not? Who are *you* to judge *me*, Jenny Bean?'

I thought Jenny would just shrivel in shame when confronted, but she's not backing down, not one step.

'You don't seem to have given any thought whatso-ever to how you're going to look after this baby. And what about pre-natal care? What if there's something wrong with the baby that can only be fixed while you're still pregnant? And that's just the baby! What about *you*, Shauna? Do you think you can just rock up at a hospital once you've gone into labour? You have to have tests done *before* you have the baby. You could have gestational diabetes. I mean, you can die of that, you know.'

Put like that, her betrayal seems reasonable – well, almost. It did get me expelled.

'You should have told me, Jenny. You should have at least *warned* me that you were gonna blab to Miss Maroney.'

'And what would you have done? Would you have gone and had all the tests?'

'Well…' I consider the question sincerely. Well, would I? Or would I have coaxed, threatened or cajoled her into shutting her mouth? 'Well, who says I *wouldn't* have had all the tests?'

Even as I say this, I know I wouldn't have had the tests if Jenny hadn't let the cat out of the bag. But so what? It's still not a good justification.

'Honestly, Shauna, I don't think you would have. I think you're so caught up in your own righteousness that you're not paying any attention to your health or the health of your baby.'

'And who the bloody hell are you to interfere?'

'Who am *I*? I am your best friend!'

'Sorry to be the bearer of bad news, but Lou-Anne's my best friend.'

251

'Well, you're *my* best friend and I felt like I owed it to you and your baby.'

I can't bring myself to forgive her or even to admit that she has a point. So I say, 'Thanks a lot, Jenny,' pretty nastily, and rush off to my next class.

By lunchtime I've had a chance to calm down and think about what Jenny said. I find her sitting by herself under the library stairs eating a sandwich. I sit down next to her and for a few minutes neither of us says anything.

'Will you help me, Jenny?'

Jenny chews slowly and swallows before replying. 'Yes.'

And that's how I get put in touch with the maternity ward at the Royal Hospital for Women, where Jenny's aunt is a midwife. I make an appointment for Friday morning, and no matter how things turn out at school, I know I'll show up. Jenny's going to come with me.

Just before English class, which is my final period of the day, Reverend Ferguson comes looking for me. She takes me outside to deliver the news. I know from the look on her face that it isn't good.

'The school board met over lunch,' she tells me, her brow pulled into multi-directional creases, 'and they've decided to let the expulsion stand. I'm so sorry.'

'Can I go to my English class?'

'I'm afraid not. I'll take you back to the dormitory now. We haven't been able to contact your parents, but Mrs Green sent a letter by express post, so they should receive it tomorrow.'

By now I know that Reverend Ferguson is on my side and doesn't deserve to have pieces of my mind hurled at her. In fact, when we get back to my room, I thank her for standing up for me.

'It's really the least I could do,' she says. She sounds like she's about to start blubbering like a baby. 'Can I touch it?' she asks, in a splintering voice.

I nod and she puts her bejewelled hand to my rock-hard bump. As if on cue, Bob the baby kicks.

'I felt that,' she says, tears welling in her eyes.

'He's naughty.'

'Do you know it's a boy?'

'Not really. I just have a feeling. I call him Bob the baby. When he was little, he was Fred the foetus.'

She laughs. 'Fred the foetus. That's cute.' She strokes my belly for a long time, which is kind of creepy and nice at the same time.

'I tried to have a baby,' she says, 'but I couldn't. I had endometriosis, only no one knew what it was back then in the seventies.' She keeps stroking me. 'I think you're very lucky to have this baby.'

'It was kind of bad luck, though. I took the morning-after pill.' I can't believe I'm talking like this to Reverend Ferguson. Who would have thought she'd have any inkling about how babies are made?

'And you fell pregnant anyway,' she says. 'Obviously Bob the baby wants to be born.'

'I think he really does.'

'God wouldn't have let it happen if He didn't think you could handle it.'

This is the first time anyone has mentioned God in relation to my baby. Reverend Ferguson, in spite of her job description, doesn't usually bring up religion during personal conversations. In our early pastoral care sessions when I first arrived at Oakholme, we just talked about my family and my old school and friends. Far from forcing God down my throat, she always waited until I asked a question.

'Do you think God wants me to have the baby?'

'Oh, yes, Shauna. Of course He does.'

'Then why is Mrs Green so dead against it?'

'Because she, like you, lives in the real world. We're all caught up in the middle of tensions. You're going to have to forgive her, no matter what happens.'

Since our first meeting, SRF's always been telling me that I have to forgive this person or that. Jamie. My parents. The police. Australia. Myself. It's so much easier said than done.

We sit on my bed and talk until the final bell rings. Self-Raising Flour tells me about her soul-destroying attempts at pregnancy and how she felt when she finally realised that it was never going to happen.

'I felt worthless. I don't feel like that anymore, but at the time I felt like I had no value. I was so angry.'

'I feel like that sometimes, too,' I tell her.

'It's not fair on women, the Western attitude to babies. Babies are a blessing and sterility's a curse. When will people realise?'

'Realise what?'

'That motherhood is feminism's best-kept secret.'

'I think that my people already know that,' I tell her. 'They know that having a baby turns you into a better person. My parents were happy when I told them I was pregnant. Well, once they got used to the idea.'

That's when Reverend Ferguson tells me about a book called *Sex and Destiny* by a feminist called Germaine Greer. She promises to bring it to school tomorrow and give it to me if I'm still here.

'I'm not leaving,' I tell her. 'They'll have to lever me out the window with a crane.'

Reverend Ferguson gives me a great big hug, and as soon as she's gone, I go to Miss Maroney's office to call Sarah Hogan-Doran.

'The expulsion stands,' I tell her. 'The school board's not giving an inch.'

'Do you want me to call my friend at *The Australian*?'

I don't have to think for too long about that.

'Yep.'

26

THE STORY GOES online at 4.22 a.m. the next morning. I stay up all night, waiting, thinking and occasionally running down to prep. hall to check the computer. When I refresh the website and the article comes up, I wake Lou-Anne and drag her downstairs.

'*Prestigious private school expels Indigenous student who refuses abortion,*' she whispers in her nasal morning voice.

'It's a hatchet job,' I say.

'Do you think it'll make a difference?'

'We'll see.'

We print the article out and lie together in Lou-Anne's bed reading it over and over again. My name isn't mentioned and neither is the name of the school. This is part of Sarah's strategy. She says that it gives me some room for 'negotiation'. If the school doesn't revoke my expulsion, we'll release names. If they revoke my expulsion, Sarah will unleash another press release praising the school for its handling of the matter, and that will kill the story.

Sarah Hogan-Doran looks meek and innocent, but in fact she's pure evil. I think she has a great future ahead of her as a lawyer. I can tell she's really enjoying herself with my case.

Not that she's taking it lightly. No, not at all. She's already looking for a barrister who's willing to act in my case on a pro-bono basis (that means for free).

'Hang in there, Shauna,' she told me at the end of our conversation last night. 'Be tough.'

And that's exactly what I'm doing. I'm going through the motions, just like I did yesterday. And I mean it about the crane. I won't leave the grounds of this school until physically forced.

By five-thirty, Lou-Anne's snoring again, but I'm too wound up to get back to sleep. I decide to pay old Olivia a visit down the other end of the dormitory. I bet she'd like to know that I've made *The Australian*.

I've been sneaking around the dormitory building all night, but as I cross the upstairs foyer, I get a sudden feeling that I'm being spied on. And not by the Reverend Doctor Sterling McBride either. He lives downstairs.

I tread as softly as my rotund figure will allow, eyes peeled and adjusted to the darkness. A distinct sniffle rends the silence.

'Who's that?' comes a strangled voice.

'Who's *that*?' I whisper back.

'It's Shauna,' I say at the same time as the voice says, 'It's Keli.'

'What are you doing out here?' we whisper in unison. Miss Maroney's room is just a few metres away from where I'm standing. I edge closer to Keli's voice.

Finally I can see the outline of her form. I wouldn't have thought it was possible for Keli to make herself small, but she looks tiny, sitting in her pyjamas with her back against the door of her dorm room. Even in the shadows, I can see her eyes shining. With tears? I suppress the urge to say, *Well, what the hell have you got to cry about, Tampon Princess?*

'Can't sleep?' I whisper.

'No,' she says, sniffing again. 'What about you?'

'Not a chance.'

'Maroney's going to hear us if we keep talking out here.'

'I know.'

'Wednesday detention.'

'Who cares?'

I'm not going to sneak into Olivia's room with Keli sitting here. I suppose I could go back to bed, but instead I decide to try something I've never done before. I guess I'm in a strange mood.

'Wanna go downstairs?'

'What for?'

'Talk.'

To my amazement, she stands up. We tiptoe together down the staircase and then sit side by side on the bottom step under the Reverend Doctor Sterling McBride's gaze. We're here to 'talk', but neither of us says anything for a while.

'So are they going to give you the boot, or not?' Keli asks finally.

'They're trying.'

'And?'

'I'll be okay, I think,' I tell her. 'I mean, either way. What about you?'

Keli gives this whimpering little sob, then covers her mouth.

'S-sorry,' she stammers. 'I know I haven't really got any problems compared to you...but...'

'What is it?'

It's lucky that it's dark, because I don't think we could talk like this if we could see each other's faces.

'Did the school send your parents your ATAR estimate in the mail?'

'Yeah. But I'd already seen it.'

'Well...me too. I just didn't know that my parents were going to be so upset about it. Now I'm upset about it too.'

Oh dear. We get to the pointy end of school and, finally, even a girl as confident and full of herself as Keli begins to fret. I can't imagine that her ATAR estimate would be sky-high, not unless the estimator was on drugs. But would that really come as a shock to Keli?

'Is it *that* bad?'

'Yeah, it's pretty bad. I won't be able to do a law degree *anywhere*, not even in a country university, not even if I pay full fees.'

'You haven't even done the final exams yet, Keli.'

I feel her shrug beside me. She knows as well as I do that you can't just pull something off at the last minute, not if you've been asleep at the wheel all year...or, let's face it, for your whole school life.

'Why do you want to do law, anyway?'

'I've always wanted to work at my uncle's law firm in Albury.'

'Can't you still do that?'

259

'Yeah, maybe as a secretary. But it won't be the same. And my parents are so cut up about my marks. They were expecting more for their money. More from me.' Keli sighs sadly. Then she says, with a hint of bitterness, 'I suppose *your* parents are happy with *your* estimate.'

In spite of a few dodgy performances recently, my estimate is somewhere in the vicinity of – hmmm, let's see – ninety-eight. And that's what I deserve. Study's a drag, and not everyone can resign themselves to the hard work. Not every-one's meant to go to uni.

'Yeah, they're happy.' I try not to sound smug.

'I guess uni won't be a breeze with a baby.' She wipes her nose with her pyjama sleeve. 'What are you going to study, anyway? Law or medicine, I bet.'

This is the first time Keli has ever asked me about my plans for the future. Suddenly, to her, I exist.

'No, I'm actually thinking about doing journalism and communications, probably combined with languages.'

'French?'

'At least French.'

'And you're going to become a journalist?'

'Maybe. It's pretty competitive these days. Even the really experienced people have trouble getting work. But there are people succeeding, and I don't see why I shouldn't be one of them.'

'What about the baby?'

'I'll study online, and by the time I'm ready to work, the baby will be ready for school.'

'You're a pretty wilful girl, Shauna. I'll give you that.'

I like the way she says 'wilful' and not something more complimentary or ordinary like 'determined', because I know she means it. And for once, she's right.

'I'll manage.' I lean over and bump my shoulder lightly into hers. 'And so will you, Keli. You're the Tampon Princess!'

We laugh our arses off – nervously at first – right there in front of the Reverend Doctor Sterling McBride. We wake up Miss Maroney, too, who wakes up half the other boarders yelling at us.

'Two Red Marks each!' she proclaims in her dressing gown from the top of the staircase, before stomping back into her lair and slamming the door behind her.

'She can stick her Red Marks,' I tell Keli. 'I'm expelled anyway.'

'Good luck,' Keli says, as we trudge back up the stairs, each of us with our own cross to bear.

'Yeah,' I reply, not really sure whether she means it. 'Good luck to you, too.'

I think about Keli later on while I'm getting ready for breakfast. It has never occurred to me before that her parents might feel disappointed with her performance at school, or that she might register their negative feelings. I've never thought about what it would be like to be average at school, and how that might play out against a backdrop of wealth and privilege and high expectations. I mean, my parents have high hopes for me, too, but they're just that – *hopes*. They're more or less delighted by anything I do. I'm pregnant at the age of seventeen and they still support me. I don't know which I'd rather be – mediocre and rich, or smart and poor. I have to say, even after speaking to Keli, I can see the benefits of being mediocre and rich! And not pregnant.

By the time breakfast is served, the article from *The Australian* has been circulated around the entire boarding house. The powers-that-be must know by now. They just *must*. I eat my breakfast surrounded by chattering friends. Everyone wishes me well. I have no idea what lies in store for me today.

'I'm going to start a campaign for you on Indiegogo,' says Bindi.

Indu rolls her eyes. 'You're going to crowdfund Shauna's baby?'

'What do *you* think we should do, Indu?' Bindi replies. 'Put in a special request to Sai Baba?'

'Works for me,' sniffs Indu.

I go to roll call with a strange sense of calm. I sit next to Jenny. She turns to me and smiles tentatively. I smile back, even though this could be my final roll call.

It doesn't surprise me when a note arrives. It comes stuck to the front cover of a great paving brick of a book called *Sex and Destiny*:

Board meeting this morning following Australian *article. Keep you updated. Chin up. SRF.*

I go to English class with Jenny by my side. Our English teacher, Mrs Arnold, gives me a cautious, curt 'Hello, Shauna' as we take our seats. She begins the lesson, never quite taking her eyes off me. I wonder what the executive order to the teachers has been? *Keep Shauna Harding in sight at all times.*

Instead of following the lesson, I dive into *Sex and Destiny*. (I'm thoroughly sick of John Donne and Charles Dickens anyway.) In its opening pages, the author, Germaine Greer, says that in the industrialised West we have created a society that does not like children, and more than that, children who don't like their parents.

The book was written over thirty years ago, but so much of what I'm reading rings true. It rings particularly true for me because I've been on the pointy end of other people's fear of children. Greer says that rich, greedy, infertile Caucasians are afraid that their standard of living is threatened by the economic demands of the over-fertile poor (*Say thanks to your dad for me, Keli*). She says that mothers, children and old people in the developed world are marginalised, and that we may never return to the riches of a family-centred world.

I realise that I am one of the over-fertile poor, part of a family-oriented black culture that white people are afraid of. It's not that I believe that white Australians are actively, consciously out to get me or Bob, but I do agree with parts of Greer's theory. When I read that opening chapter, I feel like she's talking directly to me. And what she's telling me is that I'm right to want my baby. I also know that Reverend Ferguson thinks that I'm right to want my baby. That's what she's telling me by giving me this book.

'Shauna?'

Mrs Arnold says my name for a third time before I look up from the pages of the book.

'Mrs Green would like to see you.'

Jenny squeezes my arm and mouths 'good luck'. A bit rich coming from the person who put me in it. Though I understand her reasons, I still feel raw about what Jenny did. I don't like it when someone else decides what's good for me.

At Mrs Green's office, a battle scene awaits. I swear the whole school board is crammed in there, between the door and the delicately bubbling tropical fish tank. They all stand as I enter the room. I know that the article has made a big impact. Why else would they have called in Oakholme College's infantry, cavalry and artillery? In fact, they look like relics from the First World War. It's like ANZAC day lunch at the old folks' home. They're all ancient, all crotchety, all dour. And, it goes without saying, all white.

Mrs Green, the young gun, tells me to take a seat, and as usual, I refuse. Everyone else sits back down.

'Am I expelled or not?' I ask her. The urge to get out is very strong. The sheer number of people in the room is making me very nervous.

'We think we can come to an arrangement,' says a doddery, blue-rinsed man I vaguely remember from chapel services. Reverend Bennett, maybe? I don't know. I've always just thought of him as the Blue Rinse Guy.

'What kind of arrangement?'

Blue Rinse clears his throat. 'Obviously, you were very upset by the school's decision, or you would never have approached the media.'

'My lawyer approached the media. I had nothing to do with it.'

264

'But you must have agreed to the article being written.'

I shrug. 'I suppose I *could* get my lawyer to withdraw my complaint and put out a more positive press release. You know, if the right *arrangement* were reached. I'd need to speak to my lawyer first, though.'

All the old people turn to look at the guy sitting next to Blue Rinse. He introduces himself as David Sachs, Oakholme's lawyer. He gives me his card and tells me to have my lawyer get in touch.

I nod solemnly while quietly crapping myself. I wonder how tiny Sarah Hogan-Doran will stack up against someone as experienced as Mr Sachs. But she hasn't let me down yet, has she? Her strategies have hit their target every time.

I go back to the dorms, call the Aboriginal legal centre, and leave a message for Sarah. The receptionist tells me that she won't be in the office until the afternoon.

Then I get Bindi to text my dad to let him know I'm about to call. He answers after a lot of ringing.

'Shauna?'

'Dad!'

'Is everything all right? We've had about thirty missed calls from the school. And yesterday we got a letter via express post telling us we'd better pick you up or they'd call social services!'

'Ignore it. Everything's changed since then. I've got a lawyer now, and I think they're going to let me stay.'

'How did you manage that?'

I explain how I went to the Aboriginal legal centre and met the cleverest, most devious law student on the planet.

Dad says that he hopes I sort it out soon, because they're dying of worry. Then he puts Mum on the phone.

'Shauna, love! How are you?'

Mum sounds emotional, but also excited and clear headed. She doesn't sound like she's talking under the weight of anti-depressants. I assure her that I've got an appointment with the hospital, that I'm being responsible. She wants to know if I know the baby's gender.

'I'll probably find out tomorrow. I'm going to the hospital for some tests.'

I tell her that I've been calling it Fred the foetus and now Bob the baby.

'No grandson of mine's going to be called Fred or Bob, Shauna,' she says.

Just before we hang up, Dad gets back on the phone and asks about Nathan.

'He's being a jerk, Dad,' I rage, knowing damn well that I'm being a bit of a jerk, too. 'What can I do?'

'I could speak to his parents—'

'Jesus, don't do that.'

'I think they'd want to know. If it was my son...well, I'd wanna know. Then they can talk to him. It'll give them all a chance to do the right thing.'

'I don't want to give him a chance.'

'Shauna...'

He's never quite been able to stand up to me, my old man. Sometimes I wish he would.

For the rest of the morning and into the afternoon, I lie on my bed reading *Sex and Destiny* and waiting for Sarah to call. Lou-Anne brings me a chicken burger and we eat on our beds, which is a big no-no, but at this point, who cares?

'If you want to know my opinion, I think you should never speak to Jenny again.'

'Try to see it from her point of view, Lou-Anne.'

'She couldn't hack getting beaten by a black chick.'

'It wasn't about that.'

'Promise me you'll whip her butt in every subject, Shauna. Just to teach her a lesson.'

'I'll do my best.'

'I told you from the beginning that she was bad news.'

'You did.'

Knowing how peeved Lou-Anne gets when she's talking about Jenny, I change the subject. I ask her how she's feeling about her Opera House audition, which is later this month. A well-known Aboriginal soprano called Deborah Cheetham is on the judging panel. Deborah is Lou-Anne's idol, which adds an extra layer of pressure on top of her already frayed nerves. She's too shaky to even call back her beloved Isaac, who's left three messages.

'I'm feeling bloody jittery.'

'At least your mo's grown back. That's one less thing to be in a funk about.'

She punches me in the arm.

'Is that how you treat a pregnant woman? You bash her?' I demand in mock outrage. Then I ask her how she's going to deal with her stage fright.

'Indu's aunt's going to smuggle me some Xanax.'

'So you're an opera drug cheat?'

'We've tried everything else! If I go out on stage and get nervous and my throat clams up, I'll be barking like a frog!'

'No one wants to see that.'

'Exactly.'

Sarah Hogan-Doran calls while we're still having lunch. Miss Maroney comes to fetch me with a hoity-toity expression. Once in her office, I shut the door firmly behind me and tell Sarah how the school board ambushed me and I give her David Sachs's number.

'I think they want to make a deal,' I say, trying to sound tough.

'Doesn't surprise me. That article must have scared them.'

'It has. Nothing seems to scare them more than embarrassment.'

Sarah promises to call me back when she's spoken to Sachs.

After the call, I start to feel jittery and anxious, so I go for a walk outside. One of the first people I see is Keli Street-Hughes. I don't know which of us looks the more sheepish after our tête-à-tête in the early hours, but we make eye contact.

'Shauna,' she says stiffly.

'Keli.'

'My dad saw the article in *The Australian*.'

'Did he?' I'm going for a façade of nonchalance.

'He's really disgusted by what the school's trying to do to you. He and some of the other parents are threatening to pull us out if Mrs Green doesn't change her tune.'

'Are you serious?'

'Yep.'

I'm knocked over flat with tyre tracks by this development. It's hard to know what to say – or what to do. Forgive her for all the hurtful shit that's gone down over the years and become her best friend?

Suddenly it hits me. With tongue in cheek, I grin at Keli. 'Say thanks to your dad for me, Keli!'

My words could be taken either way, but I'm hugely relieved when we both burst into uproarious laughter.

While I know I can never be friends with this girl, I marvel at how help and support can come from the most unexpected places. Imagine the man who spawned a piece of work like Keli Street-Hughes being outraged by the injustice of my situation! He doesn't even know me, but he's decided to do the right thing anyway. It's easy to forget that often people do the right thing, the brave thing, without being forced or even asked. Not to prove anything, but just to be good. Sometimes even people like Keli Street-Hughes are capable of that.

Later that afternoon, Reverend Ferguson sends a note with Lou-Anne up to our room. It says:

Shauna, please see me in my office. SRF.

I go to Self-Raising Flour's office, but it's empty.

'Shauna?' Reverend Ferguson calls out to me from the doorway of Mrs Green's office. That's when I find out that Mrs Green's resigned and that SRF is the new sheriff in town.

All the board members are gone. The only sign of them ever having been there is seven extra chairs and the unmistakable whiff of old person. In a tone so different from

Mrs Green's intimidating coolness, Reverend Ferguson explains that she's now the Acting Principal appointed by the board. She tells me that I'm no longer expelled, and that a letter to that effect has been sent to my parents.

'I am sorry for all the stress and offence this school has caused you,' she says. 'It's been very upsetting for all of us.'

She asks me when the baby's due and I tell her around stuvac.

'You're welcome to stay in the dormitory until the baby's born,' she says, 'but we can't accommodate the baby. It would be too disruptive for the other students. You'll still be enrolled at the school, and you'll still graduate, but as a day girl. I'm afraid that's the best I can do.'

'That's great.' I break into a huge smile.

'I've spoken to your lawyer, Sarah, and she says that provided that you're happy with what I'm offering, she will release a statement to the effect that the school is support-ing you. She says that with your permission, she can also withdraw the complaint against the school.'

Asked nicely by Reverend Ferguson, I'm raring to fulfil my side of the bargain.

'Okay, I'll call her and tell her to take care of it.'

I can hardly believe it. I've won. I'm still standing, and Mrs Green is gone. Maybe I should feel sorry for Mrs Green, but I don't, not after hearing the way she spoke about me and the Indigenous scholarship in general. How can someone who holds those attitudes, even privately, be trusted to act in the interests of vulnerable people? It doesn't matter how politically correct you present yourself to be, if you've given up on a particular race of children before they've even finished school, then you obviously don't understand much about education. It's all about transformation. I don't think Mrs Green ever saw me as transformed.

But I *have* been transformed. And so has Lou-Anne. On the basis of our transformation alone, the Indigenous scholarship program should be considered a success, not a failure. Why couldn't Mrs Green see that?

27

'I THINK IT's a girl,' says Dr Jacobs, the obstetrician at the Royal Hospital for Women. 'In fact, I'm sure of it.'

'No dingle-dangle?' says Jenny, which makes me crack up. That's *exactly* the kind of word she'd use for 'dick'. I can just imagine her seeing her first lover's penis and exclaiming, 'Oh, what a *lovely* dingle-dangle!'

Speaking of lovers and dicks, it turns out that Jenny is love's dark horse. While we were in the outpatient waiting room before my appointment, she revealed that she's been having a secret affair with Tom from St Augustine's! Over the last three weeks she's gone from kissing virgin to practically all the way with Stephen Agliozzo's way less handsome friend.

I can't really blame her for not telling me sooner. Things have been tense between us and I haven't been there for Jenny. I've been one hundred per cent focused on myself. To be fair, though, I do have something worth focusing on.

'No dingle-dangle,' confirms the doctor. 'And a very healthy baby as far as I can tell.'

Jenny and I share a look of relief. We both know that I should have seen a doctor a long time ago, but it's so good to be reassured that, luckily, there have been no consequences for the baby. I feel elated seeing images of my daughter's squished little self straining for room in a part of my body I could never really imagine. And to think that I baked her!

Dr Jacobs measures my baby's head circumference and length. 'She's a lot bigger than average,' she says.

'Everyone in my family's gigantic,' I say.

After the appointment, I fill out a lot of paperwork to book in for my delivery, which is just weeks away. Then Jenny's aunt Coralie, a midwife, takes us for a tour of the delivery suites. In a matter of months, I'll be giving birth in one of them. There's going to be a little girl, who didn't even exist before this year. It's incredible when you think about it, yet it happens every day. I can't get over the wonder of it, and also its everydayness. As we walk around, a smile comes over my face and I just can't shift it.

'You look excited, Shauna,' Coralie says.

'And scared,' I add.

'There's not much to be scared of at your age,' she says. 'The risks of just about everything that could go wrong for you or your baby are much, much lower than those of someone older. Even a woman in her late twenties.'

This is news to me, good news. I wonder why people act as though teenage pregnancy is the end of the world. I begin to wonder whether there is anything so terribly wrong about it for anyone other than perhaps the teenager involved.

After the appointment, Jenny and I go to the hospital café for a snack. We're dressed in civvies, so I get some funny looks. When I'm in my built-for-purpose school uniform, I get far fewer. People can't hide their shock at the sight of a pregnant teenager in regular clothes. Why is it any of their business?

'I *still* can't believe you're going to have a baby.' Jenny sips her hot chocolate and looks over the froth at me in wonder.

'I still can't believe you're going to France without me,' I reply.

Jenny has decided to start a degree in romantic languages at the University of Sydney next year. Not only will she go to Paris for a holiday during the sumptuous European summer, she's also going to do an exchange for a year at the Sorbonne or another European university. It's something I just won't be able to do, probably not ever.

As we chat about where she plans to live and her possible travel plans in Europe, I feel a deep, burning envy that I could never admit to Jenny. She'll get to remain a footloose child, while I'm forced to grow up. I'll go through the motions of being a university student. I'll research for assignments and sit exams. But the real essence of being a uni student, or at least what I'd imagined it to be – getting contentedly lost in library research for hours, meeting new people with similar interests, and going out with friends – will be for others to savour. I'll be a student in my spare time, which won't be abundant. And if I meet a man, which will be far less likely because I'll be stuck at home a lot of the time, I'll be meeting him as a single mum. I'll have to be really careful about who I let into my life.

'So?' Jenny looks at me expectantly. 'Shauna?'

'Sorry, what?'

'You *will* come and visit me in Paris, won't you?'

'What? With the baby?'

'You could leave the baby with your mum for a week or two couldn't you?'

'I guess so…'

Right at this moment, I feel like I'm going to miss out on so much that I can't even force myself to sound excited about the prospect of visiting Jenny. What would the point be? To experience, with bitterness, what great things might have been, but weren't?

'You could leave the baby with Nathan,' Jenny says casually.

I feel a sudden stab of annoyance. 'You know that Nathan's not going to be part of our lives, Jenny.'

'But you *are* going to let him see the baby, aren't you?' When I don't answer, she takes a long sip of her hot chocolate. 'I suppose it's your choice.'

'Like it was my choice to tell the school about the pregnancy,' I say quietly. Bitchily.

A strange expression comes over Jenny's face. A combination of shock and betrayal. She blinks at me from behind her glasses for a few seconds before responding.

'So you're *still* smarting, Shauna,' she says with restrained anger. 'After all this.' She gestures around the hospital cafeteria, as though I should be grateful for the stale sandwiches and soggy donuts that surround us. 'I thought you wanted help.'

'No, you thought I *needed* help.'

'Was I wrong?'

I grit my teeth. 'You can be really judgemental sometimes.'

'You can be really irresponsible sometimes,' she dares to reply.

I move forwards on my chair and its legs screech against the ground. I try to stay cool.

'You just said it was my choice whether to involve Nathan or not.'

'And it is. Doesn't mean you've made the right choice, though, does it?'

'What do you care, Jenny? It's *my* life. Why are you trying to stick your nose into everything? You're lucky I'm even speaking to you after the crap you put me in with Mrs Green!'

I push my chair back from the table, resulting in another loud screech, and clamber to my feet. People at the other tables stop talking and stare at me. I'm getting quite good at making a big, pregnant spectacle.

'Sit down,' says Jenny in a dangerously low voice. I've never heard her sound so tough. I sit. I fold my arms over my enormous boobs. When the other diners begin to go about their business again, Jenny starts talking.

'I care about you,' she tells me, still in the low voice. 'You're my best friend. And do you want to know *why* you're my best friend?'

I take a deep breath. 'Why?'

'Because you're so smart and so brave. Think about it, Shauna. Our backgrounds are really different. I'm not like Lou-Anne or Olivia. They follow you around like bad smells because you're charismatic but safe for them. You guys were *always* going to get along. You and me though, we had to get

276

to know each other, didn't we? We weren't even friends until Year 10. So I know that you probably *think* you powwow better with Lou-Anne than you do with me, and maybe in some ways you two are closer, but *our* friendship grew out of a crack in the footpath. That's why it's so strong.'

Jenny's eyes are shining with tears now.

She continues, 'So when I tell you that I care about you, I hope you know how much I mean it.'

'You think I'm going to hurt my baby by leaving out Nathan.' Now my eyes are stinging, too.

'Don't you think it would be better if she knew her dad?'

'But what if he doesn't want her...want *us*?'

'And that's the other thing,' says Jenny. 'I want *you* to have Nathan.'

I nod. 'For help with the baby?'

'For love, Shauna.'

On the way back to school, in Jenny's car (in her family you get a car when you get your licence) I think about my dad and what my life would be like without him. How could my mum have coped? Would I have made it to Oakholme? Would I even be alive?

Then I think about my parents and how they got together. They were young, clueless teenagers, too. They've had the toughest time any parent can go through, burying their son, but they're still together and they never stopped loving one another.

There was always lots of love. Always.

I want Nathan to love the baby and me, but I'm so scared that he won't. What will I do if he doesn't?

As if reading my mind, Jenny suddenly pipes up. 'There *are* other guys out there, too, don't forget.'

I smile. 'Hypocrite. I've been telling you that ever since you clapped eyes on Stephen Agliozzo. It took you a while to take your own advice, didn't it, Jenny Bean?'

28

LOU-ANNE'S BIG DAY arrives and body and mind are set to bust. Miss Della found a hideous red taffeta dress that Lou-Anne modelled in the dorms this morning like a Disney princess in a red meringue, swishing up and down the staircase. I swear I saw the Reverend Doctor Sterling McBride's eyebrows jump.

Lou-Anne and Miss Della have already left for the Opera House. Later this afternoon, Bindi, Indu and I are going to join her for the auditions for Opera Australia's Young Artist program, which are open to the public and a *huge* deal. I feel extremely nervous for Lou-Anne and I hope that she has packed a double dose of whatever tranquiliser she's intending to use to smooth out her nerves.

What to wear to the opera when you're eight months pregnant? That's what I'm contemplating when Olivia Pike walks into our room with a bouquet of gerberas. You know the type, with wire stuck up their stems to keep them erect and happy-looking.

'Hey, what's this all about?' I ask her chirpily, sure that the flowers are for me.

Olivia smiles uncertainly. 'Auntie Marilyn had them delivered for Lou-Anne.'

'Oh,' I say, slightly embarrassed.

Bindi, who's lying on her bed, smiles smarmily without looking up from her book. 'Well…she's at the Opera House right now. You can just leave them.'

Olivia stands there like a pillar of salt. 'I was actually hoping to give her the bouquet myself.'

'She won't be back until tonight.'

'But I could come with you guys.'

'Well…' Bindi looks up from her book. 'Yeah, of course you can.'

'But…' I'm not sure Lou-Anne would want Olivia there.

'But *nothing*, Shauna,' says Bindi. 'It's my brother's car and I say she can come. As long as Miss Maroney okays it.'

I shrug. 'Well, I guess so, then.'

Olivia leaves the room with the bouquet and a spring in her step. 'I'll call Marilyn right now!'

'Bindi!' I shout-whisper when she's gone.

'Oh, stop being mean!' snaps Bindi. 'You and Lou-Anne are so hard on that kid.'

'I am *not!*' I reply indignantly. 'I'm the one who convinced her to come back to school.'

'So you could torture her a little more,' adds Indu, popping out from behind the door of her wardrobe.

The two of them exchange self-righteous smiles.

'I see,' I say, mock-pouting. 'You're going to gang up on me.'

'To the contrary,' replies Indu, 'I think I've found something for you to wear.'

'I hope it's made of spandex,' mutters Bindi.

I look to Indu with interest. She smiles back coyly.

'Remember that summer I went back to Mumbai and put on fifteen kilos...'

★ ♥ ★

We arrive at the Opera House in Bindi's brother's Alfa Romeo a few hours later. All four of us – Indu, Bindi, Olivia and I – are dressed to the nines, well for us, anyway. We all feel a bit ridiculous as we walk up the stairs, the harbour glittering behind us in the low afternoon sun.

I'm cutting a dashing figure in Indu's red-and-gold 'fat sari', which she's wound around me to a reasonably elegant effect. I keep thinking it's going to fly off, but she's assured me it won't. Olivia looks particularly lovely in a denim skirt and a lemon linen blouse. Not that I would ever tell her that. She's holding the bouquet of gerberas like a flower girl.

We follow signs to the Concert Hall, where auditions are unfolding even as we enter. The disapproving faces of parents and other well-wishers snap around to chide us as we bustle in nervously. Someone shushes us. Opera crowds are scary!

Taking nosebleed seats, we have to wait about half an hour for Lou-Anne's audition. It's an incredibly intimidating atmosphere, with a spotlight on the stage and all the judges sitting in the front row. I get wicked jitters as Lou-Anne walks on in her red, floor-length taffeta dress, but what looked like a gaudy joke in the Oakholme dormitory has a stunning effect onstage. There is something about Lou-Anne's sheer scale, her wide, bare, brown shoulders, tapered waist and gigantic French roll, that makes the huge dress appear elegant.

The piano accompanist starts to play and I hold my breath.

Lou-Anne's performance is spectacular. The notes pipe and soar from her throat to the jagged, angular limits of the Concert Hall's ceiling, as if Lou-Anne herself were the musical instrument.

'How can a *person* make a sound like that?' Olivia whispers into my ear. That's exactly what I'm thinking. The coloratura is a rare and magical goddess.

I know that Lou-Anne must be nervous in the extreme, but there's no visible evidence of awkwardness while she's onstage. She blows the roof off the most famous opera house in the world. When the piece is finished and light applause descends, my friends and I in standing ovation, Lou-Anne glides to the front of the stage and bows deeply.

I can see Deborah Cheetham clapping and smiling down the front. Gratitude floods into me. On a day like today, as brilliant black judges brilliant black, I feel lucky to be black and happy to be Australian. In this moment there's nothing I would change.

After the audition, we four less-talented folk make our way out of the Concert Hall and into the foyer. Lou-Anne and Miss Della emerge from the bowels of backstage a few minutes later, each as flushed as the other with excitement and pride.

'That was amazing,' gushes Olivia, handing Lou-Anne the gerberas.

Lou-Anne's grin gets even brighter. Olivia cringes with relief. I can tell that these two tough nuts are going to be friends when I go.

When I go. It sounds like I'm about to die after a long illness, but I really do have the feeling of arriving at the end of a chapter.

'Hey, Bollywood,' says Lou-Anne, and it takes me a second to realise that she's making fun of me and not Indu. She puts her arm around me, too, so that Olivia's under one and I'm under the other. Miss Della takes a photo, which ends up getting published in the Oakholme College yearbook.

Lou-Anne accompanies Miss Della to some kind of after-party that we're not invited to. When she shuffles into the dorm at two in the morning, smelling like other people's cigarette smoke and perfume, she tells me that she has been selected for Opera Australia's Young Artist program. After she delivers the good news, we're both so excited that we can't sleep. The last time I look at my bedside clock, it's 6 a.m., and we sleep in until lunchtime. That's when I find that there's a message for me that Nathan called. I screw up the note and toss it in the bin. I don't have time for someone I don't trust. It's the end of Year 12 for Heaven's sake.

★ ♥ ★

I've arrived at the beached whale stage. I think that's the medical term for it, anyway. It's hard to sit down. It's hard to get up. It's impossible to lie front-side down, and even lying on my back is painful. I can walk, but not too close to the harbour in case someone shoots a harpoon through me.

We've just finished the third term of Year 12, which ended in typical madcap fashion with a concert where we poked fun at all the teachers – I did a great impression of SRF in

283

religious robes – and meetings about the Year 12 formal, which I, regrettably, will not be able to attend because I will have just given birth. With a boyfriend and thus a partner for the formal in tow, Jenny's been spearheading the organising committee with frightening enthusiasm. The big night will unfold at Taronga Zoo with a live band and a speech by Delta Goodrem. I'm not admitting to anyone how bummed-out I am about not going.

On the last day, all the boarders, led by Lou-Anne, decide to have a baby-naming competition. Ten names are proposed and then voted for by secret ballot, which in the boarding house can never really be secret, as everyone recognises everyone else's handwriting.

Anyway, after a noisy meeting in prep. hall, everyone comes thundering up the stairs into our room to deliver the good news. The top three baby names, in ascending order, are: Addison (as in the disease? yucko!), Piper (this is an occupation, not a name), and coming in first place – wait for it – *Keli* (very funny). When I reject the lot of them out of hand, Lou-Anne looks smug. I think she really believes I'm going to name the baby after her.

After the winning names are read out to me and I'm asked to choose between them, I announce, 'The baby shall remain nameless!' and everyone boos and hisses.

For those of us in Year 12, the holidays will merge into stuvac, and almost all the Year 12 boarders plan to stay at school the whole time. There are no more formal classes, just revision groups for those who care to attend. I'm surprised that almost everyone, even the girls who aren't academic, shows up to almost everything. Everyone's feeling the pressure but everyone's trying. I suppose that's one of the reasons that parents pay so much to have their daughters come here, to make sure their kid is in with a chance. I know only too well that at some schools in this country, only the really intelligent and self-motivated kids have that chance.

I do most of my study in bed, propped up on pillows. Indu and Bindi bring me food. Bindi's sister-in-law, Maria, makes me a dish of galaktobureko, a pastry and custard dessert, which I keep beside my bed and eat over the course of two days. Then she brings in a tray of peppers stuffed with lamb and rice. Then she delivers a tray of moussaka.

'That baby's going to come out Greek,' Bindi keeps telling me.

'I don't think it works like that,' Indu keeps telling Bindi.

I'm hungry enough to eat all day, but tragically I can only keep a plateful of food down every few hours due to my wicked acid reflux. Beryl the baby* (*not her real name) is slamming her growing self in all directions, including up against my stomach, rendering it very small and hostile to the large meals I'm dying to eat.

Beryl's also putting pressure on my pelvis and bowels, causing bottom trumpeting that becomes particularly unruly when I'm asleep. One afternoon Lou-Anne uses Bindi's smuggled phone to take footage of me in the middle of a nap with a French grammar book spread over my face. My farting is so loud and brassy that she manages to splice the soundtrack into something resembling Richard Wagner's *Ride of the Valkyries*. Think bombs dropping. Think invasion of Poland. Think *Apocalypse Now*. That's what slumber sounds like with Beryl the baby on board.

'When you're a famous journalist, you'd better write good reviews of my opera performances, or else this video is hitting the internet.'

'There's a book over my face,' I reply smugly. 'No one's gonna know that it's me.'

'What other pregnant black chick wearing an Oakholme jersey would fall asleep with a French book on her face?'

I suppose she has a point.

What's really distracting me from study, though, even at thirty-seven weeks, isn't Beryl or my friends, but thoughts of Nathan. Before the end of term my father took the liberty of calling Nathan's parents, who were apparently quite shocked by the news. It hurts me to think that the baby and I are so unimportant to Nathan that he wouldn't even tell his parents about the pregnancy. Dad says that the O'Briens want to come to visit me before the birth, but I've shut down any such plans. I suppose I'm afraid of giving them a free kick at me. I'm tired of being blamed and criticised for something that two people were responsible for.

My parents can't afford to come to Sydney on my due date and just wait around until something happens, so I'm going to call them when I go into labour, which is something else I feel apprehensive about. Medically it should be no problem because I'm so young and the pregnancy is normal. I know that *homo sapiens* have been giving birth for millennia with nothing to quell the agony but a stick between the teeth, but it sounds like hell to me. Lou-Anne and I have streamed some antenatal classes in prep. hall, but honestly, she was more into the silly breathing and noises than I was. Hyperventilating like that makes me feel sick. I think when I go into labour I'll just be screaming.

A few days into stuvac and I'm in my usual glamorous position in bed, propped up on pillows with my legs spread in front of me. It's late afternoon and Olivia's sitting on the end of my bed, wasting my time. We often hang out like this when Lou-Anne's at singing practice, comfortable in silence, talking only if we feel like it.

Then in walks Keli carrying a gigantic basket squeaking with curly ribbon and cellophane. Still far from comfortable around my gingernut-nemesis-capable-of-the-occasional-good-deed, I immediately prickle up and expect some kind of hideous prank.

'What can I do for you, Keli?' I ask coolly from my recumbent position. Olivia glances up at her and immediately looks back down.

'Special delivery for the...ah...special delivery.'

I raise my eyebrows.

'It's a present from the Parents and Citizens Association.'

She plops it between my legs. 'Aren't you going to open it?' she asks after a few seconds of motionlessness on my part.

I shrug and then begin tearing at the cellophane unceremoniously. It turns out to be a perfectly nice hamper packed with stuff for Beryl (singlets, jumpsuits, booties, a blanket and baby soap) and a few things for me, too (chocolate, a face *masque* and a funny book about what to expect when you're expecting). The most interesting thing about opening a present from Keli Street-Hughes is subtly watching her unsubtly watch me do it. She's interested in my polite reaction. *Very* interested. She's on tenterhooks as she observes me looking at things and responding to them.

I realise suddenly that that's what it was always about with Keli. Getting a rise. Getting a kick out of excluding me. I don't think her behaviour towards me was only about racism. I also don't think she likes me much now. Maybe she has a grudging admiration for me, as I do for her, but I'm not part of her world, and she's not part of mine. There's little risk of us ever becoming friends, but I know now that she was an enemy never worth having either.

When Keli leaves, Olivia immediately lays into me.

'You were *far* too nice to her. You should have thrown all that crap back in her face! Who does she think she is sucking up to you now?'

'After a couple of weeks, I'll never have to see her again. We might as well part on peaceful terms.'

Olivia folds her arms across her chest and purses her lips into the shape of a cat's bottom. I know this look. It's the face she pulls when she's sulking. I decide to throw a little shade.

'I'm actually thinking of naming the baby Keli.'

'You're *what*?'

'It's a lovely name.'

She looks so cut up that I nudge her with my foot.

'You are too easy to wind up.'

Olivia looks thoughtful for a few moments before replying. 'You will call her Olivia, won't you?'

I smile sweetly. 'Not a chance.'

29

THE NIGHT BEFORE my English exam, Olivia pops into my room with a handmade card. On the front is a flying pig shaped from pink lace with a ribbon tail and tiny black buttons for a snout. Inside the card, in Olivia's tiny, anally neat hand, are the words: *You are proof that pigs can fly. Wishing you the best during your challenging time. Olivia xxo.*

'Well, this is almost as nice as the card my cousin Andrew made for me with his own two hands,' I tease.

Olivia's mouth draws into an injured fart-shape. 'What card?'

'Oh, the card with two hundred bucks in it, so I can buy a stroller.'

Olivia slams to a seated position on the end of my bed, her back to me.

'Where could I have found two hundred bucks, Shauna? Huh? I'm not Keli Street-Hughes,' she says shrilly. 'I thought you'd *appreciate* something with a little care and effort put into it!'

I reach out my long leg and tickle her side with my toes. Olivia laughs on cue, like an automaton. When she turns around to look at me, her face is a pincushion of smiles, dimples and dental plate.

'I *appreciate* everything you do, you idiot!' I mock-abuse her lovingly. 'Don't you know that, moron?'

It's hard to believe that the rude, spiny girl who I met in the withdrawing room at the beginning of the year is now signing off with kisses and hugs. I know that I am partly responsible for her transformation. I know that I stepped up for this child, and I know that I have it in me to step up for my baby, to be a better parent than my parents were. I have the power to influence others. I know that now.

My English exam is a breeze. I only get up twice for bladder pressure, and other than that, the time just flies by. My quotations come to mind when called, and none of the questions is a surprise.

My horror day happens a few days later when I have a three-hour Biology exam in the morning and a three-hour French exam in the afternoon. Jenny's in the same boat, and we hang out together the whole day, testing each other and discussing approaches to possible questions.

As soon as French is over, I go to bed and no one wakes me for dinner. I finally stir under my own steam at about 10 p.m. to find that Lou-Anne has left a plate of pork roast on my bedside table that's now congealed. I eat it anyway, and then go back to sleep without brushing my teeth.

The next day is my due date. I attend my outpatient appointment with Dr Jacobs and she gives me and Beryl the baby a check-up.

'No signs of labour yet,' she says.

'Is that a statement or a question?'

'A statement. It's pretty common for first-time mothers to go past their due date. My daughter came nearly three weeks late.'

'That would be great,' I say. 'For me, I mean.'

'It means the baby will be very big, and possibly hard to deliver.'

'I can only think as far as my Maths exam,' I admit.

In the meantime, I try to keep my cervix clamped shut. Modern History goes well, even though I have to get up every half hour to wee. Mathematics is my final exam and I cane it, even leaving early so that I can collapse in bed. As I pass out, my final thought is that I might not have made a single mistake in maths, because I answered all the questions and still had time to go back and check every answer.

Lou-Anne wakes me up for dinner, and when I sit up I feel my whole crotch and upper thighs soak with water. I look down at my sheets and so does Lou-Anne.

'Did you wet your pants?' she asks with a nervous giggle.

I shake my head. 'Too wet to be a wee. I think my waters just broke.'

'Oh my God, Shauna! We've got to get you to hospital!'

She shouts to Bindi to find Miss Maroney, who I'm barely on speaking terms with. She arrives moments later, car keys in hand.

'Let's go, Shauna,' she says, offering me her hand.

'I'd prefer it if Bindi drove me,' I say sourly. Bindi now has her very own fifth-hand, nipple-pink Alfa Romeo since James got a promotion and bought a new car.

'You're not getting into my car like that,' says Bindi with a curl of her nostrils. I'm in too much of a panic to make a fuss about it, but I think Bindi loves her car's upholstery more than she loves me. In the end it's Miss Maroney who drives me and Lou-Anne to the Royal Hospital for Women. Once we've arrived, I call my parents. Mum cries and assures me that they're 'on their way', but if it's a race from Barraba to Sydney, and from womb to big, wide world, who knows who'll arrive first?

In a flash, I'm in the maternity ward on a hospital gurney with Lou-Anne beside me. I get wheeled into an examination room with a midwife to have mine and Beryl's vital signs taken. Everything is fine, normal. Then the midwife swab-tests the liquid oozing out of me to see if it's really amniotic fluid. It is, of course, and it means that the baby has to be delivered in the next twenty-four hours because there's now a greater risk of infection. By hook or by crook, I'm going to be a mum this time tomorrow. If I don't go into labour naturally then I'll be induced with drugs to give birth.

I feel nervous and happy and terrified as Lou-Anne and I settle into one of the birthing suites. There's a rather confronting pair of stirrups hanging from a bar over the bed, and the walls are slathered in posters detailing birthing positions and massage techniques to reduce the pain.

'You're life's about to be over, you know,' says Lou-Anne darkly. 'Look at my sister.' Then she smiles, 'But in another way it's just about to begin.'

For a few hours, nothing happens, other than Bindi, Indu and Olivia's arrival. They bring soft drinks, chips and cookies, and eat them on my behalf. In spite of my hunger, I'm not allowed to eat, in case I end up needing a general anaesthetic. We hang out nervously, cutting up and fielding dirty looks from midwives who obviously think there should be fewer of us in the room.

'Could I have gone into labour without knowing it?' I ask Lou-Anne, eventually. As she is the closest person in our group to an expert on childbirth, having witnessed her sister give birth to twins, I keep calling on her knowledge.

'Could you have stuck a besser block up your arse without knowing?' She shrugs in response to my withering look, and everyone else cracks up. 'Well, it's the same question. The baby's not going to just slide out while you smile, Shauna.'

Not much longer after her comment, and all of a sudden, the besser block action begins in a way that leaves no doubt. It strikes like an unexpected bowel-nado, uncomfortable but bearable. It lasts for about twenty seconds.

Olivia gasps, horrified, as my face contorts.

'It's okay,' I pant. 'But can I have one of those chips?'

'The midwife said no food,' intervenes Lou-Anne, grabbing the packet from Olivia.

'But Beryl says yes,' I plead.

Lou-Anne hands me one very small, very thin chip.

'Thanks for your generosity, Lou-Anne.'

'You're in for a wild ride,' she replies. 'Hopefully they'll stick a needle in your spine sooner rather than later.'

An epidural, or an anaesthetic needle in the spine, is something I've already discussed with Dr Jacobs. She said that

I can have it more or less when I ask for it, though I wonder which is worse: labour pains or a needle in the back?

A few hours later I'm in no doubt about which would be worse, because I'm in the most savage, agonising physical pain I've ever experienced. I'm talking a wheelbarrow load of besser blocks dropping and clanging and bumping around inside me. It's astounding how painful contractions can be. It's even more astounding that no one really lets you in on it beforehand. Not even my own mum gave me any clue what to expect.

Olivia and Bindi start to cry and one of the midwives asks them to leave the room and sit in the waiting area. I'm crying, too.

I look out the window and it strikes me how dark it is outside. It must be the middle of the night. I hear someone moan, 'Mummy! Mummy!', and then I realise that the scared voice is mine. I'm buzzing with pain and fatigue. My eyes close against the bright lights above me, and I can feel Lou-Anne behind me rubbing my back.

'Your mum's coming,' she says. 'They'll be here soon.'

'I want the epidural,' I manage to mutter. My lower torso is a rod of pain. It's all I can think about. From time to time I forget that there's a baby.

Indu calls the midwife and I roll onto my back. I feel the midwife put her fingers inside me to check the dilation of my cervix. I don't even care that there's a stranger down there prodding me. I stopped caring about that kind of nonsense hours ago, but it feels like years.

'Four centimetres,' she announces.

She summons an anaesthetist, whose face I don't even see. He rolls me over and I can sense him busying himself with my back. I feel a sting on my spine followed by a dull scrape. In a matter of minutes my legs feel warm and I can't feel the contractions anymore. I smile up at Lou-Anne and Indu. It's such a relief.

It's my friends' job to keep me awake now, because all I want to do is fall asleep. I drift in and out of twilight, having no idea how much time is passing. When my mum arrives, she holds my hand. I feel so happy that she made it, and I try to tell her so. Then I hear Dr Jacobs's voice.

'No more people in here,' she says firmly.

'Can I sleep, please?' I murmur.

'You're in active labour now, Shauna. It's not a good idea.'

'What time is it?'

No one tells me and it's not until much later that I appreciate the timeline. I'm in labour until sunrise, which is when Dr Jacobs realises that Beryl's head is not going to fit through my cervix.

Her face appears like a ghost's over mine.

'Shauna, you're going to need an emergency caesarean.'

I sob. She reassures me that it's not all that out of the ordinary, but I can't fight feelings of exhaustion, failure and doom. Fluorescent lights flash overhead as narrow corridors sweep past. I hear my mum call my name. Then my dad.

Then I'm being asked to count backwards from a hundred, but I can't. I see my brother's face and I'm sure I'm dead. He smiles at me.

'It'll be all right, kiddo,' he says.

Then, nothing.

30

I PUT MY hands to my belly, run my fingers over, its loose-
ness, and feel enormously relieved. It sounds horrible,
but I don't even think about the baby, except to compute
that she is gone – thank God! – from my battered body.
The sorest part of me is my throat, from the oxygen tube
I think, but the whole lower part of my body feels like it's
been under the wheels of a bus. I try to move my toes and
I can – just.

The nurses in the recovery ward are so nice. They fuss
and check on me, ask me how I'm feeling. After about
twenty minutes of slowly regaining my normal mind, I ask
about the baby.

'She's waiting for you in your room,' one of the young
nurses tells me.

Soon I'm wheeled into a tiny room by an orderly, and at
first I think I must be dreaming when I see Nathan O'Brien
with a tiny, swaddled baby in his arms. How can it be him?
I thought he didn't want us.

'What are you doing here?' I croak.

'Shauna,' he says in a shaky voice, as the orderly closes the
door behind him. 'Why wouldn't you talk to me?'

It takes me a while to answer. 'I thought you wouldn't want her. Or me.'

He walks to the bed and holds the sleeping baby to my eye-level. She has the most perfect little face, with a tiny nose and a red rosebud of a mouth. I lean over and kiss her plump, pink cheek.

'How could anyone not want her?' says Nathan. 'She's so beautiful.'

'I'm sorry. I didn't know whether I could rely on you.'

I can't move much, but Nathan lays the sleeping newborn in my arms. I gently hold her against my chest. Oh God, I think, the world can really hurt me now. It occurs to me in that instant, looking down at her face, how much my parents must have loved me and my brother, how completely. I know in my heart that they did the best they could with both of us, and that I will do the best I can with this child. I look from her to her father, bursting with love.

Finally I screw up the courage to say it. 'God, I love her, Nathan.'

'I love her, too.'

My parents come into the room and when they see me with the baby they both start crying. They're so proud of me, and I'm proud of them, too. My massively tall, bearded father looks like a dashing bushranger with his hair pulled back into a low ponytail. He's wearing his best slacks and his R.M. Williams boots. My dark-skinned mother with her wildly patterned dress and soft, generous lines is a picture of black femininity.

'Julie's driving out tomorrow to see you,' Mum says. 'She's bringing Andrew, and the rest of them will come the next day.'

Everyone clusters around me. When I open my mouth to introduce Nathan to my parents, my voice is feeble and crackling.

'Popping a baby's not the easiest thing to do, is it?' says Mum.

While Dad and Nathan get chatting, Mum turns to me and mouths, 'He's so handsome.'

'I know,' I mouth back.

We talk for ages in that little room, until Jenny's aunt Coralie comes in and boots out all my guests.

'Shauna needs rest,' she says gruffly, not knowing what an understatement that is.

When everyone's gone, she turns nice again.

'It's about time you learned how to breastfeed,' she says.

'But I'm too tired!'

'Welcome to motherhood, Shauna.'

I call my baby Olivia Jamie O'Brien, and I hope she turns out like her namesakes. She has my brother's nose and lips, and in some way, I feel like she's a little piece of him. Only the best parts.

★ ♥ ★

Over my five-day stay in hospital, my whole extended family comes to Sydney to visit. My school friends visit multiple days, too – Lou-Anne, Bindi, Indu and Olivia once in a big, noisy group, and then a more subdued visit from just Lou-Anne and Olivia, who are becoming firm friends in my absence. Jenny comes four days out of five. Self-Raising Flour visits once, but stays for three hours, her eyes locked onto my baby's face.

'This is one delicious little girl, Shauna,' she says, and I know what she means. Every now and then I get the urge to gobble baby Olivia right up.

Nathan rents a hotel room in the city and spends time with me in hospital every day, helping me wash and change our daughter. My parents can't afford to stay in Sydney long, so they go back to Barraba after two nights. It's Nathan who drives Olivia and me back up north after we're discharged from hospital.

When we walk out to the hospital car park, I see that Nathan's exchanged his souped-up aggy ute for an unspeakably dorky Camry.

'It's my mum's car,' he says with embarrassment as he opens the rear door, revealing a brand new baby seat. I hadn't even thought about that.

Nathan admits that his parents are still pretty bugged out about what's happened, but that they're looking forward to meeting me and the baby. We've talked again about what I thought his mum did to me at the Easter Show.

'You're wrong, Shauna,' said Nathan, and I could tell he meant it. 'Mum's not like that. She was so stressed out that day. She's always in a filthy mood at cattle shows.'

I have accepted that I am capable of being wrong, and that I might have been wrong about Nathan's mother. I feel apprehensive about meeting the O'Briens, but I'm trying to keep an open mind. They want to be involved with the baby, and I think I'm going to let them.

I sleep most of the way on the drive up the New England Highway to Barraba, waking only once when Olivia wants a feed. When we pull into my parents' driveway, they're waiting outside for us. I have never, ever felt so exhausted or so happy to be home.

Nathan comes in for a cup of tea, but he soon heads back to Kootingal. He plans to come and pick me up the next day so I can meet his parents at their farm, and I've agreed.

'Not a bad sort of young bloke,' admits Dad when Nathan's gone. I wasn't sure how things would go between the two of them. Dad's physical presence can seem pretty frightening.

'He's got good manners,' says Mum. 'He's well-raised.'

I realise that after days of having Nathan at my side, I already miss him.

That night after dinner, I call Jenny.

'I just wanted to thank you,' I tell her.

'What for?'

'For hooking me up with your aunt and the hospital.'

'It's a good hospital, isn't it?'

'It's a *super* hospital.' Which is true, but, honestly, that's not what I really want to thank her for. 'Jenny...look...'

I sigh, searching for the right words.

'It was nice to see Nathan with you every day,' says Jenny, as if reading my mind. 'He was really great with the baby. I know how scared you were. I know that's why you were reluctant to tell him.'

'You told me at the hospital that day that I had the scan, that I might, you know, want Nathan's love.' It's so hard to admit this. I start to choke up. 'I was so afraid of wanting it and not getting it.'

301

'You didn't think you deserved it, but you do. And I've seen the way he looks at you...'

I end the call with Jenny so I can have a cry, but it's a happy one. How lucky am I to have a friend like Jenny! A *challenging* friend. She's not sweet and unendingly devoted like Lou-Anne. Nor does she worship me like Olivia does. But she does have my back. She *has* had my back during this whole strange, wonderful, embarrassing and ugly process. She stood up to me when she thought I was wrong, and that's no easy task.

Where would I be without my friends?

I'm not only talking about my Oakholme friends either. I'm talking about my old Barraba friend, Ashley, who's full of advice about breastfeeding and getting an unsettled baby off to sleep. She's almost as excited as if Olivia Jamie were her own baby. And my over-the-back-fence friend Taylor is *smug* – the only one of our mob who's not a mum, and therefore free to do as she pleases. Lucky her. She's more the leader than I ever was.

Where would I be without these girls, common like me, posh like me?

I don't have much time to consider my question, because the peace is rent by the lusty little cry of my hungry newborn. My boobs sting at the mere sound of it. I know that these are just the first stirrings of all the pain and love Olivia Jamie O'Brien is going to bring during our time together – the rest of my life.

31

I'VE ALWAYS HATED speech night. It's such a long, stuffy, boring affair. Never-ending speeches, dull prize-giving ceremonies and lacklustre musical numbers are the norm. Usually the best thing you can say about it is that when it's over, you know you're on holidays. It's a thrill this year, though, because I know it's the last speech night I'll ever have the honour and burden of sitting through.

Things are a bit different this year with Reverend Ferguson at the helm.

For starters, she invites Lou-Anne to sing the national anthem. Lou-Anne performs it pitch-perfect and without accompaniment to rapturous cheers and a standing ovation.

Then, instead of paying some D-grade celebrity to give a motivational speech about how they got to be a D-grade celebrity, Reverend Ferguson asks me to do a speech. I am, after all, Oakholme College's first Indigenous scholarship graduate. Though at times I've been unwilling, I've blazed a wide enough trail for others to follow. I have done something good.

Self-Raising Flour gave me a lot of freedom in writing my speech. The only parameters were that I keep it under fifteen minutes and that I not mention my pregnancy, my baby or my short-lived expulsion.

'Trust me, Shauna, there won't be a person in the Town Hall who doesn't know you've had a baby. I just don't think we need to rub the noses of our more conservative parents in your outstanding fertility.'

In fact, my baby's in the audience tonight, gurgling in Olivia Pike's arms somewhere near the back, so they can make a quick exit if need be. My parents are out there somewhere, too. So are my other friends.

The subject of my speech, which I have rote-learned over many hours of breastfeeding, is about giving girls, particularly girls from difficult backgrounds, lots of chances. I talk about the kind of girl I was when I was twelve, the things that had already happened to me, and the things that probably would have happened to me if I'd stayed in my community in Barraba.

My point is that merely introducing a poor, poorly educated girl into a wealthy, academically strong school is almost certainly not enough to ensure she makes it. I talk about some of the bad things I used to do, like lying, stealing, fighting, flaking out and hiding. I say that if anyone had taken a snapshot of my character for my first two and half years at Oakholme College, I would certainly have been declared unfit to attend the school. It takes time to build character and virtue, I argue, especially when you start with a handicap. If you begin judging someone too early, you'll probably find enough fault to justify giving up on them. Sticking with difficult people in the long term is hard, but it's important.

'At the beginning of the year, I attended a Change the Date rally in Hyde Park. People were calling not only to move Australia Day, but to tear down statues of our early white explorers. The amount and intensity of press coverage for this event was astonishing. It made me wonder what would be possible if we focused as much on education as we do on the dates, words and symbols that have become popular political footballs.

'I'm not saying that history and hurt feelings aren't important, but it's too easy to spend one day a year complaining, and much harder to support someone's journey through the school system. There are no rallies or medals for outcomes in education. For students like me, though, they're much more important. Because if you have your health, a good education and a few people who are willing to give you a chance, then there are no excuses. It doesn't matter where you're from or who your family is.

'So, thank you, parents, students, staff and friends of Oakholme College, for giving me a million and one fresh chances. I desperately needed every single one of them. And I am thoroughly grateful for all of them.'

There's a tense, dangling moment of silence before thunderous applause. I walk back to my seat, a young mother in school uniform, feeling as grateful as I sound. If I could see Mr Street-Hughes, I'd probably thank him myself.

I scoop two academic prizes, Maths and French, and Jenny hogs most of the rest. Jenny is dux of the school, and she deserves to be. She's worked a lot harder than I have for years. When she walks onto stage to accept her prize, it strikes me how incredible it is that I'm friends with *la crème de la crème* of a posh Sydney private school. That must make me some kind of insider. In spite of everything that's happened, or maybe even because of it, I've cracked the code.

For the month before speech night, I'd been in Barraba. Living with my parents and the baby has been okay. I'm at the stage where I can only think as far as the next feed, the next sleep. I'm still too zonked to yearn for the excitement and sophistication of the city and I can barely get excited about my eighteenth birthday. My parents are planning to throw a big party at our house. Everyone's coming – Jenny, Lou-Anne, Big Olivia, Bindi, Indu, my family from Bathurst, Ashley and Taylor from Barraba, and, of course, Nathan.

It's going well between Nathan and me. As I keep telling Lou-Anne, I got lucky twice with the man in my life. I'm *very* fortunate, considering how random our get-together was, to have such a kind, sweet guy as the father of my child.

Do you know what he said to me recently?

He said, 'I think I was lonely before I met you and you had Olivia. Now that I have you both, I'll never feel alone.'

My heart tripped when he said that, like it does every time I lay eyes on him after a bit of a break.

I've been to the farm at Kootingal almost every weekend since the birth to hang out with him and his family. His parents, Alan and Glenda, have been scrupulously nice and welcoming, and they adore Olivia. They're still freaked out that their son has a baby, though, and I can tell they're disappointed that Nathan's decided to defer his agriculture studies in the city for at least another year. He says he's too busy, and he doesn't want to leave Olivia and me.

I haven't deferred my studies. There was no way that was ever going to happen, no matter how tired I was. Even if my ATAR isn't as high as I think it'll be, I'll probably still get into a Bachelor of Communications degree at the university in Armidale, about two hours' drive away. I'll start out online, but I might be able to attend lectures later on, when Olivia's old enough for day care. Nathan's even talked about us moving to Armidale together, but it's still very early days.

At the moment, to be honest, all I care about is sleep. I'm so wiped out that I can barely string a sentence together. I love the relentlessly growing Olivia, but she's sucked all the life out of me with that toothless, burpy mouth.

Looking after a baby is hard, but I can tell you that there are worse things in life than a teenager having a baby. I think Aboriginal girls know this better than other Australians, because we often come up so hard. We may be less worldly than other Aussie girls, but we've seen more of life, usually the disappointing side, and in that sense we're older than our years. We know that in the scheme of things, a baby is okay. For so many of us, it'll be the best thing that ever happens to us.

Before my baby existed, I'd never thought about it, but now I know that, despite popular sentiment and the ethos of abortion clinics, embarrassment is not a cause of death. Yes, I'm a bit embarrassed that I had a baby when I was seventeen, but I think I was even more embarrassed before I got pregnant.

I realise now that being poor embarrassed me. Sadly, being Aboriginal embarrassed me. My brother's death embarrassed me. Even my family embarrassed me. Not anymore. Motherhood and the love of those closest to me have helped to free me from that. I accept my past and even honour it for making me the person I am today. A good mum. An attentive girlfriend (yes, Nathan introduces me as his girlfriend!). A supportive friend. A top student.

For the rest of my life, I will love who I please, be who I am, and say what I feel.

The applause lasts long after I've descended the stairs of the Town Hall stage. I grin and blush furiously as I stride down the aisle towards the two Olivias. I'm still not great at accepting praise or gifts, but I think I've worked out the key to this. As Olivia Pike passes the sleeping Olivia O'Brien into my long, brown arms, I tell myself, *you deserve it.*

About the Author

Kathleen is an Australian lawyer and writer. She was born in rural Victoria and now lives between Australia and Europe with her husband and their four children.